Praise for Shannon Stacey

"Stacey writes whoodamn fine contemporary romance."

—*Smart Bitches, Trashy Books*

"I feel safe that every time I pick up a Stacey book I'm going to read something funny, sexy, and loving. That's exactly what I got in *All He Ever Needed.*"

—*Dear Author*

"The perfect contemporary romance!"

—*RT Book Reviews*, 4½ stars, on *Undeniably Yours*

"I absolutely adore the Kowalski series, so every time Stacey has a new release, I'm so anxious to get my hands on the newest book.... I love getting to see all the Kowalski family members happy and living their ever afters."

—*The Book Pushers*

"It is always a joy to spend time with the extended Kowalski family. And this contemporary tale is full of the love (and requisite family high jinks) that readers have come to expect from Shannon Stacey."

—*RT Book Reviews*, 4½ stars, on *Yours to Keep*

"Stacey's family drama is equal parts steamy romance and coming-of-age story, with secondary characters as fascinating as the main couple."

—*RT Book Reviews*, 4½ stars, on *All He Ever Desired*

Also available from Shannon Stacey and Carina Press

The Kowalski Series

Exclusively Yours
Undeniably Yours
Yours to Keep
All He Ever Needed
All He Ever Desired
All He Ever Dreamed
Love a Little Sideways
Taken with You
Falling for Max

The Boston Fire Series

Heat Exchange
Controlled Burn
Fully Ignited

Holiday Sparks
Mistletoe & Margaritas
Slow Summer Kisses
Snowbound with the CEO
Her Holiday Man
A Fighting Chance
Holiday with a Twist

Also available from Shannon Stacey and Harlequin

Alone with You
Heart of the Storm

SHANNON STACEY

What It Takes

A KOWALSKI REUNION NOVEL

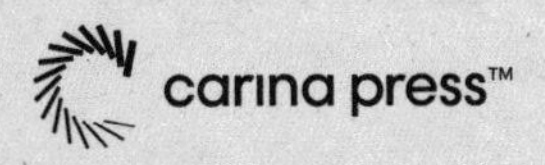

Recycling programs for this product may not exist in your area.

ISBN-13: 978-0-373-00455-3

What It Takes: A Kowalski Reunion Novel

This edition published by arrangement with Harlequin Books S.A.

www.CarinaPress.com

Printed in U.S.A.

What It Takes

A KOWALSKI REUNION NOVEL

This book is dedicated to the many readers
who have loved the Kowalski family as much as I do
and wanted more, as well as to the dedicated
volunteers who work tirelessly to make four-wheeling
a fun and safe passion for my family. Thank you.

ONE

NOTHING GOOD EVER came of a half-assed plan.

Ben Rivers stood with his arms folded across his chest, staring down at the mangled four-wheeler lying on its side about twenty feet down a pucker brush-covered hill. Though a half-assed plan was still better than no plan, he had to admit.

"The handlebars are going left and the wheels are going right," he pointed out.

Matt Barnett—who was with the Maine state warden service—and Josh Kowalski both shrugged, but it was Josh who spoke. "Yeah, you'll have to figure out how to compensate for that."

"Me? Who decided I was going down there?"

"I'm running the winch," Josh said, pointing to his ATV with its spool of heavy-duty winch cable bolted on the front.

"And I'm in charge of the investigation," Matt said, "so I can't risk breaking my paperwork hand."

Ben snorted. "And I'm the paramedic, so I should probably stay up here and be ready to patch up whichever of you idiots draws the short straw."

"Hey, I've had first aid training," Matt protested.

They laughed because they all knew Matt was a guy you'd definitely want around in a crisis, but his first aid training didn't exactly match up to Ben's years of being a paramedic in the city. That was why Drew Miller—

Whitford's police chief—and Josh, both of whom Ben had known his entire life, had called and offered him a job back in his hometown. Now that their part of the state had become a vacation destination for ATV and side-by-side enthusiasts, they needed somebody who could ride a four-wheeler, knew the area like only a native son would, and could offer advanced medical care while victims were slowly carted out of the woods to a waiting ambulance or helicopter. Ben had fit the bill and his phone had rung at a time he was staring down the barrel of burnout and looking to make a change.

"If Matt wasn't here we could just push it off the tree it's hung up on and let it roll the rest of the way down the hill into the pond," Josh said.

"We'd never get the equipment we'd need for extraction down there," Ben said.

"That's between the owner and his insurance company."

"We're not pushing it into the pond," Matt said firmly. "Do you want the lecture on water contamination, wildlife impact and EPA fines or can we just go with *because I said so*?"

Josh groaned. "Hell no, I don't want a lecture. And you know I was kidding, but since you won't let us do it the easy way, we'll watch you do it the hard way."

Matt looked at Ben. "Rock, paper, scissors?"

"I saved the rider. You save the machine."

The game warden snorted. "Saved the rider? You cleaned the scrape on his elbow and gave him a Band-Aid."

"Hey, infected wounds are no joke." He managed to say *wound* with a straight face, but it wasn't easy.

The rider had bailed when the machine started to

roll, throwing himself free. He'd skinned his elbow when he hit the ground and he'd be finding new bruises for a couple of days, but he'd been lucky and Ben's services hadn't really been needed. Unfortunately, the information that the rider wasn't still on the ATV when it rolled over and went off the trail and down a hill wasn't relayed to the dispatcher right away and hadn't been relayed to Ben at all. So he hadn't saved anybody, but that wouldn't stop him from trying to pawn the physical labor off on one of the other guys.

In the end, both Matt and Ben ended up over the edge while Josh ran the winch. After they secured the steel cable to the frame of the ATV, they had to guide the ATV as Josh reeled the cable back in. It was slow work, and they had to constantly move to make sure they were never in a position to be swept down the hill on the odd chance the winch cable snapped.

By the time they had the four-wheeler back on the trail, Ben was sweaty and cursing himself for not leaving as soon as he'd slapped a Band-Aid on the machine's rider. Instead, he'd hung around after Andy went back after a truck and trailer, the so-called victim riding behind him since Andy had a two-up, chatting. Then the chatting became a discussion of how to retrieve the ATV and here he was.

"Now comes the hard part," Josh said, and Ben's groan was almost drowned out by Matt's. "We have to get it two miles to the closest spot Andy can get the truck and trailer to."

"We're not driving it, that's for sure." Matt was circling the ATV, taking pictures. He'd taken some while it was hung up on the hill, too, as well as a few of the marks on the trail leading up to the spot it rolled over.

It looked to Ben like the rider had simply caught a rut wrong and it was a straight-up accident, but that was Matt's job.

"I don't see why we don't leave it and let the guy who owns it worry about it," Ben said. "You'd have to be one tricky son of a bitch to steal it in the condition it's in."

Josh shook his head. "Because guess who's going to get asked to bring him back out here and then get the machine back to the road? I'm here now. And you guys are here. I'd rather do this with you than a guy who managed to roll his machine on a dirt road."

"There *are* ruts," Matt pointed out.

"How are you planning to get it to the road?" Ben asked Josh, hoping they could move the process along so there was at least the hope of having lunch in the near future.

"It's only a 500, so my machine can take the weight. We're going to put the front wheels up on my back rack and strap the shit out of it. Then, nice and slow so I'm not doing accidental wheelies, I'm going to pull it out to the road."

Ben laughed, shaking his head. "Sean and I did that once. He made me ride all the way back on the front rack of his machine to balance the weight of mine on the back."

"I remember when you guys pulled in the yard. Worked, didn't it?"

Ben looked at Josh. "We were young and stupid."

"And now we're older and wiser, so nobody's riding on the front rack. It is going to take all three of us to get that front end up high enough, though."

Matt snorted. "Aren't you glad you took this job, Ben?"

He laughed, but he *was* glad he'd taken the job offer. Sure, he was sweaty and his arms were going to be sore and he could only hope there hadn't been poison ivy or oak on that hill, but he had no regrets.

Coming back to Whitford had been the right decision and he had a feeling things were really going to start looking up.

LANEY CASWELL HAD been looking to make big changes in her life, and almost being able to touch both walls of her new home at the same time certainly qualified as a big change.

The camper was small, but it had a bed, a tiny bathroom with a tinier shower, and outlets for her coffeemaker and charging her phone. What more did a woman starting over in her midthirties need?

Today was the first full day of her new life at the Northern Star Lodge & Campground, she thought, feeling pretty damn proud of herself. The divorce had taken forever, but the papers had been signed and it was *finally* final. Throw in the camper's hot water heater being just big enough to rinse all the soap and shampoo away, and things were looking up already.

A knock on the camper door startled her, and she would have laughed out loud at herself except she knew campers weren't exactly soundproof and she was trying to make a good impression on her new employers. After setting her coffee mug on the small square of Formica that made up her kitchen counter, she opened the door to find one of those bosses smiling up at her.

"Good morning, Laney."

"Good morning." Laney guessed Rose Miller—who she'd been told to call Rosie, like everybody else did—was in her very late sixties, though she wouldn't ask, of course.

"Now that you've spent your first night in the camper, I thought I'd stop by and see if everything went okay, or if there were any problems."

It was awkward standing above the woman, so Laney stepped down onto the metal step and then the ground. After separating the two door panels, she closed the screen door and then folded the exterior door all the way back. There was a small hook bolted to the side of the camper that would hold it open. The camper had been closed up for a while and every little bit of fresh air would help.

"I didn't have any problems," she said. "Everything seems to work fine, the bed is comfortable and my coffeemaker went off at the time I set it to. Thank you for the welcome basket, by the way. The muffins were amazing, and the banana bread was the best I've ever had."

"You're welcome." Rosie smiled. "And you can't ask for much more than a comfortable bed and fresh coffee in the morning. Andy's off doing some chores and I thought maybe you'd like to take a walk with me and see a little more of the place."

"Of course." This was going to be her home until fall, and she was looking forward to exploring it.

"Your flamingo is adorable, by the way," Rosie said.

Laney looked at the silly yard ornament she'd set into the ground next to her step and smiled. The wooden flamingo was bright pink and it had a funny, painted cartoon face. It also had thin plastic wings that would whirl if the winds were strong enough. It was something neither her family nor the Ballards—including her ex-husband—would have allowed on their lawns, and Laney loved it.

"Thank you. He's definitely a cheerful guy."

They walked around the campground area of the property. There were two cabins, and a dozen sites with sewer and electric hookups, not counting hers. Her site was closer to the line of trees between the camping area and the lodge, and had a view of the new pool.

When they walked past the field behind the campsites where the campers could park their ATV trailers, Rosie waved to her husband, who was mowing with a zero turn mower. He blew her a kiss and Laney swore she heard Rosie giggle.

During her very informal interview, which had been a conference call with Rosie and Josh Kowalski, Rosie had made a joke about being a newlywed and then explained to Laney that she and Andy had only been married for a couple of years.

Just thinking about it made Laney smile. If Rose could find true love and happiness at her age, that meant there was still plenty of time for Laney. She could take her time making her life into what *she* wanted it to be and then maybe, in the distant future, she'd be lucky enough to find a man who would want to share it with her.

First she had to figure out what exactly she wanted her life to be, of course. And that's why she was here, in the middle of nowhere Maine, with nothing but her clothes, a few prized possessions, and a tablet loaded up with movies her ex-husband hadn't wanted to watch and books she'd never gotten around to reading. She was going to live simply, consume things she enjoyed and find her true self.

She felt as if she was starring in one of those movies, invariably based on bestselling books, in which women went on epic treks of self-discovery to distant and exotic lands, except in Laney's case, she'd trekked to Maine to live in a box on wheels for a few months.

The Northern Star Lodge & Campground was her distant and exotic land. Or distant-*ish*, since she'd started her journey in Rhode Island. But the difference between the decade she'd spent being Mrs. Patrick Ballard in a big house in Warwick and now couldn't be measured in miles.

"Let's go out front and I'll tell you where we keep some of the things you might need, like extra propane tanks."

Laney had already figured out that *out front* meant the lodge itself and the lawn and outbuildings surrounding it, and *out back* meant the camping area and field. As soon as they walked through the gap in the trees, though, she saw two guys—one of them being Josh—standing next to a trailer bearing an ATV that looked a little worse for wear.

"Who's that with Josh?" she asked, knowing she'd be meeting a whole lot of new people in the days to come.

"That's Ben Rivers," Rosie answered. "He grew up in Whitford, but he moved away to the city years ago. Now he's back, which makes his mama happy, let me tell you. Ben's a good boy."

Laney bit back a laugh at the idea of the man standing across the yard being described as *a good boy.* He looked about her age or maybe a little older, with dark hair and a scruffy jaw. He wasn't as tall as Josh but Laney could tell he was at least a couple inches taller than her, so he was probably five-ten or five-eleven. Very faded jeans and a navy T-shirt hugged his body, and he was wearing battered work boots.

But it wasn't his appearance that caused Laney to be amused by the word *boy.* Whoever Ben was, he carried himself with the kind of confidence and authority that came from life experience and feeling secure in his place in the world.

Must be nice.

And then he turned his head to look at her, one eyebrow arched as if silently asking why she was staring at him. She felt her cheeks warm before his gaze shifted to Rosie beside her. He smiled, and his face lit up in a way that made Laney's pulse quicken.

How ridiculous to feel as if she could burst into flames just seeing a man smile, and not even at her, she thought. It had been a very long time since she'd had that kind of reaction to a man and, while she was glad everything felt as if it was in good working order, she wasn't here for that.

She was here to work so, as Rosie spoke to her, she tore her gaze away from the handsome *good boy* and tried to pay attention.

TWO

BEN WAVED TO Rosie Davis—no, it was Miller now, he reminded himself—but as she turned to keep walking, he couldn't stop his gaze from returning to the woman with her. She was close to his own age, with long light brown hair that had been highlighted either naturally by the sun or very professionally from a bottle.

Probably by the sun, he thought, noticing how tan her long legs were and the color across the apples of her cheeks. She'd been spending a lot of time outside. As he watched, Rosie pointed at each of the lodge's outbuildings, as if explaining what each was. It seemed like an odd thing for a camper to be interested in.

"Who's that?" he finally asked Josh. "The woman with Rosie, I mean."

"Her name's Laney. She's going to be helping out for a while."

"It's quite the expansion you guys have done here. The campground. Cabins. A pool. Now an employee who's not family." The lodge had been in the family for several generations, and it was Josh's dad who'd turned it into a snowmobile lodge. They'd managed to get by for many years on the seasonal business, but when the economy tanked, they'd found a way to go year-round by hooking the town into the nearby ATV trails.

Josh nodded. "It's crazy how much business the trails have brought to town. We've had at least a half a dozen new businesses in the last couple of years. And since we expanded and added the campground, it's harder to keep up. I mean, technically there are four of us, but Katie has the barbershop and she's having a baby in three months. Rosie's been taking care of this lodge my whole life and Andy helps with the campground, but she's almost seventy and he's at least that. I don't want them working that hard."

"You can't do it alone."

Josh shook his head. "Not and keep up with the club business. Since I'm the president and Andy's the trail administrator, that takes up a good chunk of our time. It makes sense to have somebody who can help out in a general sense and focus on just the guests."

"Is she from around here?"

"No, but she was willing to live on-site in a camper until after the long Labor Day weekend, accepted the salary we offered and Rosie liked her."

Ben suspected it was the last qualification that had sealed the deal. Rosie had been hired by Frank and Sarah Kowalski back when he was a kid and he couldn't remember when Sarah had died, but he'd been young. Rosie had not only been taking care of the lodge for Josh's whole life, but she'd been like a mother to him and his brothers and sister, too. Accepting help wouldn't come easy to Rosie, so her actually liking whoever they hired was vital.

"You ran a background check, right?" he asked, because there had to be a reason why a woman his age would take on a job probably better suited to a college kid looking to earn a paycheck while saving money on rent over the summer.

Josh snorted. "The chief of police is Andy's son and my brother-in-law. What do you think?"

"I'm going to buy a whiteboard to start keeping track of that stuff." Ben shook his head. Josh was married to Andy's stepdaughter, Katie. And Andy's son, Drew, was married to Josh's sister, Liz. The bottom line, though, was that anybody looking to work at the Northern Star would be thoroughly vetted.

"I'm going to leave the wheeler right on the trailer," Josh said. "He brought it up in the bed of his pickup, but in its current condition, he'd be better off borrowing the trailer from me."

But they had to unhook the trailer from Josh's truck, and it was an old one. That meant lifting the hitch off the ball by hand and setting the tongue on a heavy-duty jack stand Josh grabbed from the barn. Because nothing was ever easy, it slipped—a rough edge cutting the palm of his hand—and he let loose a few choice swear words.

"We probably own twenty pairs of leather work gloves between us," Josh said, brushing rusty paint flakes off his hands.

Ben frowned at the cut, carefully brushing a few paint flakes away from it. "I've got at least three in my truck right now."

"Me, too." Josh laughed. "I appreciate the help."

"No problem. I figure if I pop over and make myself useful enough, eventually Rosie will bake me up some of that banana bread I love. There are some things a man never forgets and Rosie's cooking is one of them. Your wife inherit that gene from her mom?"

"No. Cooking is not one of Katie's stronger skills." After taking a deep breath, Josh looked toward the break in the tree line that marked the beginning of the camping area. "I guess I'll go see what's happening with this guy and let him know his machine's back. For all I know, he decided to head to the hospital."

"I doubt it." Ben looked at his hands. "I'm going to go in and wash up, since I want to run a little soap over this. I'll catch you later."

He was halfway to the house when he realized he was on an intercept course with Laney, who must have been done walking with Rosie. He could have hesitated or veered off toward his truck, but he'd meet the woman at some point. It might as well be now.

Ben saw the moment she saw him—the hesitation in her step—but then she smiled and kept walking until their paths converged. "Hi, I'm Laney Caswell."

"Ben Rivers." He started to hold out his hand, and then stopped, twisting his wrist to show her his palm. "I'd shake your hand, but that trailer back there got the better of me."

Frowning, she leaned closer to look at it. "That cut needs to be cleaned."

"Yeah, I'll get to it."

"I know exactly what that means when a man says it. You'll probably spit on it and wipe it on your jeans when I'm not looking."

"Or slap a little PVC glue on it," he teased, unable to help himself.

"Rosie had a first aid kit in the kitchen," she said. "I'll take care of it for you."

Ben could tell her he'd been on his way to the kitchen already. He could tell her he was pretty well qualified to deal with a small cut on his hand. Instead, he nodded and gestured for her to lead the way.

"Wash your hands and then have a seat," she said firmly before going into the pantry.

By the time he'd done as he was told and then sat down, Laney had found an ancient plastic storage bin marked FIRST AID in big letters on a piece of masking tape. She carried it over and popped the lid. "Rosie told me she's had this box for thirty years because regular first aid kits weren't enough for the Kowalski family."

"She wasn't lying." He held out his hand, palm up on the table, so she could look at it.

"You've known them a long time, then?"

"My whole life. I ran with Josh's brother Sean, mostly, since we're the same age, but we all grew up together."

"There's something in this," she said before rummaging in the box for tweezers. Then she opened an alcohol wipe and cleaned the slanted tips, which he appreciated.

"Probably a paint chip. The trailer's seen better days. And before you ask, my tetanus is up to date."

When she laid her fingers across his, holding them flat, Ben felt a frisson of awareness up the back of his neck. He was aware of how soft her hands were. That her hair smelled like roses. Her eyes were blue and she had long, makeup-free lashes the color of dark maple syrup.

Then she went after the paint chip and he hissed at the sharp pain. She paused for a second, then kept going. "I have to get it."

"I know. I'm okay," he said. But he liked the sound of her voice and wanted to hear more of it. "You should talk and distract me from what you're doing."

"I'm trying to concentrate. You talk and that'll distract you."

"Okay, so Josh said you're not from around here, but he didn't say where you're from. Still New England, I'd guess from the accent." She nodded, but didn't say anything else. The corners of her mouth tilted up in a small smile, though, so he felt comfortable prodding a little more. "Yankees or Red Sox?"

She snorted. "Red Sox. How is that even a question?"

"Rhode Island, then?"

"Yes. Warwick." She stopped poking at his cut to look up at him. "How did you guess that from a baseball team?"

"I've got a pretty good ear for accents, so I'd already narrowed it down to Connecticut or Rhode Island. Somebody from Connecticut would know why I asked the question, since they're infected by Yankees fans from New York City, so I went all in on the Ocean State."

"Good call. Okay, I got the paint out, so go wash your hands and then I'll put some gunk on it."

He chuckled as he walked to the sink. "Gunk? I take it you can get that over the counter?"

"It's fancy medical terminology."

Her laugh was cute and Ben was reluctant to turn the water on because it might drown it out. But he needed to wash the cut, so he grabbed the soap, gritted his teeth and got on with it. Wincing, he patted it dry with a paper towel, trying to think of something he could say to make her laugh again.

But when he turned back around, Laney wasn't even smiling. Her cheeks were bright pink and her lips were pressed together. "What's wrong?"

"I had noticed that your shirt says WFD on the front, but I didn't realize what it stood for. But it says Whitford Fire Department on the back, with *paramedic* under it in big capital letters."

"Yeah."

"I don't suppose there's any chance at all you bought that shirt at a yard sale or stole it from a Laundromat?"

That made him laugh, even though he had no idea what she was talking about. "No, it's mine. Even though it was Josh—because he's president of the ATV club—and Drew Miller, the police chief, who not only offered me the job, but talked me into taking it, I'm officially employed by the town through the fire department."

She sighed, shaking her head. "So you're a paramedic?"

"Yes. Is that a problem? You look…not happy about it and I can't figure out why."

"Maybe because I told you you'd probably spit on your cut and wipe it on your jeans and made you come in here and the entire time you're actually a trained medical professional." She rolled her eyes. "I feel kind of stupid right now."

"Don't." Ben hated seeing that look on her face. The embarrassment and self-deprecation he saw there made him want to comfort her—to touch her—so he crossed his arms to keep his hands confined. It took everything he had in him not to wince when his palm brushed over his shirt because he was an idiot. "Professionals aren't always the best at taking care of themselves. And there *was* a fifty-fifty chance I was going to wipe it on my jeans, though I would have washed it out eventually."

"You probably wouldn't have spit on it, though."

He laughed. "Probably not."

Her expression cleared, leaving nothing but that smile he liked. "Sit back down and let me put a bandage on it. Paramedic or not, it's harder with one hand."

Doing as he was told, Ben sat back at the table and offered his hand. "Usually I'd skip this part, but I'm afraid if it gets infected, you might try to give me a shot."

"Funny." She opened the tube of ointment and set it aside. "So you grew up here, but Rosie said you moved to the city. She didn't say which city, though."

"I've been in the Lewiston-Auburn area for the last eight or nine years, though I started on the coast. It kept me pretty busy."

"This will be a big change of pace for you, then," she said, opening the wrapper for the adhesive bandage. After squeezing a little ointment onto the pad, she reached for his hand.

"It seems that way but, really, this job has its own set of challenges. The city was busy, but I had a fully stocked ambulance, paved roads and the magic ability to make all the stoplights green. Here, I'll have fewer calls, but I have to find my patients out in the woods, treat them with what I can fit in the cargo boxes on my ATV and then figure out how to get them to either an intersection an ambulance can get to or a clearing where a helicopter can land."

Instead of holding his hand down this time, Laney took his fingers and lifted it. He watched her brows draw together and caught her bottom lip between her teeth as he tried not to laugh. Laney seemed to have a good sense of humor, but she'd been feeling embarrassed just a few minutes ago and he didn't want to bring that back.

"This isn't going to stick well," she said as she laid the bandage across the cut and pressed the adhesive against his skin. "Maybe I should wrap it with gauze to hold it on."

"It'll get me home and even if you wrapped it, I'd have to change it when I shower anyway."

"Are you sure?"

She was still holding his hand and though he knew she was doing it thoughtlessly because she wasn't done fussing over him and she was talking, he liked it. It was weird, since he didn't know this woman, but there was something about her that made him want to change that.

"I'm sure. I need to get back to the station and do some paperwork before I head home, so there will be plenty of time for that medical gunk to soak in."

She let go of his hand, but she laughed again, which was just as good. "I guess I don't have to give you aftercare instructions."

"No, but if I need advice, I know where to find you."

She smiled up at him as he stood. "I'll be here for the summer."

Ben forced himself to thank her again and then walk out the door, when he really wanted to pour them each a glass of lemonade and go sit out on the front porch with her.

There would be plenty of time for getting to know Laney Caswell.

ONCE THE KITCHEN door had closed behind Ben, Laney bent forward and let her forehead hit the big wooden table with a thunk.

I'll be here all summer.

Had she really sounded as breathless as she had

in her own mind? Seriously, she couldn't have issued a more obvious invitation short of breaking out card stock and a calligraphy pen.

She should put the first aid box away. Then she should look at the list Rosie had left for her on a side table in the living room, which detailed the daily housekeeping tasks for the lodge and campground. Andy had wanted to introduce Rosie to a couple who'd stopped by to visit some friends who were camping there, so she'd sent Laney to look over the to-do list so they could discuss it later. And then she'd gotten sidetracked by a sexy paramedic with an injured palm and a wicked grin.

Instead of doing the things she should be doing, Laney sat there with her head on the table, thinking about Ben's hands.

He had strong hands. Not rough, but the skin on his fingertips was thick and he had calluses across the pads. And his forearms…

She sighed, a sigh so deep it seemed to come from her toes, and then thumped her head on the table again. Never in her life had she been attracted to a man's forearms. But she'd played hell concentrating on the arm stretched out to her when she kept glancing at his left arm. He'd rested it casually on the table and the first time she'd tried to grab the paint chip with the tweezers, the fingers of that hand had curled into a fist. The action made the muscles in his forearm tense and Laney's mouth had gone dry.

It was a miracle, really, that she hadn't stabbed him with the tweezers. Either he hadn't noticed her reaction or the subsequent shift of her body to move his left arm out of her sight line, or he'd been too polite to mention it.

Hopefully the paramedic wouldn't be spending too much time at the Northern Star, she thought as she raised her head and stood. After taking alcohol to the tweezers again, she put the first aid box back in the pantry and threw away the garbage. She'd come here specifically to learn to be alone—to bring back that confident, self-sufficient inner woman she'd spent ten years shushing in order to make her husband happy—not to find another man.

She didn't have any trouble finding Rosie's list. It was on the side table next to a beat-up old rocking chair that had a basket of knitting on the floor beside it. Laney was willing to bet that when guests were hanging out in the living room to watch the television or socialize, they knew without being told that chair wasn't for them.

The list was long and doubt rose up in Laney's chest like acid reflux. She hadn't worked since she was twenty-five years old and was informed by her mother-in-law that women in the Ballard family didn't work. They tended to their husband, homes and children—in that order, based on Patrick's mother's attitude—without distraction. The fact children had never come once seemed like a curse, but now was a blessing.

If she failed at this, she wasn't sure what she would do. Not that she couldn't find another job. But this one was about more than a paycheck. She *wanted* to be here. And she might not have any employment history since quitting her job at the jewelry store where Patrick bought his watches, but she had skills.

And one of those skills was keeping an immaculate house. A very large house, as a matter of fact. And maybe she'd never had to clean rooms for paying guests, but making a bed was making a bed.

Feeling more centered, Laney read down the list item by item. Needless to say, she'd have to spend a couple of days shadowing Rosie to learn how she liked things done and where everything was kept, but she was a fast learner. Her duties in the campground included cleaning and stocking the bathhouse and cleaning the two cabins after checkout, but mostly she would report things to Josh or Andy.

"I didn't scare you away, did I?"

She hadn't heard Rosie come in and she started, though she managed not to yelp. Turning, she smiled and shook her head. "Of course not. This is a beautiful place and I'll do my best to help keep it that way."

"It *is* beautiful, isn't it? It always has been, though it got a little shabby a while back because money was tight. The boys worked really hard at not only fixing up the house, but connecting the property—and the entire town, really—to the ATV trails. Nobody expected that to take off the way it did, but now we're busy year-round instead of just snowmobile season. They expanded the camping area and added the two cabins and the pool last year, and we not only have reservations through Columbus Day weekend this year, but several bookings for Memorial Day weekend next year."

"I'm looking forward to being a part of it. Oh, and before I forget, I used the first aid box, but I cleaned the tweezers before I put it back. I hope you don't mind."

"That's what it's there for. Did you have a sliver?"

"No. Ben cut his hand helping Josh and there was a paint chip in it. I got a little bossy with him about taking care of it and *then* found out he's a paramedic." Her cheeks heated again, even though it wasn't that big of a deal.

"It wouldn't matter if he was a brain surgeon, honey. Men are the worst when they're hurt or sick and the only way to deal with them is to get a little bossy." Rosie's face softened as she smiled. "My only child might be a girl, but I raised four Kowalski boys along with their sister. Trust me on that one."

"You worked for their mom?" Laney prompted, trying to remember the little bits her cousin had told her.

"I did. She let me bring my Katie with me, so it was perfect. Then she died suddenly back in eighty-seven. An aneurysm. I stayed on and did the best I could to help Frank take care of them. He passed away in 2002. The kids were all scattered around, so it was Josh and I for years, doing the best we could. A few years ago, he broke his leg and I called Mitch—the oldest—home to help out and when he saw how run-down things had gotten, they all came together. Mitch and Liz are both back in Whitford. Ryan's in Brookline, Mass, and Sean lives in New Hampshire. You'll get to meet them all."

Laney's head was spinning, so all she did was smile and nod. There was a lot of family history here on top of the town being a very small, tightly knit community. Her plan was to smile and nod *a lot* and keep her mouth shut.

"Let me give you that tour," Rosie said. "And don't worry about remembering everything right off. We keep things pretty simple and I'm not going anywhere."

The rooms for guests were all in one wing, which had been added to the original house years before, though they were free to make themselves at home on the ground floor of the lodge. The exception was a room off the living room, at the opposite end from the guest wing. A very polite *keep out* sign hung on the closed door, and Rosie told her that was Josh and Katie's room.

Upstairs was Andy and Rosie's room, an office, and a couple of bedrooms used by visiting family. Downstairs, in the basement, were shelves of supplies and the commercial washer and dryer. As far as the kitchen, that was Rosie's domain. She liked to bake for the guests, but there was no expectation Laney would cook, since meals weren't part of the package.

"I know it seems like a lot, between the lodge and the campground," Rosie said when they were back in the kitchen. "But we're not just throwing you in the deep end. We're all here, so you're not alone."

There was something warm and maternal about the woman that made Laney feel as if she could be honest with her. "I wouldn't have come here if I wasn't willing to do the work, but somehow I feel like the hardest part of my job is going to be making you let me do it."

"It might be. I've been taking care of this place for a very long time." Rosie smiled, her eyes crinkling at the corners. "But I had a couple of bouts with pneumonia several years ago and now I have Andy, so I *might* be ready to slow down a little."

Before Laney could reply, the kitchen door opened and a woman around her age with a blond ponytail pulled through a battered Red Sox cap walked in. She was visibly expecting and besides the fact she resembled Rosie, she knew Katie—Rosie's daughter and Josh's wife—was six months pregnant. And she wasn't around all the time because she owned the barbershop in town, which had been her dad's before he died.

After introductions were made, Katie grabbed a cookie from the jar on the counter. "I'm glad you're here, Laney. I assume you were warned my mom can be stubborn?"

She laughed. "Andy warned me she might try to get me to sit and eat cookies and drink lemonade while she does the work, but I can be pretty stubborn, too."

Katie had her mother's smile, and Laney was once again struck by how lucky she had been to find herself in this place. She liked these people, and they seemed to like her. That was already more than she'd had going for her the last few years.

By the end of the season, she was going to be happier, stronger and ready to go make a new life for herself.

THREE

THE NEXT MORNING, Ben woke feeling groggy and not well rested. He wasn't sure why—and he couldn't remember anything he'd dreamed about—because if there was one thing he'd mastered over the course of his life as a first responder, it was sleeping well when it was time to sleep.

After throwing back the sheet, he sat on the edge of the bed and scrubbed his hands over his face. Then he swore a blue streak and looked at the cut on his hand. After cleaning it again, he'd decided to leave it uncovered because what kind of damage could he really do to it in bed?

Apparently, the rubbing it over a bristly jaw kind of damage.

A glance at his clock told him he could make it to Sunday breakfast if he hurried. Despite the rough night, he made quick work of his morning routine and threw on some sweats and a T-shirt. His mother's breakfasts were worth the effort.

At five minutes before nine, he jogged down the stairs that led to where his SUV was parked in the driveway. Then he crossed behind his dad's work van and his mom's smaller SUV to get to their back door.

When his parents had expanded the garage, making it a little deeper and adding a second bay, they'd also turned the space over it into a studio apartment for

Ben's younger brother. Jimmy had done his time at a trade school and then returned to Whitford to work for their dad's plumbing business, turning Rivers Plumbing from a one-man to a two-man show. Because nobody was ever going to get rich being a plumber in Whitford, Jimmy had been happy to live over their parents' garage. His wife, Chelsea, had been happy to live there, too, until she'd gotten pregnant and they'd rented a house of their own. For three years it had been occupied by a friend of his dad's until he decided to move south to warmer pastures.

As luck would have it, the apartment was empty when Ben got the call offering him the job. It was close to the fire station, the rent was cheap and he already knew he liked the landlords, so he didn't bother looking for anything else. At some point he probably would, since living with his parents wasn't one of his long-term goals, whether he had his own entrance or not.

But right now, with the scent of coffee and bacon greeting him as he stepped into his mom's kitchen, it didn't seem like a high priority.

"Morning, son," his dad said, smiling at him from the stove.

"Morning." His mom was buttering toast, and he kissed her cheek. "What can I do?"

"Refill our coffees and pour one for yourself, please."

Ben dumped the cold remains from their mugs and rinsed them before grabbing the carafe. His dad at the stove meant scrambled eggs made with more than the average amount of black pepper and American cheese melted on top. And thick, toasted slabs of his mom's homemade wheat bread and crispy bacon to go with it.

Definitely worth rushing.

"I was going to call you," his mom said, "to see if you were coming down, but I'm always afraid I'll wake you up when you've just gone to sleep because of a call."

"I'd have to be some kind of exhausted to turn down Sunday breakfast. And I told you before, if I'm really beat, I can set my phone to allow the dispatcher and the fire and police stations to call me, but silence everything else. You can call or text me anytime and if I really need the sleep, I'll get back to you when I wake up."

"Maybe someday I'll listen," she said.

"Don't hold your breath," his dad said, following the words with a wink at his wife.

She laughed and waved a hand at the table. "Funny. You two sit down and get out of the way so I can dish this up while it's hot."

Thirty-nine years, Ben thought as he obeyed, sitting in the same spot he'd been sitting in since they moved into this house the year he turned twelve. If he was thirty-eight, they'd been married thirty-nine years now and it would be forty years in September, since their anniversary was the same day as their birthdays.

Alan and May Rivers had first met when their respective friends had thrown them parties at the same roller rink. Sharing the same birthday had been an icebreaker and they both claimed it had been love at first sight. He proposed on their next birthday and they were married the birthday after that. The rest of the family had expressed some teasing disappointment their first child hadn't been born on August 20th, but Ben was more than happy to let his parents keep that spotlight on themselves.

They'd both be turning sixty later this summer, which made Ben wonder if they should have some kind of a party. Sixtieth birthdays. Fortieth wedding anniversary. It seemed like a celebration of some sort was in order. Not a big bash like they'd—God willing—be having in another ten years, but forty years together was an achievement worth a cake, at least.

As he dug into his breakfast, he wondered if he'd missed his chance for a fortieth anniversary cake. Since he wasn't even dating at the moment, he'd be at least forty before he got to the altar, which meant he was looking at being eighty for that milestone. Doable, maybe, based on his family tree, but he was going to have to start making space in his life for a relationship.

"Got anything planned for today?" his dad asked when they'd finished eating.

The question sounded deceptively casual to Ben's ears and he suspected he was going to get wrangled into helping his dad with some random project from his mom's "honey-do" list. And, while he didn't mind working alongside his dad, he wasn't committing to anything without some idea of what she was getting them into.

"I've got a few things to square away at the station today, but that's about the only thing." It wasn't really a lie, but the amount of things he had to square away and the amount of time it would take would depend on the alternative. "How about you?"

"Thinking about stripping the asphalt shingles off the old shed out back and replacing it with metal roofing. Had some leaks over the winter and it'll be a good practice run since we've only got another few years in this house roof."

"I can give you a hand today and stop by the station later in the afternoon." That kind of manual labor, Ben didn't mind. But the first weekend he'd been back, he'd gotten suckered into snaking a clogged drain for his mom's widowed friend because Jimmy was busy and he'd spent hours fighting his gag reflex. There was a reason Jimmy became a plumber and Ben was a paramedic. Blood he could handle. The black slimy stuff that lived in clogged drains, not so much.

"You have a cut on your hand," his mom pointed out. "Make sure you put a padded bandage on it and wear good leather gloves over it."

Under the sweet maternal concern was an edge of command that made him think of Laney and smile. She'd been cute as hell bossing him around yesterday, and he felt bad she'd been embarrassed to find out he was a paramedic. He hadn't really been hiding it, but he probably should have mentioned it when she accused him of waiting for her to turn her back so he could spit on his open wound.

"What's making you smile like that?" his dad asked before giving him an arched eyebrow look over the rim of his coffee mug, as if he thought Ben might be smirking at his mother's concern for him.

"I was just thinking about the woman I met yesterday. She helped me clean the cut, that's all."

"Really?" His mother didn't even bother to hide her piqued interest and he wondered just what kind of smile he'd had on his face—the amused kind or the sappy, slightly goofy kind. "Where did you meet her?"

"At the Northern Star. I guess they hired her to help out around the place and she'll be living in a camper on the property…or something." He added the last part just to make it sound like he didn't know too much about her.

"Oh, her name's Laney, right?" his mom asked, and then continued without pausing to give him time to answer. "We haven't met her yet, but it's been all over town that Josh hired somebody to take some of the workload off of Rosie. She's been taking care of that lodge—and the family—for so long, I'm not sure how she's going to take having somebody else doing any of the work."

"I'm sure Rosie will get used to not having to make beds or scrub toilets pretty quickly," his dad said, and Ben nodded his agreement.

"Well, maybe," his mom said. "Women tend to like things a certain way, you know."

"We know," they said together, earning them each a withering glance from her before she gave in and laughed.

"How old is she?" his mom asked, dashing his hope she'd move on to a new subject. "She must be single if she can live in a camper for the summer, right? What does she look like?"

With both of his parents looking at him expectantly, Ben almost didn't dare open his mouth. What did she look like? She had blue eyes that really stood out when her cheeks were pink with embarrassment. Her hair was long and he wanted to run his hands through it and see if it was as soft as it looked. She was pretty and she was funny and, though he wasn't absolutely sure, he had to agree with his mom that Laney was most likely single.

"She's pretty, I guess. About my age. I have no idea if she's single or not. I didn't talk to her very long."

He stood and carried his plate to the counter while his mom made a vaguely disappointed sound. Maybe he'd run into Laney again and get to know her better, or maybe he wouldn't. But he knew from growing up in Whitford that he did *not* want his mother or any other woman in town involved in it.

But as she shooed them out of the kitchen so they could get to work on the shed roof—and let her watch shows she streamed on her tablet while she took longer than necessary to clean the kitchen—Ben admitted to himself he wouldn't mind running into Laney again.

And since she'd be living on the Northern Star property for the summer, he wouldn't have to try very hard to make it happen.

ROSIE HAD WARNED Laney that Sundays had a tendency to get interesting around the Northern Star. Technically checkout time was at eleven, but some campers left at the crack of dawn to avoid traffic, some stayed until eleven and a few would even stay later. And if they asked up front, Josh would allow campers to pack up and park their trucks and campers along the edge of the field—out of their way—and then ride for the day, if they wanted.

It was a lot, Laney thought, as she waved goodbye to the next-to-the-last of their departing campers—a family of four who'd had some trouble packing things back into their SUV the same way it had all come out. It was almost noon, but they'd been very apologetic, so she'd told them to take their time. She'd already picked up on the cardinal rule of the campground—if you were good people, the rules were fluid. If you weren't, the rules got a lot more strict and included a late checkout fee. While Laney preferred things to be cut and dried rather than up to her discretion since she wasn't the boss, that wasn't how they did things here.

Now there was just one more cabin to be vacated and they'd have no guests until Friday. The week after would see the end of the school year for most of New England's schools and then they'd be busy all week, but it was still mostly weekend business at the beginning of June.

She was about to go and check on the couple in the cabin, but then she heard him yelling something and decided to give them a few more minutes.

"Laney!" She turned to see her cousin, Nola Kendrick, walking toward her.

Laney smiled, relieved to have an excuse not to think about the grumpy guest in the cabin for a few minutes. "Hey, Nola."

"Are you busy right now? I thought everybody might be gone and we could sneak a quick lunch together. Most places have checkout at eleven."

"We have a couple on their way out of the cabin, but I'm giving them a little extra time because he seems to be having a bad time of it." And she was definitely hungry. "I can grab a quick lunch, though I'm not sure what I have."

"I brought turkey sandwiches from the diner." She lifted the bag Laney hadn't paid any attention to. "On wheat bread with mayo and cranberry sauce, like we used to eat when we were little."

The shared memory warmed Laney's heart and made her feel less alone than she had in a long time. Born the same year, Laney and Nola had been as close as cousins who only saw each other once or twice a year could be. Nola's mom, who was Laney's mother's sister, had met her future husband at a concert in Old Orchard Beach and run off to someplace in Maine none of them had ever heard of to marry him. Their visits to Rhode Island had been somewhat regular until Laney's grandmother died and then they'd dwindled away. Luckily, Facebook had eventually come along and Laney and Nola had reconnected.

Maybe Nola was part of the reason she'd taken a chance on this job, Laney thought as they walked toward her camper. She not only got to earn money while living the simple kind of life she wanted, but she could spend time with somebody who'd known and loved the younger version of Laney Caswell.

Once she'd grabbed them each a cold drink from inside, they sat in her folding camp chairs in the shade of her awning to eat.

"I ordered two Adirondack chair kits online," Laney said. "Hopefully they'll be delivered soon and I can build them before your next visit, so we'll be more comfortable."

"I'm sure you could have borrowed a truck if you wanted to go buy a couple of chairs."

"I know, but they're a lot cheaper if you build them yourself. And it'll be a fun project for me." She took a bite of the sandwich, and then chewed slowly to savor the taste. Once she'd swallowed, she looked at her cousin. "This is even better than when we were kids."

"The diner has the best food. Seriously, everything they make is delicious."

Laney knew the Trailside Diner was owned by Paige Kowalski, Josh's sister-in-law. She'd bought the place some years back, when the town only saw snowmobile business, and the diner was one of the many businesses benefitting from the ATV traffic. Mitch and Paige had a two-year-old daughter, plus Rosie had mentioned Paige was seven months along with their second child.

"How are things going here? Do you like it?"

"So far, so good. Everybody's nice and the work isn't too much." Laney rolled her eyes. "I should have had you write up notes on everybody in town, though, so I wouldn't have looked like an idiot fussing over a cut on Ben Rivers's hand because I didn't know he's a paramedic."

Nola's eyes widened. "You met Ben? And fussed over him?"

"I didn't fuss over *him.* Just the cut on his hand. Entirely different."

"I had such a crush on him when I was in the ninth grade. He was a junior and had no idea I was alive, of course. But he's been in the town hall a few times and I swear, he's even hotter now than he was then."

"You should ask him out," Laney said, thinking that was the perfect solution for any budding attraction she felt for the man. If her cousin was interested in him, he was totally off-limits to her.

"Nope. I mean, he's a great guy and he's not hard to look at, but there isn't any real spark. He's not making up reasons to come into town hall to see me and I'm not taking my time doing whatever he needs just to keep him there, if you know what I mean."

"That's too bad."

"I could set you two up on a date, though," Nola said, looking only too happy about it.

"No." Laney didn't even hesitate. "I'm not dating. And please spare me the *get back in the saddle* speech.

I want to enjoy my own company for a while, just me and books and movies and my little camper."

"Fine." Nola gave an exaggerated sigh of disappointment. "Speaking of the camper, is that going okay? I remember seeing a picture of your house on Facebook and there isn't even a house like that in Whitford, never mind a camper. I hope you weren't expecting one of those big fifth-wheel models with the master bedroom suites and a fireplace."

"It *is* small, but I like it." She laughed at Nola's skeptical look. "No, really I do. I've had a lot of expensive things in the last ten years and they didn't really mean anything to me. Now I'm limited to things that really matter to me and being limited space-wise means I have to think about what's important and what's not."

"I was so afraid you'd get here and wonder what the heck I'd gotten you into."

"I'm happy I'm here. I promise. I mean, I have no idea what will happen at the end of the season, but I'm enjoying right now and I'm glad to have the time with you."

Nola smiled, her honey-blond bob swishing around her neck as she nodded. "Me too. But keep in mind, the Northern Star is open year-round. The lodge anyway, for the snowmobilers."

Before Laney could point out that she wasn't spending the winter in a camper and she wasn't sure Whitford was where she would put down actual real estate-type roots, there was a loud crash from the direction of the cabins and then a woman screamed.

SAM JENSEN, WHO headed up Whitford's extremely small volunteer fire department, was stretched out on the couch behind the engine, watching a sports talk show on the screen hung on the opposite wall when Ben walked in.

"Do you actually *have* a home?" he asked when Sam turned his head to look at him.

"Yup."

"Seems like a waste of money since you're here whenever I show up, no matter when it is."

Sam shrugged. "I'm the only one who doesn't have a wife and kids, so why make one of the other guys sit here and watch TV alone. It doesn't matter to me which couch I park my ass on. And what are you doing here, anyway?"

"I helped my dad strip some roofing this morning, but I needed a break." He held up his hand, which he'd left uncovered after giving it another cleaning. The cut wasn't pretty, but it seemed to be healing okay.

"Ouch. And on the right palm, too. Bet that's hell on your sex life."

"I hope you're better at fighting fires than you are at comedy."

"Luckily we don't have too many of those around here. Help yourself to something from the fridge if you want."

The fire station still blew Ben's mind, even though it had been weeks. It was a rectangle, with the front two-thirds taken up by the engine and the utility truck, and the back third reserved for an equipment locker, two couches and a TV, a sad excuse for a kitchenette area and a bathroom. The only way it could be further removed from the city stations he was used to would be for them to park the trucks in somebody's backyard under a carport.

"I can't believe this town doesn't have a real ambulance," Ben said as he unscrewed the top off a bottle of lemonade with his left hand and settled onto the other couch.

Sam shrugged. "A lot of small towns out on back roads don't. It takes so long for an ambulance to get here and then get back to the hospital that people are used to throwing people in their cars or trucks and driving like hell. I know it's wrong and it's dangerous, but it *is* faster. And those people, who've been handling emergencies a certain way for generations, are the ones who vote on the town budget."

"So they'll approve an ATV with lights and sirens for me and a UTV with a rescue sled for the fire department to take out into the woods, but not an ambulance for their families."

"Honestly, most of the money for you and the incredibly long list of crap you need to do your job came from Max researching and writing the hell out of grant requests."

Ben had met Max Crawford a few times and he seemed like a decent guy. He was a little awkward with strangers, but he liked to talk sports, so they didn't have any trouble making conversation. He worked out of his basement and there were some rumors he was a serial killer, but Ben thought the rumors that he painted brass locomotives and stuff for model railroaders were more credible. Most importantly, Max didn't ride off-road at all, but he liked doing his part for his friends and the town, so he handled all the paperwork and that made him everybody's best friend.

"That UTV they got you guys is going to come in handy," Ben said.

"Yeah. I don't know how Max scored *that* donation from the manufacturer, but we owe him big-time."

For years, the standard way to extract a victim from the trails had been a four-wheeler towing a rescue sled on wheels. After placing the victim on a backboard, he or she had to be secured in the sled and then one of the first responders had to perch on the side of it and hope they didn't hit any big bumps. The new UTV was a four-seater with a utility back, but it had been modified so the right half of the backseat and dump body were replaced with a sled. It was still a bumpy, painful ride out for the injured, but it was safer for them *and* the first responders, especially the one who could sit next to the victim in the backseat instead of trying not to fall off the side of the sled.

Max had scored Ben a utility ATV with a light, sirens and cargo boxes that stored the most vital of emergency supplies. Because he was an experienced rider and didn't have to wait for other volunteers to arrive, he could go like hell through the woods and offer critical care until the other guys showed up.

"You miss the city much?" Sam asked.

Ben considered the question for a moment, then shook his head. "Not really. Other than the fact Whitford's seriously lacking in sports bars, it was a good change for me. A little weird not having set shifts and just...being on call 24/7, but it's good."

"If you need time off, just give me the heads-up and between us and the warden service, we can cover things. And you're pretty safe making plans for Tuesdays and Wednesdays, as a rule."

"Yeah, I figure Friday afternoons and Saturdays will be my busiest times. Except for holiday weekends, most people are just packing up and heading home on Sundays."

No sooner had he said the words than the alarm sounded and their cell phones rang at almost the same time. Leaving Sam to communicate with dispatch and go from there, Ben answered the call from Josh as he ran to his SUV. It wasn't marked, but it had lights and sirens and was fully outfitted for almost any emergency.

"Here at the lodge," Josh said as soon as he answered. "The cabins, actually. Guy was loading his wheeler and rolled it over backward on himself."

"Don't move him." He turned on the siren and hit the gas.

"Laney's got his head braced so he can't move. He lost consciousness for at least a minute. He's somewhat coherent, but having trouble breathing."

Ben listened to the voices on his radio as he gave instructions to Josh that amounted to keeping him immobilized and as long as he was breathing, not to touch anything.

"They've dispatched an ambulance, but I'm almost there. Sit tight."

God only knew how long the private ambulance service from a few towns away would take to get there, Ben fumed as he drove. At least twenty minutes and, unless the victim's injuries were severe enough to merit a helicopter, the hospital was an hour away. And if he'd suffered head or spinal trauma, there was a good chance the ER docs would only stabilize him before transporting him to Maine Med for treatment.

He turned up the drive to the Northern Star Lodge and drove past the house and out back to the campground. After killing the siren, he pulled up near the people gathered—he could see Josh, Andy and Rosie with an upset woman, with two people on the ground—and shut off his engine. Then he hit the button to open the lift gate so it was open by the time he got to the back of the SUV. After grabbing his bag and a cervical collar, he walked to the man lying in the dirt.

Laney was kneeling above the victim's head, her fingers laced under his neck and his head gripped between her knees. She looked up as Ben crouched beside her and they made eye contact. She was calm and ready to follow any instructions he gave her, so he got to work.

He'd wait for the ambulance crew before attempting the backboard, but he needed to stabilize the head and neck.

Slowly and carefully, he slipped the C-collar around the victim's neck. Laney pulled her hands out of the way, but kept her knees on either side of his head until Ben let her know she could get up.

After checking his pulse, Ben looked down into the man's face. "What's your name?"

"His name's Corey," the woman said, and Ben had to stifle a sigh. That wasn't really helpful.

"Corey, can you tell me how old you are?"

"Twenty-eight."

"Good, and do you know where you are?"

"Maine."

The Connecticut plates on the truck let Ben know Corey had a basic awareness of where he was, though he would have liked more specifics. "Tell me what's going on. How's your breathing?"

"A little better, I think. Maybe I just had the wind knocked out of me."

"What about pain?" He checked Corey's pupils and did a visual inspection of his extremities. Then he took shears out of his bag and sliced his T-shirt up the front so he could look at his torso. There was some bruising already showing on his right shoulder, but his chest and abdomen didn't look bad.

There was no obvious trauma, but the head, spine and internal organs were the real problem in this kind of accident. It's what he couldn't see that concerned him.

"I feel like an ATV fell on top of me."

Ben smiled, encouraged by the attempt at humor, as he slid the blood pressure cuff onto Corey's arm. "I guess I don't need to ask if you remember what happened, but why don't you give me a little more detail."

As Corey started listing off places that hurt in varying degrees, Ben relaxed a little. Considering the size of the quad Josh had righted and pushed out of the way, it started to look like today was Corey's lucky day.

"I'll feel it tomorrow, for sure," Corey said, "but I don't think anything's busted. I could probably sit up."

"You lost consciousness, which is always a concern, so we're going to hang out just like we are until the ambulance comes. We'll get you on a backboard as a precaution and after the doctors have looked you over and done some scans, they'll tell you when you can sit up."

They heard a siren in the distance and Corey's wife, who'd calmed down a lot, seemed to grow agitated again. "Is that the ambulance? Will they let me ride with him? What about the truck and our stuff?"

"That's not the ambulance yet," Ben told her. "That'll be the guys from the fire department, just in case I needed help."

He probably should have called in and let them know not to come, but he'd been busy and hadn't thought of it. They'd brought the utility truck, rather than the engine, and he saw that Sam was driving as they pulled up next to his SUV. The guy riding shotgun was Dave Moody, who'd served as the EMT for the Whitford Fire Department for years but, because it was a volunteer position, had never invested the time and money into becoming a paramedic. He was over fifty and had no interest in off-roading so that—besides the fact Ben was qualified to offer more critical care than an EMT—was a big reason they'd decided to add his position.

"You can ride in the ambulance or you can drive the truck," Josh was saying to Corey's wife. "As long as you're calm and feel up to it, since the hospital's almost an hour away. If you want to go in the ambulance, we can make arrangements to get the truck to you sometime later today. As for your stuff, it's fine here. We won't throw it—or you—out in the street just because it's past checkout time."

She smiled, but her husband groaned. "I was rushing because we were late checking out. The tires slipped and it pissed me off, so I hit the throttle. But I didn't take the time to put a strap on the ramps, so they kicked out and the damn thing came over backwards on me."

"You're not the first person to do that," Andy told him. "You got lucky, though. It could have been a lot worse."

"Sit tight," Ben told Corey before standing up and walking over to Sam and Dave. "I probably should have called in and canceled your response, but you were already on the road by the time I knew I didn't need help, anyway."

Sam shrugged. "I was watching a repeat of a repeat of a sports talk show, so it's all good."

When they went over to introduce themselves to Corey and talk to the others, Ben stretched his back and watched as Laney said a few words to Rosie before walking toward him.

"Thank you for keeping his head still until I could get a collar on him," he said when she was close enough so he could speak to her without raising her voice.

She stopped, giving him a little smile. "That's more or less all I know how to do in an emergency. Don't let them move their necks."

"Or spit on open wounds." When she laughed, he saw everybody turn to look at them—except Corey, of course—but he didn't care. She had a great laugh. "But seriously, you did great."

"Thanks. I really hope this doesn't happen a lot. It was terrifying to be honest, and I was just going to my camper to get some water."

He looked over his shoulder at the small camper that sat slightly apart from the other sites. "The one with the flamingo?"

When she looked at the wooden flamingo, she smiled and then looked at him. "Yes, that's mine. I know it's silly and I spent too much on it, but it was the first thing I bought for myself after my divorce."

"Do you always smile like that when you look at it?"

Laney looked back at the flamingo and once again, her lips curved into a smile. "I guess I do."

"Then it was worth every penny you paid for it."

Her eyes softened and her lips parted, but whatever she'd been about to say was lost when they heard a siren wailing in the distance and getting closer.

"I guess you should get back to Corey," she said.

"Yeah."

She walked by him and only the fact there was a group of people watching him kept Ben from turning and watching *her* as she walked away.

FOUR

THE FOLLOWING EVENING, Laney sat cross-legged on the ground with pieces of Adirondack chairs in front of her, a very poorly drawn instruction sheet in her lap and brand-new tools on the grass next to her.

A little after noontime, Rosie had asked her if she'd mind doing errands for her now and then, which of course she didn't. Today she'd needed a few things from Whitford Hardware, so Laney had taken her almost-new Camaro—one of the few material possessions she'd fought for in the divorce—and headed into town.

In addition to the odds and ends on Rosie's list, she'd bought herself a small toolbox that seemed to have the basic necessities and would fit in the tiny cabinet under the sink in her camper. She'd also learned that Dozer, who owned the hardware store, was the father of Lauren Kowalski, who was married to Ryan—the brother who was a builder and lived in Brookline, Massachusetts.

She was going to ask Rosie for one of her many notepads and literally start a list so she could keep track of who was who. Navigating Whitford was turning out to be a Six Degrees of the Kowalskis game.

Then he asked how their guest had made out after his accident, and it helped cement in Laney's mind just how small a town she was living in. She'd heard the jokes about small-town grapevines, of course. She just hadn't realized how true they really were.

"His scans were clear, so they gave him some pain meds and let him go. Josh let them stay in the lodge overnight at no charge, and then he and Josh finished loading up their stuff so they hit the road this morning. With his wife driving, of course," she'd told him.

Now she had some free time, so it was time to put together the two chair kits she'd found propped against the side of her camper with a note from Andy. *Holler if you want help.*

It was sweet, but she was determined she'd put these chairs together all by herself. Maybe it was silly and stubborn of her, but she'd stayed in an unhappy marriage for far too long because she was afraid she couldn't make it on her own. Now she was going to prove she could and if there was something she couldn't do for herself, she'd do without it.

Putting together two chairs the same bright pink as her flamingo couldn't be that hard, she'd told herself. Of course, she'd underestimated the weight of the slats and how hard it would be to hold them in place while trying to tighten a nut on a bolt.

Two hours later, one was done, she had the base of the second chair together and was working on the back when she heard a vehicle pull up to the lodge and stop. She couldn't see it through the line of trees that separated the house from the camping area, but she knew they weren't expecting any guests, so it was probably a friend or family member stopping by to visit.

She was studying the instructions, wondering whether the person who'd done the sketches had been sober, when she heard a voice beside her. Looking up, she was surprised to see Ben standing there and her pulse quickened. He sure did spend a lot more time at the Northern Star than she'd expected.

"Hi," she said when she realized she'd been staring up at him for a few seconds too long.

"Hi. So I stopped in at the town hall to drop off the monthly log because they track statistics to include in the annual town report and—okay, that's all boring. The bottom line, I mentioned I was coming out here to look over some aerial maps because we think there are some places we could talk landowners to grant me emergency access even though they don't want the actual trails to cross their land and… I guess that wasn't the bottom line. I'm rambling."

"No, you're not." The tips of his ears were pink and she was fascinated by how adorable it was. "You're talking to me and yes, I find it interesting."

"Oh, okay. We're trying to find a few places I can use as shortcuts to cut down on my response time to some of the out-there spots on the trail system, and I mentioned that to Nola because she always asks how things are going, and when I said I was coming here, she asked me to bring you this."

He handed her a sealed envelope, and then walked around the back of the partial chair. "Quite a project you've got here."

"I probably should have taken a nap after the first one." She peeled the flap off the envelope and pulled out a folded paper.

Inside was a short, handwritten note. *I think you should go for it.*

All of a sudden, her cheeks felt warm and she wanted to hide the words against her chest or crumple the paper so there was no chance Ben could read it, even though he'd probably have no idea what her cousin meant by it. Instead she refolded the paper and slid it back into the envelope. Then she pressed the flap down the best she could before lifting the toolbox and sliding it underneath.

"Everything okay?" he asked.

"Yeah." She looked up at him, her mind flailing for some reasonable explanation why Nola would ask him to deliver something to her. "Just some information I needed about getting a Maine driver's license and plates for my car and…stuff."

Please don't ask me why she didn't just call or text the information, she thought as soon as the words left her mouth.

"Cool. Do you need some help with this chair?"

"No, thank you. I've got it."

"Want some company?"

"Sure." She wondered if he'd make it five minutes before he leaned in and tried to tighten a bolt for her before just building the rest of it himself. "Want a drink?"

He held up an insulated tumbler as he sat in her folding camp chair, shaking it so the ice rattled. "I have one, thanks. Do you need a fresh one?"

Laney kept her face down, looking at the instruction sheet, so he wouldn't see her smile. He was so polite, but she didn't want to imagine him in her camper. He wasn't as tall as Josh, but he had broad shoulders and she could picture him filling the space. If they were both in there, they'd brush against each other trying to get by…and her imagination needed to change the subject before she started blushing again.

"No thanks," she said. "I'm good."

"Okay. Yesterday's accident aside, how are you liking the Northern Star? And Whitford in general, I guess."

"I haven't seen too much of Whitford yet. The market and gas station, and the hardware store. And obviously I'll be going to the town hall soon."

"You haven't eaten at the Trailside Diner yet?"

"No, but Nola brought me a sandwich from there yesterday. Right before the accident. It was really good."

"Their dinner menu is even better."

Was he working his way around to asking her out to dinner? It had been so long since she'd dated, she wasn't sure if she was reading too much into a friendly conversation. But it seemed her next line would naturally be *I'll have to try it sometime* and then he'd say *"how about tomorrow night?"* or something like that.

And she had no idea how she felt about that.

BEN WASN'T SURE what to make of Laney. There was something open and friendly about her that made him want to talk to her, which was why he was sitting in the shade of her awning right now. But at the same time she seemed to keep a part of herself walled off—the part that had her refusing help with the chair and tensing up at the mention of having dinner at the Trailside Diner.

All he really *knew* about her was that she was Nola Kendrick's cousin, she stayed calm in emergencies and she really liked flamingo pink.

But he thought maybe she'd come to Whitford, Maine because she'd been unhappy where she was. And if it had been a guy who'd made her unhappy, that might explain why his talking about dinner at the diner made her lips press together and her grip on the papers in her lap tighten.

She thought he was going to ask her out and that wasn't a look of interest or anticipation. That was more of an *oh, crap* look, which was never the reaction he was looking for when he asked a woman to have dinner with him. If that's even where the conversation had been heading, since he hadn't come over here intending to ask her out. But when he'd replayed the conversation in his head, trying to identify the source of her tension, it had sounded like it. And he certainly wouldn't mind spending an evening in her company, but she clearly wasn't ready for that.

"If you go there, make sure you check out the specials board," he said, hoping to put her mind at ease. "You'd be surprised by some of the good stuff they come up with."

It worked, proving his theory. Her jaw relaxed and she looked up at him, making eye contact. "I'll keep that in mind."

She picked up one of the slats that made up the back of the chair and put it in place. Then, after putting a bolt through it, she reached for the socket wrench. The board slipped and the bolt fell out. After wiping her forehead with the back of her hand, she lined them up again. Then, while holding the bolt with the socket wrench, she had to tighten the nut with a crescent wrench.

It was killing him to watch, but he took a sip of his lemonade and pretended he was interested in watching the leaves on the distant trees swaying in the light breeze. It not only kept him from interfering, but it kept him from staring at her long, tanned legs in her cutoff denim shorts, too.

"Okay, maybe I could use a *little* help."

Yes. He got out of the chair and sat in the grass across from her. "Tell me what you need me to do."

"I can't hold the boards in place and tighten the bolts, so if you could just hold them for me, that would be great."

She was giving him the easier part of the job and it was on the tip of his tongue to point out it would be faster and smarter for him to run the socket wrench. But for whatever reason, putting these chairs together herself was important to her, so he kept his mouth shut and did what he was told.

"I know it would be easier if you were doing this part," she said when they'd put on a second slat. "You're a pretty patient guy, and I appreciate it."

"They're your chairs. We'll build them however you want." He was going to let it go at that, he wanted to know more about this woman. "It seems important to you. That you do it yourself, I mean."

"My divorce was finalized a few months ago and it was a long process after a long marriage, and I realized I'd spent so many years trying to make other people happy, I really didn't know how to live my *own* life anymore. Or what I even want my life to look like. So now I'm here, doing things myself." She took a deep breath, and it sounded shaky to him. "It sounds silly when I say it out loud."

"It's not silly."

"When I was young, I was independent and confident and… I don't know. I guess I spent so many years shushing her that she disappeared. I want to find her again."

"I don't think you'll have to look very hard." When she looked at him, he smiled. Then he held up his hand so the cut on his palm faced her. "I've already met her."

She blushed, but she didn't drop her head and, after a few seconds, she laughed. "Later on I kicked myself for being so bossy, though."

"Don't. And it wasn't just the forced first aid, you know. Josh told me you weren't shy about handling the situation when the guy flipped his ATV, either. You *are* a strong, confident woman and no amount of shushing will change that."

"My ex-husband never saw it."

"Probably because he wasn't a strong, confident *man*." Ben shrugged. "Also, he's an idiot."

"I agree." She grinned as she picked up the socket wrench. "Luckily, he's also in my rearview mirror."

"So you guys didn't have any children?"

She looked down at her lap, fiddling with the socket. "No, which I guess is a blessing."

He tilted his head sideways so he could see her face. "I hope you'll forgive me for being personal, but you don't look like you think it's a blessing."

"It *is* definitely a blessing," she said, lifting her chin. "Having that connection to my ex and his family for the rest of my life would have been miserable. It's just a painful topic because I spent ten years being criticized for not giving him children."

"I'm sorry. I shouldn't have gone there."

"No, it's okay." She smiled and he was relieved it didn't look forced. "I saw all the doctors. Had all the tests. Nothing medical turned up."

"And his tests?"

"He didn't have any because there's no way *he* had a problem."

"Ah. One of those guys." Ben shook his head, fighting back an irrational anger on her behalf. "That must have sucked for you."

"It did, for a long time. But looking back, I'm glad we didn't have children because I might never have left." After lining up another slat so he could hold it, she put a bolt through and started the nut by hand. "So how come *you* don't have any kids? Assuming you don't. I guess I should have asked that first."

"I don't have any and it's my own fault, I guess. I focused on working hard and playing harder because there would be plenty of time later to have kids. Women moved on to guys who were ready to settle down, but that was okay. There would be plenty of time, right?" He shrugged, a wry smile twisting his mouth. "Now I'm thirty-eight years old, alone and wondering where the hell the time went."

"And I'm thirty-five and starting all over so I'd like to think you're right and there's still plenty of time."

"At least you have great chairs," he said as she tightened the last bolt.

"We're finally done?" She pushed herself to her feet, wiping grass off the back of her shorts.

He nodded, even though he wanted to take the wrenches from her and give each of the nuts an extra twist to make sure they were tight. "They definitely brighten up the place. I like them."

She grinned, her hands on her hips as she looked at them. "Thank you. I'll be able to sit and read and still keep an eye on the pool area."

His cell phone vibrated and he pulled it out of its holster to read the text. "Josh is wondering if I got lost between the driveway and the house."

"I totally forgot you were supposed to be looking at maps with him."

"So did I." And he didn't care in the least.

"I…do you think, before you go, you could just tighten the bolts a little more for me?"

Nothing would make him happier. "Sure."

He took the tools and made quick work of tightening the bolts. She'd done great, but it would make him feel better knowing they were snug. When he was done, he handed the tools back. "All set. Barely took any, really."

"Thank you for your help. It was nice to have company."

"Anytime. I'll see you around, I'm sure."

Ben practically had to force himself to walk back to the lodge. He'd lost interest in looking at aerial maps tonight. What he really wanted to do was sit in the pink chairs with Laney and continue their conversation while enjoying the night air.

ON WEDNESDAY EVENING, Laney tossed the empty plastic bowl from her microwaved dinner and got ready to walk to the lodge. It wasn't the most satisfying meal she'd ever had, but she'd been too tired to cook something and, despite invitations from Rosie, Andy, Josh and Katie, she wasn't comfortable joining them for their family dinners in the house.

She'd already learned that family was everything at the Northern Star and she respected that, but she was here to work. They were her employers, not her family, and it was best for her if she didn't blur that line.

And she'd had her fill of families in the last few years. Her family, other than Nola. Her in-laws.

She'd been surprised when Josh invited her to the monthly meeting of the Northern Star ATV Club tonight, which was her reason for going to the house. She'd never even ridden one, but he'd explained it was a good idea for her to know what was going on since she would spend a lot of time interacting with campers who *did* ride. And some of what they would cover tonight would be relevant to her.

Ben's SUV was in the parking area, along with a half-dozen or so other vehicles, and she cursed the jolt of anticipation she couldn't deny she was feeling. She wanted to see him again.

Every time she looked at her pink Adirondack chairs, she thought of Ben. His face was more expressive than he realized, and she knew how badly he'd wanted to take over the project. But he hadn't. He'd waited until she asked for help and then still kept quiet while she fumbled with the tools.

It had been sweet. And then, when she'd asked him to do a final tightening on the bolts, he hadn't looked smug or made a big deal of it.

He was also easy to talk to. Almost too easy, she thought. She'd come very close to asking him if he'd like to come back after his meeting with Josh and try out one of the chairs. But she hadn't for the same reason she'd panicked when he started talking about the diner.

She wasn't here to date. She had absolutely no interest in sharing her life with a man right now, even one as attractive and kind as Ben Rivers.

Of course that didn't stop her gaze from going directly to him when she walked into the living room, where she'd been told the meeting would be. The room was full, but Ben was leaning against the doorway to the dining room, his arms folded across his chest as he spoke to a man Laney didn't know.

Ben saw her and smiled, uncrossing his arms to wave to her. She waved back and then took a seat in one of the dining room chairs somebody had moved into the room. Looking around, she tried to guess who some of the visitors were.

The man talking to Ben looked enough like Josh that she guessed he was one of his older brothers, but it wasn't until a little girl ran up and hugged his leg that she figured out it was Mitch Kowalski. And the woman chasing the girl despite being even more pregnant than Katie had to be his wife, Paige.

Andy was handing a little boy over to a man in a Whitford PD T-shirt, so she knew that was Drew Miller, his son. Rosie had told her their grandson had just turned one. And she'd laughed as she told Laney she was a double-grammy to little Jackson because she was Drew's stepmother, but also because she'd practically raised Liz. After looking around the room, Laney spotted a woman with dark, curly hair and blue eyes who was talking to Rosie, but keeping a close eye on the baby. She guessed that was Liz Kowalski Miller.

Taking a deep breath to calm herself, Laney pulled up the app on her phone in which she kept various notes relating to the Northern Star. It had a photograph of the task list Rosie had written out. She also had a list of the inventory it was her job to keep track of, along with other miscellaneous notes. Starting a new one with *ATV Club Meeting* at the top helped with the feeling of being overwhelmed. Nobody expected her to memorize every person in the town and family right off the bat. It would take her a while to get to know everybody, and right now all she needed to do was take note of anything during the meeting that might be relevant to her job.

Finally, Josh called the meeting to order and everybody in the room quieted. They went through typical club business, like a treasurer's report and reading minutes from the last meeting. There was talk of trail maintenance and a landowner who wasn't thrilled a group of side-by-sides cut across his lawn. Then it was time for new business and Josh talked about how he and Ben were exploring the possibility of finding a few emergency-use-only shortcuts through the woods.

Laney glanced at Ben when Josh said his name, and was surprised to find him looking at her. Their eyes met for a few seconds and then he turned his attention back to Josh. Flustered, and hoping nobody would notice, Laney looked down at her phone and pretended to read her notes.

"And one last thing," Josh said. "Some of you know this is happening, but for everybody else, Rosie and my aunt Mary decided to move the annual Kowalski family camping trip to the Northern Star this year. The invasion begins the Wednesday before the Fourth of July and they'll be here for two weeks."

Laney still wasn't sure exactly how many Kowalskis there were, but she knew there were a lot of them. She'd just started this job, and the place filling up with the bosses' family members was a whole new level of pressure.

"I'll make you a list, Laney," she heard Rosie say and even though everybody in the room laughed, she was pretty sure the woman wasn't kidding. She liked lists.

"The reason I mention it," Josh continued, "is that it coincides with heavy traffic times on the trails, especially the holiday weekend. It'll probably be best if we coordinate ahead of time who's willing to do trail patrol and when so we can keep everything under control, even if Andy and I are spending less time than usual out there."

"I baked some goodies today," Rose said. "And once the meeting proper is over, everybody who's willing to volunteer some extra trail patrol time can come on in the kitchen and we'll look at the schedule while we eat."

Laney joined in the laughter as they all recognized they were being blackmailed by baked goods. And if the welcome basket she'd found in her camper when she arrived was anything to judge by, it would work, too.

"Oh, that wasn't the last thing," Josh said. "The actually last thing is a new face in the room. Most of you know Laney's staying here for the season to help us out, so I want to introduce her because if Andy and I aren't around, she'll be taking care of things."

Laney smiled when everybody turned to look at her and gave a little wave in everybody's general direction, but she was relieved when Josh announced they were done and there was a mad rush for the kitchen.

She heard Ben's voice as he walked out of the room with Rosie. "You know, technically I'm part of trail patrol 24/7, since I'm always on call. How many cookies does that get me?"

"Does that count the two I know you stole before the meeting even started?"

He laughed, and Laney felt her mood lift just at the

sound. She loved his laugh. As she stood, tucking her phone into the back pocket of her shorts, he turned back to her.

"You're going to come have some cookies, right?"

"I'd have a hard time doing trail patrol since I've never been on a four-wheeler in my life."

His eyebrow arched. "Never?"

"Nope."

"There are ATVs all over this place. I can teach you."

Now it was her turn to raise her eyebrow. "Teach me what? How to ride one?"

"Yeah."

"I don't know if I'd like that." Obviously she'd seen others driving them around the property since she arrived, including the guy who ended up underneath his, but she hadn't felt any sudden need to try it herself.

"You might not. Or you might love it. No way to know until you get on one." He grinned. "Something new to experience this summer."

"You're playing dirty now."

"Oh, I can show you dirty." He paused and the tops of his ears turned pink. "Uh, mud puddles. ATVs in the mud. You get dirty."

Laney laughed to let him off the hook, though she knew it was going to be a long time before she could get those words out of her mind. "I'll think about it."

"You know where to find me."

She definitely did, since it seemed like he was there every time she turned around. Or closed her eyes.

"Hey, Laney," she heard Josh call to her. "Come meet some people."

While she ate cookies and focused on trying to

memorize names and faces and connections to the Northern Star, Laney couldn't quite shake her awareness of Ben, even in the crowded kitchen. He talked with people and held Jackson for a while. Snuck a cookie to Sarah and got a stern talking-to from Paige. And the one time she dared look directly at him, he caught her looking. And he winked.

Oh, I can show you dirty.

She wondered how many warm, fresh chocolate cookies she could eat and still button her shorts.

FIVE

Ben wiped his hand across his face, but it did nothing but grind the dust and grit deeper into his skin. It was hot and humid for late June, and right now he wanted nothing more than to ride his quad out to the Northern Star and dive into their pool. But Rosie would slap him sideways if he jumped in as filthy as he was.

Or Laney would.

Oh, I can show you dirty.

It was three days later and he still felt his face get hot when he remembered that moment. As soon as the words had left his mouth, he'd realized how it sounded and been afraid Laney would take it the wrong way.

And maybe she had, but she hadn't slapped his face. Or gotten tense and turned away. Something had flared in her eyes and her lips had curved into the hint of a smile as she looked at him. The unintended innuendo hadn't offended her. It had intrigued her.

And he couldn't stop thinking about it. Even now, sitting on his ATV in front of the fire station with his helmet on his lap because he couldn't summon the energy to get off the damn thing, he was thinking about that look on Laney's face.

"Hey, you planning to sit there until Whitford gets a takeout joint that'll deliver?"

Ben turned to see his brother Jimmy leaning against the brick wall of the station and remembered they were supposed to have dinner. "How much do you think it would cost me to have a pizza delivered?"

"Considering the nearest place is probably twenty minutes away, time and the price of gas, maybe a hundred bucks." After a few seconds of silence, Jimmy cocked his head. "You're not actually considering it, aren't you?"

Ben laughed. "Not really, but it sure sounds good. I'm starving."

"Then get off the machine and we'll walk over to the diner."

That was the plan they'd come up with, but Ben hadn't been exhausted and so sweaty the dust was turning to mud on his skin. "I have to replace the supplies I used and bring the ATV inside before I can go."

"Then get moving. And no, you're not getting a rain check. The boys are driving Chelsea crazy lately and you wouldn't believe how hard it was to get a night out. I have to help her clean closets this week. *And* put up shelving in the basement for all the bulk crap she buys with coupons."

With a groan, Ben climbed off the ATV and hung his helmet off the handlebar. "I have to eat, anyway. The fact you'll have to organize your wife's shoes just makes it that much sweeter."

"How the hell did you get like that, anyway? Did you stop and roll around in the dirt on your way back?"

"We responded to an accident. Family in a four-seater got hit by a guy on a quad. They were okay, but the mom got a dislocated shoulder because she saw it coming and reached back like she was going to brace the kids or something. But the guy took off and they said he was drunk, so we left Dave and the other guys to handle the mom and took off after him. Drew just put new tires on the PD's quad and the tread was throwing up dust like a damn cloud."

"Who the hell gets drunk at lunch and then goes out on the trails?"

"The same guy who's eating dinner in a cell tonight because we know the trails and he doesn't. We split up because we knew Matt was coming in from another direction and he ran out of places to go."

"At least it wasn't worse."

Ben couldn't begin to count the number of times he'd said that to himself over the course of his career. He knew what worse really meant, and today it definitely could have been worse.

Even though the injuries had been minor, he still had to do the preliminary paperwork and a quick inventory. Then he backed the ATV down between the engine and the wall into a small space they'd cleared for it. Because of the drugs he was able to carry and dispense, the machine couldn't be left unattended unless it was in the station, but the engine and the utility truck ate most of the space.

Then he did the best he could do washing up in the sink and called it good. Jimmy had told his wife he'd try to be home in time for the bedtime routine, so it would take too long for Ben to shower and change. And Paige had built the diner's business on being snowmobile and ATV friendly, so they wouldn't mind a little dirt.

When she'd bought the closed-down restaurant, Paige had redone the inside but kept a cool retro look. Black-and-white marble. Red vinyl. With good coffee, great food and friendly staff, it was no wonder she'd made a success out of the formerly dismal and ultimately abandoned establishment.

Rumor had it she'd also invested in the Northern Star when the family realized the ATV trail access was going to not only save the lodge, but make money if they expanded. And her investment was separate from that of her husband, Mitch, who owned one of the top controlled demolition companies in the country. Ben wasn't sure how much of that particular rumor was true, but he did know that the family had jumped through all the legal hoops to turn the Northern Star into a structured business, which then grew into the Northern Star Lodge & Campground.

Tori was working tonight, he saw as he walked through the door. The pretty brunette was married to Max and they had a six-month-old daughter named Chessie, who'd be at home with her daddy. Max worked from home and Tori actually did, too, since she did some kind of graphics work with book covers or something. But she liked getting out of the house, so she'd picked up shifts at the diner before she and Max got together and she kept on doing it.

Her cousin, Gavin, was cooking, and as soon as Ben saw a glimpse of him on the other side of the pass-through window, his mouth started watering. Gavin'd gone away for a while to cook in Kennebunkport, but then one day he'd come back and Ben didn't know the story of why. But he didn't really care. The man was an amazing cook.

"Hey, guys," Tori said, setting menus down in front of them. "Rough day?"

Ben shrugged. "Could have been worse."

"Coffee or something cold?" They both asked for

coffee. "By the way, Gavin made chicken parmesan tonight and that might sound boring, but you would not believe how amazing it is."

"Sold," Ben said.

"Ditto. We're easy," Jimmy said.

"That's not what your wife says," she retorted, and she was laughing as she walked away.

"Speaking of being easy, Mom says you've met Laney."

"Have *you* met her?"

"No, but everybody in town knows they hired help for Rosie and her name is Laney." Jimmy paused while Tori set down their coffee mugs and a dish of creamer cups, and then he leaned forward. "And according to Mom, she's about your age, pretty and held your hand or something."

Ben rolled his eyes. "She didn't hold my hand. She cleaned my cut."

He held it up so Jimmy could see for himself, and then turned it so he could see it. The lighting here was better than it had been in the station's bathroom and he probably should have cleaned it better after it took a beating today. It was a little sore.

"But the pretty part is true?"

Ben nodded, then took a sip of his coffee to avoid saying more. But Jimmy just watched, waiting him out. "Yeah, she's pretty. She's also divorced and has no interest in getting involved with anybody right now."

"Huh. Seems to me a woman your age who was stuck in an unhappy marriage for a while would want to have a little fun."

"Well, she doesn't," Ben snapped, a little more harsh than he intended. But he'd spent too much time trying to convince himself he and Laney were a bad mix to want to listen to his brother joke about it. "And I'm not looking for a little *fun* at this point in my life. I'm almost forty, so if I have a relationship, it's going to be with a woman who wants the same things I do, like a home and kids and maybe a dog."

"Jesus, my kids are up my ass about getting a damn dog. Chelsea already told me if I bring home a puppy, she's going to set my pickup on fire and she may or may not let me get out of it first."

Jimmy kept going—something about garbage cans not being brought in—but Ben wasn't really listening. And he wasn't looking at him, either, because the view over Jimmy's shoulder was of the door.

And Rosie walked through it, with Laney right behind her.

LANEY WAS SO focused on what Rosie was saying, she made it halfway through the diner before she spotted Ben. Luckily, Rosie also stopped, so it wasn't awkward.

But Ben was rumpled and had sleepy eyes and was very, very dirty. And though she never would have guessed it about herself, Laney found it incredibly sexy.

Or maybe it was the way he looked at her—with a directness and intensity that made her shiver—before he shifted his gaze to Rosie.

"Good evening, ladies."

"Heard you had a rough day," Rosie said to Ben after smiling a greeting to the other man.

"Could've been worse." When Rosie nodded, he looked at Laney. "Laney, this is my brother Jimmy. Jimmy, this is Laney."

He turned in the booth to smile up at her. "Nice to meet you."

"You, too." The resemblance between the two brothers wasn't as pronounced as it was in the Kowalski family, but they had the same smile.

"I've heard a lot about you," he said, and her gaze flicked to Ben, whose eyes were fixed on his brother, and then back.

"Not much to tell yet," she said. "I haven't been here very long."

"I'm surprised to see you guys in town on a Saturday evening," Ben said.

"Josh and Andy are holding down the fort," Laney said.

"I've been trying to do some planning for the family vacation and I can't get two minutes to think in that place," Rosie said. "Katie came home, and then Drew and Liz were there and I decided if they were all going to hang out there, I'd just leave. And I made Laney come with me so she could drive and help me make lists."

When Laney looked back at Ben, she wondered if the day had been harder than he'd let on. His eyes were tired and a little red, and they didn't really crinkle when he smiled like they usually did.

But she knew from Andy that today's injuries had been minor and they'd caught the drunk rider before he could hurt anybody else. So maybe he was just tired and hot. And hungry, since their silverware was still wrapped.

"We had to do some errands in town and you know how I love to talk. And then we went to the market and Fran talked Laney's ear off."

That had been both of them, not just Fran, but Laney hadn't minded. The Whitford General Store and Service Station was owned by Butch and Fran Benoit, with Fran running the store and Butch taking care of the gas pumps and oil changes, along with the occasional tow. Laney had been in there several times, but it wasn't until she went in with Rosie that she got to find out just how much Fran loved having company at the store during the day.

"You boys enjoy your dinner," Rosie said, which was Laney's cue they were going to start moving again.

"It was nice to meet you, Jimmy," she said. "I'm sure I'll run into you again soon, Ben."

"Seems that way," he said, and this time when he smiled it reached his eyes.

Laney was glad Rosie walked to the empty table farthest from Ben and his brother. She wasn't sure how well she'd be able to concentrate on whatever lists she was supposed to be helping Rosie with if she could hear Ben's voice. The problem, though, was that the booths made an L-shape following the coffee counter—except for an opening to the back dining room and restrooms—and she could see his back in her peripheral vision.

So she saw when Jimmy glanced at her and then leaned across the table with a grin on his face to say something to Ben. And she saw Ben try to cuff him upside the head, but his brother was too fast. And she heard them both laugh.

"I hope you don't mind me dragging you all over town," Rosie said after they'd ordered, which had taken longer than usual, since it required an introduction to

Tori. She was married to Max, who she'd met at the ATV club meeting.

"Of course not. And you're not exactly dragging me. It's nice to get out and meet people sometimes. I'm not sure how much help I'll be with your lists, though."

That made Rosie laugh. "Oh, I don't really need help with any lists."

"Oh." She was confused because, besides errands, working on the lists in peace and quiet was the excuse Rosie had given everybody for why they'd flown the coop.

"I just wanted to get away for a while and the easiest way to do that is to give them a believable reason. If I said I didn't feel like making them supper and they could eat leftovers or sandwiches for a night, or that I wanted different walls to look at, they'd start wondering if I don't feel well or if there's something wrong."

"That makes sense in a sneaky kind of way."

"I've spent most of my life taking care of that house and the family in it but trust me, I know how to take care of me, too." She paused and then gave a little shrug. "Okay, so I tried to hide pneumonia and I'm still adjusting to having you helping me, but I know how to get a night off."

"Everybody needs a break now and then."

"And that's why you're here with me. I get the sense you're going to have trouble letting us know you want a day off or a few hours to yourself because there aren't really any set hours. So I brought you with me to show you how it's done."

Laney laughed. "So if I tell you I need to find a place to work on some lists, you'll know I've run off to have some fun."

"Exactly."

They did talk about Rosie's lists while they ate cheeseburgers and fries, though. They went over where the family members would all be in the campground—who had campers, who would be in the cabins and the older kids in tents—which made Laney's head spin. Some had babies and toddlers and they discussed the pros and cons of putting them near each other. On the one hand, their parents would be more tolerant of crying children. On the other, if the crying children got other children crying, it could be a mess.

"Maybe, other than need based on the size of the campers, we should let them figure that part out," Laney suggested.

"I guess you're right. But they'll all be arriving at different times, so it would be so much easier if we already knew where everybody was going."

"Have you talked to Mary about it?" Laney paused, frowning and reaching for the notebook so she could see the names. "That's Josh's aunt, right? The grandmother of all the babies?"

"Yes, that's Mary. And don't try to memorize this list ahead of time," Rosie told her. "You'll just give yourself a headache. It'll be a lot easier when everybody's here and you have faces, trust me. And not only have they been doing these annual camping trips for years, but they all feel right at home here, so those two weeks should actually be easier for you."

"I don't know if being in charge of the happiness of my boss's entire family will be easy, but at least I shouldn't have to help them hook up their sewer lines." She gave an exaggerated shudder to make Rosie laugh, but Andy showing her how that was done hadn't been one of her favorite days at the Northern Star.

"Honey, you're working yourself up for nothing. We raised those kids right and there's not one of them who can't fend for themselves, and they know if anybody tries to throw their weight around with you because of the last name, they'll get Mary's wooden spoon upside the head." Rosie nodded. "And yes, she keeps extras in her RV for these trips."

Even as she smiled at the visual of a woman smacking a grown man with a wooden spoon, in her peripheral vision, Laney saw Ben and Jimmy sliding out of their booth. Ben, probably stiff after the day he'd had, stretched and her self-control failed her. She turned her head to watch him and all she could do was hope she made no audible sounds of appreciation as the muscles in his arms flexed.

He spoke to a couple of people on his way out, but right before he got to the door, he turned and looked back. His eyes met hers and he smiled before giving her a wave.

Laney waved back and then turned her attention back to her last few fries as he walked out the door, hoping Rosie wasn't going to make a big deal out of it. Maybe older women in small towns all being obsessed with matchmaking was a stereotype and she wouldn't have to explain to Rosie why she wasn't going to date Ben or anybody else while she was in Whitford.

Rosie did give her a speculative look, but then she flipped to a clean sheet in her notebook. "I know Mary will make sure they all bring enough food for an army, but let's make a list of extra supplies and staples we should have on hand. And maybe some activities for the younger kids."

Breathing a sigh of relief, Laney chewed on a french fry and tried to think of what little kids might want to do in a campground for two weeks.

LANEY STARTED HER Sunday at five o'clock in the morning. She could have slept later, but she'd discovered that she liked making herself a cup of coffee and taking it back to bed. Curled up against a mountain of pillows, she'd sip her coffee and read until it was time to get dressed.

She'd tried taking her coffee and book outside to her pink chair one morning, but the mosquitoes were vicious in the early morning hours and she didn't want to douse herself in bug spray while still in her pajamas. The bugs had even changed a lifelong habit of showering in the morning. Because it was almost impossible to be outside in the evening without bug spray, she'd started showering once she was in for the night and getting ready for bed. Sometimes that meant crazy hair in the morning, but that's what ponytail holders were for.

At quarter of six, she got dressed and ate a banana before grabbing her keys to the supply closets and stepping out into the damp morning air. They were far enough north so it was still chilly that early in the day, but it would warm up quickly. Quietly, so as not to disturb the sleeping campers, she hit the big bathhouse. Cleaning bathrooms wasn't her favorite part of the job, especially since dirty riders and water tended to make for muddy floors and sinks. But quickly and efficiently, she cleaned each bathroom and made sure the toilet paper, paper towels and soap were stocked.

She'd go through them each a few times over the course of the day for quick problem checks, but she liked to do the thorough cleaning before anybody else was awake.

Next she unlocked the gate in the fence around the pool area and used the skimmer to scoop out a few leaves and some bugs that had drowned overnight. Like the bathhouse, she'd do a few checks on the pool over the course of the day.

Finally she did a quick stroll through the campground, avoiding the camper in the back with the dog so he wouldn't bark, making sure everything was okay. Nothing had changed since she'd locked the pool and done her final walk-through the night before, making sure campers hadn't left food or garbage out where bears might be tempted to help themselves and checking to make sure campfires abandoned by sleepy guests were burning down safely.

It was a long drive to Whitford from almost everywhere so Saturdays, people tended to get up earlier than they might normally on vacation in order to get on the trails in time for a full day of riding. On Sundays, it varied. Some got up even earlier so they could ride for several hours before checking out. Others slept in until it was time to pack up and leave.

Today there were a few early risers, so she left them to their coffee and walked to the lodge. Rosie always had muffins or banana bread or some other treat, along with a carafe of coffee, and Laney would have some breakfast and visit with her. Then the real work of the day started.

Guests at the lodge were told up front it wasn't a hotel. Nobody was going to go in every morning and make their beds and pick their towels up off the floor.

If they needed something, they could ask. Otherwise, there were fresh bedding and towels when they arrived and it was changed and the rooms cleaned after they checked out. They cleaned the shared bathrooms every morning, though, and the living spaces always needed picking up.

Today, Katie was in the kitchen with her mom, and she waved when Laney walked in. “Mom made apricot oatmeal bars and they go fast, so grab one.”

“Is that why you’re up so early?”

She snorted. “I had to pee. I’m only six months pregnant and Paige is seven, but I swear I have to pee twice as often as she does.”

“Or maybe it just seems that way because you complain every time you have to stop what you’re doing to pee and she doesn’t,” Rosie said, which startled Laney until she saw the affectionate smile. More teasing she wasn’t used to.

Her parents hadn’t been the teasing type, so if her mother had said those words, they would have been meant as a criticism. And with no siblings and a few cousins she didn’t like very much, she didn’t know what it was like to have that teasing relationship with another adult like she’d seen between Ben and his brother last night.

Laney poured herself a coffee and grabbed an apricot oatmeal bar. She’d never heard of such a thing, but she was a fast learner and one of the first things she’d learned was that if Rosie baked it, it was good.

A stitched sampler hanging on the wall caught her eye. *Bless This Kitchen.* “Did you make that, Rosie?”

The older woman looked where she was pointing,

and then smiled. “No, Sarah did. Josh’s mom, back when Sean was just a baby.”

“Sean’s the brother who lives in New Hampshire?”

“Yeah, he’s the middle of the five. He never really loved this place and hated having strangers in his house. He went in the army and then, when he got out, he went to New Hampshire to see Leo and Mary and his cousins. Of course, he met Emma and stayed there, but he comes to visit now and then.”

“I can’t believe they’re *all* going to be here in a week and a half,” Katie said. “It’s going to be crazy. Plus, half the town will probably be here off and on to see them. Like Ben. He and Sean were good friends growing up.”

Laney was careful not to show any reaction to that statement, but *uh-oh* echoed through her mind. On the ride home from the diner, she’d told herself she needed to keep her distance—both mentally and physically—from Ben. She had books to read and movies to watch when she wasn’t working, and it shouldn’t be too hard to avoid running into him if she was actually trying. Sure, he was at the lodge sometimes, but she could find other things to be doing.

But if one of his childhood best friends was going to be staying in the campground for two weeks, he was probably going to be around more and not less.

Uh-oh, indeed.

SIX

Sean

SEAN KOWALSKI LOOKED at the massive pile of what looked like everything they owned sitting on the front lawn and shook his head. “We can’t possibly need all this stuff.”

“We’re going for two weeks,” his wife replied. “We have a three-year-old.”

“People are going to think you got mad at me and threw all my stuff out the window.”

Emma gave him a sideways look. “They know better. If that was the case, the pile would be on fire.”

He laughed and stepped close enough to loop his arm around her waist and pull her up against him. “Good point. I hope you’ve talked to Cat and Russell and have some idea of where they are, because it’s supposed to rain later.”

“It’s not supposed to rain until *much* later, and they’ll be here anytime. She sent me a text about twenty minutes ago.”

Sean hoped the weather forecast was right, because given a choice between carrying that pile back inside only to carry it all out again or setting off on vacation tomorrow with wet belongings, he wasn’t sure which he’d choose. It was bad enough they were going to not only have to fit that entire pile into the camper, but make sure everything was stowed securely so they weren't dodging projectiles like a bad arcade game going down the road tomorrow.

Emma's grandmother and step-grandfather were taking two weeks off of their RV-ing-around-the-country life to house-sit for them, which Cat would love since it had been her home for most of her life and was the house that she'd raised Emma in. And he, Emma and Johnny would be taking their RV to Maine.

"How many texts have you gotten from Aunt Mary?" he asked.

"Sixteen."

"This week?"

"Today." She laughed. "And those are separate from the group text with *all* the women. I swear I've had to remind them that Maine has stores every day this week."

"And Aunt Mary reminds you they only have a small market in town and—"

"I'll pay twice as much than if I just buy it now and take it with me," she finished for him.

"Plus, if I know Rosie, she'll have been baking and cooking and we're all going to have to eat so much food, we won't be able to ride our four-wheelers. Or swim. We'll just sink to the bottom of the pool."

"I think I've gained weight just from *thinking* about spending two weeks with Mary and Rose."

Sean bowed his head to kiss the side of her neck. "I'm sure we can come up with ways to burn off those extra calories."

"There's nothing sexier than being surrounded by your entire family." She laughed when he nipped at her earlobe, but he winced when she yelled to Johnny.

"Stop taking toys out of the pile or you won't have them at Nana Rosie's house!"

Johnny threw his favorite dump truck back in the pile and looked at them, scowling. "Put it in Daddy's truck."

"We're not taking Daddy's truck," she said, and Sean guessed by her tone they'd already had this discussion a few times today. "Or Mommy's. We're taking Grammy's camper, so when she and Papa get here, we'll put your toys in the camper, okay?"

"He's going to run himself ragged playing with his cousins," Sean said. "We'll be lucky if he can stay awake through supper."

"I'm hoping a family-wide afternoon nap rule is put into effect. I think we'll all have fun, though. It'll be nice to relax. Did you finish up that job today?"

"All done." They maintained separate businesses—the landscaping business Emma had established before they even met and his building business—but they often worked in conjunction. Since she specialized in low-maintenance landscaping for summer homes and camps, he offered decks, stairs and docks, and they were able to save clients money and aggravation by being a package deal. And they were able to coordinate their schedules so one of them was usually home with Johnny, though he'd visit Aunt Mary or one of his aunts if they were in a time crunch.

Emma's phone chimed and she groaned, dropping her head against his shoulder. "You know that stretch of road on the way that has no cell phone reception? When you get there, drive really, really slow, okay?"

He laughed, but then his phone chimed, too. He pulled it out while Emma was typing out a reply on hers. "Crap. It's Uncle Leo, making sure I packed all of Johnny's riding gear. Is that somewhere in the pile?"

"Yes and, once again, he's only three. His riding gear consists of a helmet and a pair of goggles."

"Okay." He typed out a response for his uncle, mentally cursing his cousin Kevin for deciding Leo needed a cell phone in the first place. "Is *our* riding gear in the pile?"

"Everything that was on the list is in the pile."

He could hear the rising annoyance in her voice, but he couldn't help himself. "Okay. Was our riding gear on the list?"

"Sean, really?" She stepped back so she could put her hands on her hips—phone still clutched in one—and glare at him. "Feel free to take your grown ass over there and look at the damn pile."

Grinning, he closed the space between them and, cupping the back of her head, lowered his mouth to hers. He kissed her until the tension eased from her body and she moved a hand from her hip to his.

"Sometime during the next two weeks, we're going to sneak away. Just the two of us. There's a spot we can get to, *mostly* on legal trails, that I want you to see."

"Mostly legal? Your brother is president of the ATV club. Your sister's married to the police chief. You need to behave."

Before he could respond, they heard a horn and turned to see an RV coming up the drive. It wasn't huge, since it was only Cat and Russell and they didn't want to tow a car, but it would be plenty of space for the three of them. The pile, he wasn't as sure about.

"Grammy and Papa," Johnny yelled, pointing at the

RV. Then he grabbed a bag from the pile and started dragging it toward pavement.

Sean sprinted across the yard and scooped up his son, bag and all. "Not so fast, kid. Let them park."

"I want Nana Rosie."

"Me, too, but we have to wait until tomorrow. You're going to sleep in your bed tonight and when you wake up, we'll have breakfast and then go to Nana Rosie's."

He felt as anxious to be there as Johnny did. They hadn't been to Maine as a family since a quick trip over during the Christmas holidays, and he was looking forward to sitting by the campfire with his family.

He'd hated the lodge growing up and had gotten out of Whitford as soon as he was of age. But when he'd gotten the call it was in trouble a few years back and then seen for himself the state it was in, he'd realized how much it really meant to him. Saving it had renewed the close bond with his siblings he'd lost, and he didn't feel the old resentment anymore when he thought of the Northern Star. And as Johnny got older, Sean was looking forward to taking him back and watching him experience the adventures he had as a child.

Russell, Emma's step-grandfather, walked over and they shook hands. Then the older man looked at the pile in the yard. "What did you do wrong and when's the bonfire?"

"YOU'RE NOT GOING out by the Northern Star tonight by any chance, are you?"

Ben glanced over at Drew Miller who, as the police chief, was often buried in paperwork. That appeared to be the case today, since there were mounds of papers on his desk and he was crankier than usual. Ben had stopped by his office to drop off some papers from Sam, which hadn't made Drew happy as he already had enough of the stuff. And now it looked like Ben was going to get shuffled off on another errand.

To the one place he'd been avoiding for a week and a half.

There was a connection happening between him and Laney. It was that connection that had compelled him to turn back to her before he walked out of the diner, and was the reason she'd been looking at him when he turned. That quick smile and wave goodbye had felt like the most natural thing in the world to him.

But he knew Laney wasn't looking for a connection, and the last thing he needed to do at this crossroad in his life was fall for a woman who had no idea what she was going to do—or probably where she'd even be living—come the changing of the season. So he'd stayed away from the lodge, hoping that the budding connection would fade with a little time and distance between them.

Judging by the jolt of excitement he felt at the thought of having a solid reason to head out there, he'd been wrong.

"Wasn't planning on it," he replied, thinking Drew would say *never mind* and he wouldn't have to rely solely on his own self-control to keep him in town.

"Because you were too busy planning to sit in my office and drink my coffee all day?"

"I've only been here fifteen minutes. But yes, that's my entire plan. I even wrote it in big letters on my calendar so I couldn't fit anything else in."

When Drew sighed and scrubbed his hands over his face, Ben felt his resolve weaken. He looked stressed and tired. “I need my dad’s signature on a few papers and they have to be original, not scanned. And Liz has classes online all evening, so Paige has Jackson, but she runs out of steam early now that she’s so pregnant. Two toddlers are a bit much, especially because Jackson doesn’t stay where she puts him anymore.”

Liz was taking some kind of business marketing course online so she could take over the website and social media for the lodge. The family had been paying the woman who handled the website for Mitch’s demolition company to do it, but the lodge’s needs—and the money being paid out—had grown with the expansion and Liz taking it over worked out best for everybody.

“I can run them over,” Ben said, relenting. He’d find Andy, get the signatures, and get out.

Maybe. It would probably be rude to leave without at least saying hello to Laney. And it had been long enough so it wouldn’t hurt to check the bolts on her Adirondack chairs and make sure none had loosened up. She might not think to do that.

“I owe you one. Liz has been trying to get a lot of her work done in advance because her family’s coming tomorrow and she doesn’t want to spend their entire vacation on her computer, so I’ve been trying to juggle *all* the balls this past week.”

Ben wondered if Laney would be busy, with the extended Kowalski family showing up the next day. But knowing Rosie, they’d probably been ready for days. “I’ve got a few more things to do and I don’t want to stray too far because Dave had some kind of an appointment this afternoon, but then I’ll take a ride out there. You need them back tonight?”

“No, but by ten tomorrow morning at the latest. I

can swing by the station in the morning if you're going to be there."

"Sounds good." He took the manila envelope Drew fished out of the pile.

"Sean will be expecting you to stop by. He's mentioned it to Liz a few times."

Ben's first thought was how much he was going to enjoy kicking back and catching up with one of his oldest friends. Right on its heels, though, was *more time with Laney.* "Yeah, I'll be around. Especially if there are s'mores."

"I've been camping with this family. Trust me, there will be s'mores."

When he left Drew, Ben walked back to the fire station and put the envelope on the passenger seat of his SUV so he wouldn't forget about it. It wasn't likely, if for no other reason than he couldn't remember the last time he'd gone an hour without Laney crossing his mind, but he didn't want to drop the ball.

Once Dave texted him to let him know he was back in town and available for calls, Ben went home to grab a quick bite to eat. That led to him helping his dad change the HVAC filters in the basement, so then he needed a shower. So maybe he didn't exactly *need* one and it only meant extra clothes in the laundry hamper for the day, but he almost managed to convince himself it had nothing to do with Laney and the fact he'd probably be seeing her.

And the anticipation he felt was almost scary, he realized as he pulled out of his driveway. His plan had backfired and instead of the attraction he felt for her fading, he was even more anxious to see her.

If he was smart, he'd pull up to the lodge's door, get

Andy's signature on the papers, and then drive away before he was tempted to do something stupid.

THE NORTHERN STAR was as ready as it could be for tomorrow, and there was literally nothing left for Laney to do. After making sure Rosie didn't need her for anything, she'd decided to go for a walk to clear her head. She'd begun walking a little bit each day, treating it like a form of meditation, and it was quickly becoming a favorite part of her routine.

With peace, quiet and plenty of area to explore, she got a chance to sort through her thoughts and just enjoy being by herself. Usually she went out a little earlier in the day so she could eat dinner before doing her evening chores. But there were no guests tonight, so she'd waited until it cooled off. It meant more bug spray, but less sweat.

But now her feeling of serenity was slipping because up ahead she could see a fence with a brightly colored mailbox she didn't recognize.

Laney didn't think she was lost, since she hadn't turned off the road or taken any forks, but she should have paid a little more attention to what she was doing. She'd walked a lot further than she'd intended to and the sun was definitely getting lower in the sky. Not that she was afraid of the dark, but she'd rather not have to find her way back by the flashlight function on her phone. And she wasn't sure she even had enough battery life to get there.

She was almost back to the path that cut from the main road through the woods to the ATV trail, which had an access into the back of the lodge's property, when she heard a vehicle coming. It was still light out, but the sun was low enough so it would be a lot darker in the woods, so she'd decided to stick to the asphalt until she got to the main driveway. But for a second, she thought about ducking into the trees, anyway.

The vehicle passed her and at the moment she recognized it as Ben's SUV, the brake lights lit up. After it stopped, the backup lights came on and, hugging the shoulder of the road, he backed the SUV to where she stood.

She crossed the street as he put the window down, unable to keep from smiling at the sight of his face. He hadn't been around for a while, and she'd only thought about him a few dozen times. Per day.

"Hey, Laney. Nice night for a walk."

"Yeah." She was close enough to smell his aftershave through the open window, and to see the top of an aluminum can showing from a koozie in the cup holder. "I walked a little further than I meant to."

"I'm on my way to see Andy. Want a ride?"

"No, thanks. It's good exercise."

"It'll be getting dark soon. And you just said you didn't mean to walk so far."

"I'm okay, really. I only accept rides from sober drivers, but thanks."

"Ouch." His eyebrow shot up and he took his drink out of the cup holder. Then he slowly slid the foam koozie off, revealing a soda can. "You know what they say about assuming things, sweetheart."

She felt her cheeks grow hot, and she wasn't sure if it was from embarrassment or a reaction to the way he called her "sweetheart" in that low voice of his. She'd object to the term if he used it again, but for now she let it go. "Sorry. I've listened to too many country songs over the years, I guess. They're always cruising down back roads with a cold one in the center console."

"Yeah, I'm not really country song material."

She didn't agree, regardless of his beverage choices or lack of cowboy boots. "Can I change my mind about the ride?"

"Of course."

She walked around the front of the SUV and, after he stuck an envelope that had been sitting there above his visor, she climbed into the passenger seat. It looked like any other huge, fancy four-by-four, except for the bags in the backseat. The back cargo area, though, she'd bet was a different story. Once she was buckled, he put the vehicle in Drive.

"I'm sorry I thought you were drinking and driving," she said. "I have a way of putting my foot in my mouth when it comes to you."

He glanced over at her, grinning, before turning back to the road. "If I'm on vacation or officially off the books for the night, I might have a couple of beers, but otherwise I rarely drink. Never when I might be driving. I've responded to too many of those calls to take a chance."

"I always thought people used those koozies to hide the fact they're beer cans, not sodas."

"Some probably do. I use them because they keep my soda cold longer and I hate when it's hot and the cans sweat and I get condensation on my hand and in the bottom of the cup holder."

She bit back the apology that sprang to her lips. She'd already said she was sorry and Ben didn't seem all that perturbed by it.

"Ready for the big day tomorrow?" he asked, and she appreciated the subject change.

"As ready as we can be, I guess. Although, every time I turn around, Rosie thinks of one more thing. Maybe that's why I walked so far." She chuckled. "Earlier today, she remembered the inflatable pool she'd bought online for the babies. She put the box in the barn, but forgot to put blowing it up and filling it with water on any of her lists."

He was wearing shorts tonight, she realized. And the sun might be on its way down, but there was still plenty of light for her to appreciate the well-toned curve of his calf muscle. She'd seen him in jeans and in navy cargo pants, but this was the first time she'd seen his legs. Her fingers practically itched to skim over the light sprinkle of hair, so she turned her gaze back to the windshield.

"You haven't been around much," she said, and then she wanted to slap herself in the forehead. She hadn't meant to say that out loud.

"I've been busy, I guess. And I've been helping my dad with some yard projects my mom's been after him to get done."

"Do you live close to them? I mean, I know Whitford's a small town, but it seems to have a lot of land area and the houses are spread out."

"I live in the apartment over my parents' garage."

She smiled, but didn't tease him about living with his parents. She wasn't sure her teasing would come across as that, and she'd already stumbled with the drinking and driving thing.

"I guess that makes you a handy yard work assistant," she said. "Being so close."

"Too handy sometimes."

When he turned on his blinker and started braking, she realized they were already back at the lodge. The realization they'd be parting ways in a few moments made her wish she could think of something to say, but nothing came to mind. Instead, they drove in silence until he pulled up to the side of the barn and killed the engine. Then, as she got out, he took the envelope from the visor and did the same.

"Thanks for the ride," she said. "I'd still be out on the trail in the woods if you hadn't come along."

"You would have been fine." He turned and smiled at her. "But it was nice to have company for a few minutes."

She thought that would be the end of it, but when she started walking, he fell in beside her. "You don't have to walk me to my camper. I promise it's safe, and it looks like you have business in the house." She waved a hand at the envelope.

"Oh, I know you're safe. I was thinking, though, that I should check the bolts in your chairs. Sometimes they loosen up during initial use and it's a good idea to give them each an extra tightening just to be sure."

"Oh." She hadn't even thought of that. "They'll just loosen up on their own?"

He shrugged. "They don't necessarily loosen up, but sometimes they seem fully seated until you use the chairs and the boards shift. It'll only take a minute."

When they reached her camper, she went inside to grab her tool kit, and when she went back outside, she found him sitting in one of the chairs. He had his head tilted back and smiled up at her.

"They're surprisingly comfortable," he said.

"Yes, they are." She wondered how long he would stay and talk if she sat in the other chair. But he'd tossed the manila envelope in that seat and, when he saw the tools in her hand, he pushed himself to his feet.

It only took him a couple of minutes to check the nuts on both chairs. There were a couple he tightened, and then he held the socket and crescent wrenches out to her.

"They look good," he said. "Now I don't have to worry about the chair collapsing under you because I didn't tighten them enough the first time. It's been bugging me, so I'm glad it's taken care of now."

The visual of landing on her butt in a pile of pink wood made her smile, even though a small part of her was recognizing that Ben didn't just take care of people who were having medical crises. He was just the kind of guy who took care of things—and people.

Don't you worry about it, Laney. I have everything taken care of.

The last voice she wanted in her head right now was her ex-husband's. Yes, he'd taken care of everything. He'd handled everything to the point it took Laney a lot of years to realize he wasn't taking care of things out of love and concern for her. He either didn't believe her capable of taking responsibility or he'd wanted to ensure he had total control over all aspects of their lives. Either way, once Laney recognized she'd become a shell of the woman she'd once been, she'd tried to take back control over her life. Patrick had resisted and so she'd divorced him.

On the surface, Ben and her ex-husband appeared to have nothing in common. But the idea of being taken care of again scared her. Especially since she was enjoying taking care of herself so much.

Then she took the tools from him and their hands touched, and she forgot about that voice inside of her who was leery of Ben Rivers.

As her fingers curled around the metal, his fingertips skimmed up the side of her hand until they got to her wrist. Then he gave her a gentle tug—so tentative it was almost an unspoken question—and she answered by moving forward.

Her body tensed in anticipation of his kiss, and she closed her eyes as his mouth covered hers. One of his hands was still holding her wrist, but the other cupped her face. His mouth wasn't forceful against hers, but it wasn't too sweet, either. And as he kissed her, a rush of desire she hadn't felt in many years swept through her.

But then he broke off the kiss, and Laney opened her eyes to see him looking at her mouth and he wasn't exactly frowning, but he didn't look happy.

"I'm sorry, Laney." His hands fell away from her and he took a step back. "I shouldn't have done that."

Ouch. "Don't be sorry."

"No, I shouldn't have done that." He blew out a breath and then scrubbed a hand over his face. "I mean, I...dammit. I'm screwing this up."

He looked miserable, so she felt sorry for him and decided to help him out. "Are you trying to tell me you didn't want to kiss me and accidentally did, or that you're worried I didn't want to kiss *you*?"

"Oh, no. I wanted to kiss you. I wanted to so much it seemed like kissing you was all I've thought about lately. But I have no idea if you wanted me to."

"I did," she admitted, because she wasn't going to let

him beat himself up over something they both wanted. "But, that doesn't mean it was a good idea. I'm not… looking to date anybody, you know?"

"I do know." His smile was genuine, reaching his eyes. "Okay, so I'm not sorry I kissed you. But I'll try not to do it again."

That should have made her happy, but she knew her smile probably didn't look as real as his had. "We'll probably be seeing a lot of each other and it'll just be easier that way."

Easier in some ways, maybe, but Laney knew when she crawled into her bed tonight, she was going to think about his kiss and ache for more.

"I have to go see Andy for a few minutes, and then I'll be out of here." He grabbed the envelope off the seat of the chair. "I'll probably be by in the next couple of days to see Sean, though."

"It's going to be a fun couple of weeks. I hope."

"It will be. I just don't want to make things awkward."

"Ben, it's fine. It was a kiss. A really *great* kiss but, still, we don't have to let it make things awkward between us. I don't want that."

"Me, either." He slapped the envelope against his palm and looked as if he was going to say more, but then he sighed. "Good night, Laney."

"Good night."

She watched him leave and, once he'd disappeared beyond the trees, she pressed her fingers to her mouth.

It hadn't just been a great kiss. It had been amazing, and she wanted more. She wanted to know what his hair felt like sliding through her fingers. She wanted to run her hands over his arms and his back, and feel his taut muscles.

Instead, the next time she saw him, she was going to smile and make conversation, because no matter how much she wanted him, she hadn't been lying. She wasn't ready to date anybody. Not the kind of dating that was meant to become a real relationship, and she had a strong feeling that's where Ben was in his life.

But she wasn't there yet.

SEVEN

LANEY WAS SERIOUSLY regretting her choice not to sacrifice any of her camper's precious refrigerator or cabinet space to alcohol. She didn't drink a lot, but if there was ever a time she deserved a reward cocktail at the end of a day, it would be the extended Kowalski family's arrival day.

It seemed as if every time things calmed down, another vehicle rolled in. Multiple vehicles, actually, since there were not only the campers, but also trucks pulling trailers loaded with four-wheelers.

There were a *lot* of four-wheelers, which made sense due to the fact there was a *lot* of family.

Leo and Mary had arrived first in a big diesel pusher that looked to Laney like an RV version of a luxury yacht, and she was thankful they hadn't shown up last. The vehicle didn't really have a tight turning radius. Other than helping Andy in making sure he didn't run over any electrical or sewer hookups, there wasn't much for Laney to do other than meet them. She knew Leo and Frank—Josh's father—were brothers, but Leo had ended up settling in New Hampshire with Mary.

As the rest began trickling in, Laney was thankful she'd taken a copy of the campground map and marked down names and a few notes so she could sneak a peek as they arrived.

Josh had already spoken to her about Joe, who was

Leo and Mary's oldest son. He was some kind of famous horror author, and she'd had explained to her in no uncertain terms that he was an extremely private person and that what happened at the Northern Star stayed at the Northern Star. He and his wife, Keri, along with their five-year-old daughter, Brianna, would be staying in one of the cabins.

Terry, Joe's twin sister, and her husband, Evan, had an RV. Mike and Lisa, with their two younger sons had another. And Kevin and Beth, with six-year-old Lily and two-year-old Gabe rounded out Leo and Mary's kids. They had an RV, but it was smaller and at the last minute, they'd opted for the second cabin to give the kids more floor space.

As for Josh's siblings, Sean and Emma would be arriving with their son in a big RV at some point. His brother Ryan and Lauren, his wife, would be coming up from Massachusetts and taking one of the guest rooms in the lodge. And Rosie had decided to keep the other rooms open for the family who lived in Whitford. Mitch's wife was very pregnant and they had a two-year-old, and Liz had one-year-old Jackson, so they might want a place to have nap time or change after the pool. Rosie also wanted the beds empty in case anybody had more beer than they'd anticipated and shouldn't drive home.

Laney also had a list of the older kids who had jobs and social lives that got them out of spending two entire weeks with their family. Ryan and Lauren's son, Nick, and Stephanie—Terry and Evan's daughter—plus Joey and Danny, who were Mike and Lisa's two oldest boys, would be showing up just for the long Fourth of July holiday weekend and planned to stay in tents. Rosie had warned her that once it started getting dark and their phone batteries started getting low, they might try to sneak into the lodge for the night—especially Stephanie—and that it was okay.

"Overwhelmed yet?"

Even before she turned, Laney recognized Leo's voice. He wasn't a big man, but he had a very big voice. He also had the pretty blue eyes both sides of the Kowalski family shared, while Mary had given her kids her dimples.

"A little bit," she admitted, since he wouldn't believe her if she denied it. "But you guys don't seem to need me for much, anyway."

"We've been camping a long time," he said. After a few seconds, he snorted. "Camping. My old man would cuff us upside the head if he heard us call what we're doing camping."

"Your RV definitely isn't primitive. But it *is* in a campground, so technically…"

He laughed. "Sometimes the wife and I joke about living in the RV and renting out the house because it's a lot nicer. I think we're joking, anyway. So who are we missing?"

That made her laugh, since it was *his* family he was asking about. "Sean isn't here yet. And, according to Rosie, Ryan and his wife should be here any time."

"It'll be good to be all together here at the Northern Star. My brother would be damn proud to see what the kids have done with this place."

Leo was proud. She could hear it in his voice. And she hadn't seen it during the rough years, of course, but she could see how much work and love had gone into making it the place it was now. "I'm sure he would."

Two little girls ran up to Leo, each grabbing one of his hands and talking at the same time. "Come see what we made!"

They looked close in age to Laney, and both had dark hair and blue eyes, but she could tell them apart by the dimples. Brianna, who was Joe and Keri's daughter, didn't have them while Lily, who was slightly older and belonged to Kevin and Beth, did.

"My granddaughters don't waste any time," he said. "It was nice talking to you, Laney."

"You, too."

Once the girls had dragged Leo away, Laney decided to duck into her camper for a quick break. Everybody was visiting and putting the final touches on their sites, so she didn't think they'd need anything from her for a while. She'd gone through the lodge a final time that morning, making sure everything was clean and ready for guests, so until it was time to help guide Sean and Emma into their site, there was nothing for her to do.

Of course, thinking about Sean's imminent arrival made her think about Ben. And thinking about Ben made her think about that kiss.

She'd be seeing him soon. Maybe tonight or maybe tomorrow, but he'd be stopping by and she was going to have to pretend she hadn't been thinking about the kiss since last night. No staring at his mouth. No blushing when they made eye contact.

After grabbing a can of mixed fruit from her fridge, Laney opened the shopping list app on her phone and typed in *chocolate*. Maybe it wasn't quite the reward a cocktail was, but she didn't think alcohol and Ben would be a good mix for her.

Emma

"I WANT NANA ROSIE."

She'd lost count of the number of times Johnny had said that since they left their driveway, but since they'd just passed the *Welcome to Whitford* sign, Emma smiled at her son. He'd turned to see her the best he could, since his car seat was buckled into the shotgun seat, and she was behind him on the RV's couch. "Just a few more minutes, buddy."

"I want to play trucks with Gabe."

"We have your trucks," she said. Again, not for the first time. "Are you excited to spend two whole weeks with your cousins?"

He actually clapped his hands, which made her and Sean both laugh. He had a lot of play dates with Lily and Gabe, and with Brianna, but it was never enough for him. He was an energetic little extrovert and he got bored having just Mom or Dad in the house. So they "borrowed" his cousins as often as they could, and they'd had a few discussions about letting him go to day care part-time just to have time to play with other kids.

Mostly they'd been trying to give him a little brother or sister, but he was three now and it still hadn't happened.

Emma watched as the trees whipped by the windows, trying to put the brakes on that train of thought. Not only did she want to focus on enjoying the next two weeks, but she'd be spending them with some *very* perceptive women and she didn't want to talk about it. She and Sean hadn't even really talked about it yet, other than a few passing remarks here and there.

"We're here, Johnny," Sean said at the same time Emma felt the RV slow. "It's time for the Kowalski family vacation!"

"Of doom," Johnny added, clapping his hands again.

They were laughing when the lodge came into view, which Emma took as a good sign. She couldn't stop herself from looking over the landscaping, which had fared well since her last visit. The flowers were Rosie's choice and some of the trees and shrubs had been there as long as the house, but Emma'd spent some time helping them with the rest of the property. Drainage and borders when they'd expanded the parking areas, and to make an area where they could power-wash ATVs without worrying about erosion.

"I'm going to park out here so we can say hi and find out where we're putting this thing," Sean said.

"And put it in place without *somebody* yelling to get out," Emma added, having to speak up since Johnny was already demanding to be released from the car seat.

Sean shut off the engine and, by the time Emma popped the buckle to release Johnny, he had the passenger door open and caught their son as he jumped down. "Let's go find Nana Rosie."

Emma slid into the driver's seat and out that door, since it was the easiest way to exit, so she was a few steps behind them. A knot of emotion lodged in her throat as she watched her two men—one tall and strong, and the other so little in his father's arms—walking toward the lodge. Sean was already pointing things out to Johnny, like the tree he'd fallen out of when he was five and the window he'd accidentally broken trying to teach himself golf in the front yard.

For Emma, the Northern Star Lodge was where they'd be spending their two-week vacation. To Sean, this was home. Not the place he lived, but the place he was *from*.

When he reached the front door, he stopped and turned back to wait for her. Sean was practically beaming, his blue eyes framed by laugh lines that she loved to kiss sometimes, even though it drove him crazy. He looked like he was about to say something, but then the door opened and Rosie was there.

She threw her arms around Sean, wrapping up Johnny in the process, and Emma watched Sean hug the woman who had been like a mother to him. Rosie squeezed back until Johnny protested, and then it was Emma's turn.

"I'm so glad you're finally here! I can't believe how big this guy has gotten since the last time I saw him." Rosie kissed Johnny's cheek, making an exaggerated *mwah* sound that made him giggle.

"We got started later than we intended and then stopped a few times," Emma explained. "He's at that age where he doesn't want to be strapped to a seat for very long and I was hoping he'd nap some, since I know the kids will be wound up tonight, but he was too excited to see everybody to stop talking long enough to fall asleep."

"Well, I think Johnny and I will go have a quick visit in the kitchen while you guys get your RV settled. I'm not sure where Andy got off to, but Laney's out in the camping area and she'll know the best way to pull you into your spot."

"I'm looking forward to meeting her," Sean said. "Josh likes her and you know we were all in favor of you having some help around here. Not that you need it, but you deserve it."

Rosie smiled, and then patted his cheek. "I like her, too, and thank you. Now go get set up so we can put up the canopy for the kids to play under if the sun's too hot or it's raining. You have to drive through the grass where it's going, so we can't do it until you're parked."

"Nana Rosie, where are the cookies?" Johnny asked, because he knew she'd have some in the jar.

"Be good," Emma told him, and then she went back outside with Sean.

He reached out and grabbed her hand as they walked, lacing his fingers through hers. "I can't believe how good it feels to be back here."

"I can't wait to park my butt in a camp chair and do nothing." She sighed. "For a few minutes, anyway. Johnny's going to keep us on our toes."

"That he will." He leaned closer, bumping her shoulder with his. "But between Aunt Mary and Rosie and all his aunts, I bet we'll manage to sneak away for a few minutes now and then."

"To a camper surrounded by your family?"

They'd reached the RV, so he let go of her hand, but he slapped her ass before going around to the driver's side. When they were both inside, he paused before turning the key. "Guess you'll have to be really quiet."

"Oh, I think *you* are the one who'll need to be quiet." When he raised his eyebrows suggestively, she laughed and gestured for him to get going.

She had a camp chair to park herself in.

BEN PARKED HIS SUV across the front of Josh's truck and Katie's Jeep, figuring if he blocked them in, nobody would be able to block *him* in. There were a lot of vehicles in the yard already, but he had no idea if all the family had arrived or not.

He knew Sean had, though, since he'd sent Ben a text message earlier. Come meet my wife and son. We'll crack a beer.

It had been years since he'd seen Sean. A lot of them, though he'd probably have to sit with a pen and paper to actually figure out how many exactly. But they'd been almost inseparable until adulthood, when Sean joined the army and Ben headed to college and then the city.

As soon as he opened his door, he could hear laughter from the camping area. Rather than going through the lodge to see if anybody was in there, he cut across the yard and headed for the trees. And as he walked, he braced himself.

Not for the chaos of the family gathering, but for seeing Laney again.

He'd kissed her. He hadn't planned it and he didn't regret it, but it had weighed on him since last night. They had chemistry. It was undeniable, and the kiss had felt like pouring gasoline on burning embers. The need for her had flared, hot and strong.

But then he'd remembered too late that they weren't looking for the same things in life, and he'd pulled back. And then he'd botched the apology, though she'd taken it well. So things would hopefully not be *too* awkward between them, but he was going to have a hard time looking at her and not wanting to kiss her again. They'd agreed, though, that it wasn't a good idea.

And that's what he was telling himself for the umpteenth time—kissing Laney again would *not* be a good idea—as he walked down the dirt drive into the camping area into somewhat organized chaos.

"Ben!"

He would have recognized Sean Kowalski anywhere, but seeing him was a bit of a shock. They'd both put on some years and seeing Sean made him keenly aware he'd aged exactly the same amount.

It didn't matter. It was good to see him. "How the hell have you been?"

They shook hands and then Sean dragged him to each cluster of family milling around. He said hello to the Kowalskis he knew and was introduced to the ones he didn't. The kids managed to be still long enough for Sean to name them all, but then he scooped a little boy into his arms, truck and all.

"And this is my boy, Johnny."

"He's a handsome little guy," Ben said, and he couldn't look away as Sean kissed the top of his son's head before setting him back down.

The last time he'd seen Sean, they'd barely been adults and now here he was with a kid of his own. He looked, not just content, but really happy. And even though he was happy for his old friend, Ben couldn't help but compare his own life to his. Same age. Same beginnings. But Ben was living in an apartment over his parents' garage with no sign of a wife on the horizon, never mind kids.

"You have good timing," Ryan said, holding up a beer in one hand and a soda in the other. "We're getting ready to fire up the grills."

"It doesn't take a smart man long to figure out what

time Rosie likes to put supper on the table." He took the soda and popped the tab. "Thanks."

"How are you liking being back in Whitford?"

"It's a big change, but a good one. I'm glad to be back."

"I know the town's glad to have you." Ryan opened the beer Ben hadn't chosen and took a long swallow. "I think if things keep growing the way they are around here, the state's going to have to consider some kind of regional medical center that's centrally located for the trail system, even if it's a small one."

"Whitford's kind of centrally located."

Ryan nodded. "Yes, it is."

Ben asked how business was and they talked about the custom home business Ryan owned down in Brookline. While Ryan was older than him, if you were friends with one Kowalski, you got to know them all. Sean had been in the middle—Mitch, Ryan, Sean, Liz and Josh—but the five of them were only spread out over seven years, so they'd often traveled as a pack. Along with Katie, of course. Rosie's daughter fell in age between Sean and Liz, so she'd practically grown up at the lodge. Ben still couldn't believe Josh had finally smartened up and married her.

"Oh, Ben," Rosie called, waving at him. "Have you seen Laney?"

"No." The question had taken him off guard, but he hoped like hell he didn't look guilty. He hadn't seen Laney, but it wasn't because he hadn't been scanning the people, looking for her. "I haven't seen her anywhere."

"Can you do me a favor and go check her camper?

The burgers are almost done and she should come have some since we made enough to feed the entire county."

There was no reasonable explanation he could offer as to why somebody else should go knock on Laney's door, so all he could do was nod. "Sure. I'll go find her."

After excusing himself from the guys, who were talking about the possibility of luring a private medical clinic to the area, he walked toward the front of the campground, to Laney's camper. Josh had chosen the spot well, because she could see almost everything through the tinted windows. But he'd angled it so her door and awning—and her cheerful pink chairs—were on the side facing away from everybody else. That gave her some privacy during her downtime and also didn't give the guests the feeling she was watching them all the time.

When he turned the corner, he stopped short at the sight of Laney. She was sitting in one of the chairs, with a tablet propped on the arm. She had earbuds in and, as he watched, she smiled at the screen. A big smile, as if she would have laughed if she knew nobody would hear her.

When he took another step, she must have caught the movement in her peripheral vision because she started. When she realized it was him, she tapped the screen and then pulled the earbuds out.

"Hi, Ben. I didn't hear you coming." She held up the earbuds. "I guess that was obvious."

"I didn't mean to startle you. What are you watching?"

"A sitcom that's been on for years, I guess, but I just

started watching it a few nights ago. It's ridiculous, but it makes me laugh."

He loved her laugh and found himself wishing he could watch it with her. "Rosie sent me to find you. It's almost time to eat."

"I can smell the burgers." She stood and wrapped the cord for the earbuds around the tablet. "Does she need help bringing stuff out? Like condiments and stuff?"

"I don't think so. It looked they have everything on one of the picnic tables."

"Oh. Well, I'll go ask her what she needs, then."

"Laney, she doesn't need anything. She wants you to go eat. And I hope you're hungry because there were three grills going. There are a *lot* of burgers. And hot dogs."

She looked at him for a long moment, indecision written all over her face. It probably wasn't easy working for people like Rosie and Josh, in what was their home. If she was the kind of person who liked well-defined lines between employers and employee, she was going to have a hard time adjusting.

"I…don't know what to do," she blurted out, and then her cheeks turned pink. "Is she just asking because it's polite, and I should be polite and say thank you, but I have dinner plans?"

He could almost feel her anxiety, and he felt like maybe somebody—like an asshole ex, maybe—had made most of her decisions for her in the past. "You can do whatever you're comfortable doing. I *can* tell you Rosie's not just being polite. You're part of the Northern Star, so she's going to take care of you, even though you're an employee. But she also won't be offended if it would make you more comfortable if I tell her you already made yourself some supper and are watching TV. What do you *want* to do?"

She caught her bottom lip between her teeth and Ben had to force himself to focus on her eyes. "Those burgers do smell awfully good."

"Then let's go have one. Or maybe five or six." When she gave him a shocked look, he laughed. "Seriously, you are not going to believe how much food they cooked."

Ben waited for her to put the tablet inside and then they walked back toward the area near Terry and Evan's RV where they'd gathered all the picnic tables together. It felt good to have her next to him, as if he wasn't quite as alone, even though they weren't a couple. And maybe, in another time and place, it would have been a date.

In this time and place, though, it wasn't. But at the very least, they'd become friends, and that would have to be enough since Laney had made it very clear she didn't want more.

EIGHT

"You were not kidding about the food," Laney said in a low voice to Ben.

"The really amazing part is how much of it is gone," he whispered back and she chuckled.

Somehow, without her realizing what was happening, she'd ended up sitting on a picnic table bench next to Ben. She had been sitting there talking to Beth, who did the office work for the sports bar her husband owned, and then Kevin had spotted Ben and waved him over to ask him a question about the ATV trails. After they'd talked for a couple of minutes, it had seemed natural for him to sit down. And then Mitch and Ryan had joined them, so Ben had scooted closer to her.

So here she was, in a crowd of people, so close to the man she'd kissed only twenty-fours ago that their legs kept bumping together. And the last time they'd bumped, he hadn't bothered moving, so his thigh was resting lightly against hers. Normally, she would chalk it up to six adults sitting at a picnic table, but this was Ben. And when it was him touching her, incidentally or not, she noticed.

A child's wail went off suddenly, like a siren, and Kevin and Beth both turned their heads toward where the kids were all eating together. Then, as Laney watched, they turned back to each other and played a fast game of rock, paper, scissors. Her paper covered his rock and after being denied a chance for two out of three, Kevin got to his feet and headed toward the kids.

"Gabe has a bit of a temper and he's stubborn as hell," Beth told her. "People try to tell me it's the terrible twos, but I haven't met a Kowalski yet who's outgrown it."

"Hey," Mitch and Ryan said at the same time.

Beth smiled sweetly at them. "Are you denying it?"

When they refused to answer, Beth laughed and Laney found herself laughing, too. The family dynamics were fascinating to her. The Kowalskis were nothing like her family, and they especially weren't like the Ballards. It wasn't that Laney didn't love her family, and she knew they loved her, but they weren't very expressive about it. And they often spoke of family as a duty. An obligation.

If the Kowalski family was any more expressive, they'd be too much. They were loud and funny and, even when they were insulting each other, the affection they felt for one another was always evident.

Watching them with the kids really made her ache, though. If she'd had children, that's how she would want them raised. Everybody kept an eye on them, but they weren't forced to sit still and behave. They had rules, of course. She'd already seen Lily get a talking-to from her grandmother and Lisa had reined her teenagers in when they got too rowdy too close to the grills. But they were happy kids, obviously loved, and they were given the freedom to be themselves.

Watching them made her even more painfully aware that she'd always thought she'd have children by this point in her life, but these kids also reinforced that her lack of conception during her marriage might have been a blessing.

"You okay?"

It was Beth who asked, breaking into her thoughts, and Laney smiled at her. "Yes. I was just lost in thought there for a minute."

Kevin came back and stepped over the bench to sit back down. "Johnny stole one of Gabe's chips, so Lily gave him one of hers, but hers was barbecue-flavored and he did not like that."

After a few more minutes of chatting, Laney realized she was starting to feel a little too comfortable at the table. Everybody was very friendly, but it wasn't only that. It was sitting with Ben, legs touching, that made her feel almost as if she was a part of something she actually wasn't. She liked boundaries and she needed to maintain some not only between her and the family she worked for, but between her and Ben. They'd survived one kiss without too much awkwardness, but she didn't want to be sending him mixed signals.

"I'm going to help clean up," she said, getting to her feet. "I need to burn off some of the million calories I just ate."

"Calories don't count if the food was cooked on a grill," Kevin said, and Beth laughed.

Even if she hadn't known the families camped together at least once every year, Laney would have been able to guess by their level of organization. It wasn't long before the paper plates and napkins were tossed, and the condiments were all on trays that were easy to carry back to the campers.

"I'll take that to the Dumpster on my way back to

my camper," she told Ryan's wife, Lauren, who had just pulled the full trash bag out of the can. At least she wouldn't have to lecture this group on how much raccoons, skunks and bears loved garbage and carelessly stored food.

"Just throw it on one of the four-wheelers," Lauren said. "The keys are still in most of them."

"I told them not to be lazy about the keys." Mary shook her head. "We have too many little ones now to be leaving keys in the machines."

"I'll remind everybody. But Laney, you can go ahead and take one of them."

"I don't know how to drive a four-wheeler," she confessed. "I've never even sat on one before."

Not only Lauren and Mary, but a few people who were nearby turned to look at her, but it was Keri who spoke. "Never? Oh, you have to learn. I only learned the summer Joe and I got together—at the annual camping trip, no less—and it's a lot of fun."

"I can't believe Josh or Andy hasn't had you practicing," Mary added. "It seems like being able to drive an ATV around would make some of your work easier."

Laney thought of Ben's offer to teach her and couldn't stop herself from looking over at him. He was not only close enough to hear the conversation, but he was watching her to see what she was going to say. "I'm definitely going to learn. Maybe once things settle down a little."

Ben's lips curved into a smile and she thought he might have given her a quick nod. The other women started talking about who would be the best one to teach her—and it seemed like a tie between Andy and Ryan—but Laney just let them talk. As much as spending time together complicated things, she couldn't really see herself trusting anybody but Ben to show her how to ride one of those things.

And from the looks of it, he was still willing to teach her.

"Evan's got that campfire roaring already," Keri said. "I was hoping we'd get to relax for a bit before s'mores time."

"We'll relax," Mary said, "and bring out the marshmallows when we're ready. And when somebody reminds him we want more hot coals and less raging inferno with these kids."

"I'm going to get some stuff done," Laney said. She might be able to do a quick check of the bathhouse while they were distracted with marshmallows. "I'll just carry the garbage bag. It's not that heavy."

"Make sure you're back for s'mores," Lauren said. "Probably about forty-five minutes or so. We have to let the fire burn down some, but we don't want to wait too long to jack the kids up on sugar."

"Oh, I'll probably just go in for the night."

"And miss the s'mores?" Mary shook her head. "They're the best part of camping."

"I've never had one, actually."

"You've never had a s'more?" Lauren cocked her head. "How is that even possible?"

"We never went camping that I remember."

Keri laughed. "Sometimes, in the winter, Brianna and I put on a movie and toast marshmallows over a candle and make s'mores in the living room. Very important to use unscented candles, by the way. Learned that one the hard way."

"You don't want to miss the s'mores," Mary said, and Laney knew the issue was settled.

"I'll definitely be back, then," she said, and through the corner of her eye, she saw Ben smile.

Sean

THERE WERE TIMES in Sean's life that made him wish there was a pause button so he could treasure a moment longer. Moments like Emma and Johnny working in the garden together, singing silly songs. The way Emma laughed when Sean told her a stupid joke.

And this moment, when Johnny was trying to feed Emma a s'more and marshmallow was stuck to her chin and she was laughing too hard to bite into the graham cracker and chocolate. He was frowning in concentration, and maybe a little bit of annoyance, and while Johnny looked like him, the expression was so Emma, Sean couldn't help smiling.

"You are one lucky son of a bitch," Ben said from the chair next to him.

"That I am." They were all lucky, he thought, looking around the fire. Liz was feeding Jackson little bits of lightly toasted marshmallow while the other kids made s'mores with the help of various adults. It was a messy business and occasionally dangerous if you didn't want to get slapped with a molten marshmallow flung off the end of a stick being waved around, but he knew none of them would rather be doing anything else. "So you never got married, huh?"

"Nope. Gave too much to the job and not enough to the women who were willing to try to make a go of it with me."

"Now you've got a little more free time and you can find yourself a nice hometown girl." As soon as he said it, Ben's gaze shifted and Sean didn't miss it.

He'd had a hunch his old friend might be interested in Laney, and the way Ben looked at her now confirmed it. She was on the other side of the fire, holding Gabe on her lap while frowning at the ends of her hair, which had marshmallow stuck in it.

"Laney fits in well with everybody," he said, fishing with a more obvious bait.

Ben looked at him, nodding slowly. "Yeah, she does. She's a nice woman, so I'm not surprised."

"What's her story, anyway? Rosie said she was divorced and looking to leave…where was it she's from?"

"Rhode Island."

"Right. And she ended up here in Whitford, huh?"

Ben frowned. "She's Nola Kendrick's cousin, which I'm pretty sure you already know, since it probably came up during the family meeting about hiring her."

Sean decided to dial it back a little. "That's right. Honestly, Josh does such a great job of running this place now that I don't always pay attention as well as I should on the conference calls. Which I hate, because it's confusing keeping track of who's talking."

Emma, who'd finally managed to swallow a few bites of Johnny's s'more, walked toward them. She was holding their son's hand since they were close to the fire ring, and grimacing at her other hand, which was covered in marshmallow and chocolate.

"Tell Daddy we need help cleaning up," she said when they were standing in front of him.

Johnny pulled his hand free from his mom's so he could hold them up. Judging by the amount of marshmallow and chocolate on the two of them, he had to wonder if they'd gotten any in their mouths. "We might need a hose."

Johnny laughed, since they often joked about using a hose on him after he'd been playing outside or working with Emma in the yard. And sometimes they weren't joking. When Emma nudged him between the chairs, he took off running toward the camper with Emma on his heels.

"The bathhouse, Johnny. Don't you dare touch Grammy's camper with your hands like that."

"I better go help," Sean said.

"I'm going to get going, anyway," Ben said. "It's been a long day and I ate way too much. If I don't leave now, I might fall asleep in this chair and I don't trust you guys."

Sean laughed as Ben stood up, and then shook his hand. "You'll be around, though, right? We'll be hitting the trail tomorrow."

"I might see you out there."

Sean didn't miss the glances and waves Ben and Laney exchanged before he said a general good-night and walked away from the fire. Then he heard Johnny squeal and he put his friend's love life out of his mind. If he didn't get to the bathhouse and help Emma, it was his own love life he'd be worrying about.

He found them in the bathroom, with Emma trying to balance Johnny on her raised knee so he could reach inside the sink. But he was too heavy for that now, so he grabbed his son around the waist and lifted him.

"I'll hold him and you scrub him."

Emma made quick work of Johnny's hands and face with the warm water and soap, and Sean dried him off while she washed herself up. Then, while she dried her hands, Sean looped his arm around her waist and pulled her close so he could kiss the back of her neck.

"Are you having fun so far?"

"Yes, although I'm freaking exhausted and it's only the first day."

"There was also the driving and the set-up. But I'll take him to the camper and get him in his pajamas. If I read to him for a while, he'll probably nod off. You brought the baby monitor, right?" She nodded. "Then you go get Terry to make you a drink and sit in front of the fire for a while. I'll bring the monitor out with me when he's asleep."

She turned in his embrace so she could kiss him. "That sounds like one hell of a plan."

"Then maybe later we can fool around a little."

After a nod toward their son, who was trying to scrub chocolate off of his shirt with a wad of paper towel, she shrugged. "I might let you get to second base."

"Tell Terry to make it a *stiff* drink."

She kissed him again and then bent down to kiss Johnny. "It's time to go in the camper and read with Daddy."

Sean knew his son was wiped out when he didn't put up a fight. He just took his hand and walked with him toward their RV. Emma looked back at them, silhouetted by the campfire behind her, and he blew her a kiss.

Yes, he was definitely one lucky son of a bitch.

LEAVING THE NORTHERN STAR without specifically seeking out Laney to say goodbye felt wrong to Ben, even though he knew it was the right thing to do. The smile and wave across the campfire had to be enough, since anything more would have attracted attention and she wouldn't want that. He had a feeling if Mary and Rosie decided to do some matchmaking, Laney would feel uncomfortable pretty quickly.

His apartment was dark when he let himself in, and so quiet he turned the television on just to have some background noise. Most of the time he didn't mind being alone too much, since he was used to it, but he didn't usually spend the evening surrounded by happy couples. Tonight, though, the apartment felt so empty he was surprised the voice of the sports reporter on the television didn't echo.

After changing into a pair of cotton sleep pants, he stretched out on his couch with the remote and started flipping through channels. He found nothing that was engrossing enough to make him stop wishing he had somebody to talk to.

He could picture the others going back to their RVs and talking about the night. Laughing at something one of the kids had done. Sharing little tidbits they'd heard through the family grapevine. Talking about their plans for the next day's vacation.

Ben fell asleep to an infomercial for some gadget that would roast a chicken in a fraction of the usual time and woke with a sore neck to the early morning news.

After setting the coffee to brew, he jumped in the shower, hoping the hot water would ease the pains of a restless night on the couch. He should have just gone to bed, but he'd been afraid he'd lie awake, thinking about Laney and how lonely he was.

Ben dressed in cargo pants and his paramedic T-shirt because, if he did decide to meet up with the guys and ride, he'd still technically be on duty. He still hadn't made up his mind about that, but he thought he might go out for a little while. It would be the guys, which meant he wouldn't feel like a third wheel, or a fifth wheel or whatever wheel he'd be. And he could burn off some energy, which wouldn't hurt.

He heard voices in the driveway, so he went downstairs to see his parents for a few minutes before going to work. They were the early-to-bed-and-early-to-rise kind of people, so he always had a better chance of seeing them at the beginning of the day than at the end.

They were discussing whether or not the driveway needed resealing, and less than two minutes later, Ben wished he'd found a way to sneak out without them seeing him. It wasn't likely he could have gotten in his SUV and driven past them, but he could have tried.

"We can just seal the cracks again," his dad said for the fourth time since Ben hit the bottom step.

"Our driveway already looks like it's duct taped together thanks to years of that," his mom argued. "I think we need to redo the entire thing. Ben, what do you think?"

He hated when she did that. In his mind, he heard *which parent is your favorite at this moment, Ben?* "What does Jimmy think?"

"We haven't asked Jimmy," she said. "And you live here, so you get a vote."

He really hoped he wouldn't be living over his parents' garage for so long that the longevity of the driveway surface was relevant to him. "I think you should have some kind of cook-off and whoever wins gets to make the driveway plan."

His dad scowled. "What the hell is that supposed to mean?"

"You make those ribs that make grown men eat until they throw up and maybe some coleslaw. Mom can offer up some cornbread. Maybe a strawberry-rhubarb pie. Jimmy and I can judge and whoever wins…wins."

"You just want ribs and pie."

Ben shrugged. "Just trying to come up with a fair plan because I'm a good son like that."

"What do you really think?" his dad asked.

"Honestly? It's starting to look like a patchwork quilt, so either this year or next year, depending on your finances, you should consider having it repaved."

"Maybe I should raise your rent," his dad growled.

"Then I'd better to get to work so I can earn more money." Ben kissed his mom on the cheek, seeing his opportunity for escape.

"We know you're salaried," his dad called after him, and Ben laughed.

Sam was at the fire station when Ben walked in, which was no surprise. Dave and Jordan were also there, hanging around. There tended to be a lot of hanging around in Whitford, which was a good thing, since people usually only called them when they were having a really bad day. But it was still an adjustment for Ben, who was used to spending most of his shifts on the run.

Now there were no shifts. If there was a problem, they showed up. Otherwise, they maintained equipment, trained and—in the case of some of the others—worked other jobs. For Sam and Ben, there was a lot more hanging around than anything else.

"Hey, Ben," Sam said, once he'd had a few minutes to shoot the shit with the guys. "Got a second?"

"Sure." There was technically an office, but it was more like an oversized closet with a cheap desk shoved in it, so they went outside. It wasn't totally private, but the other guys were arguing about whatever was on the TV screen and not paying them any attention. "What's up?"

"They'll be a lot of traffic this upcoming weekend, what with it being a holiday and all. We'll probably have more ATV calls than usual."

"I figured as much. It's the same in the city, except for the ATVs. A holiday means more parties, more driving under the influence. More accidents. And being the Fourth, more drownings and more injuries from fireworks and sparklers."

"Rumor has it you've been spending a lot of time at the Northern Star lately."

"Rumor has it, huh?"

Sam shrugged. "It's a small town."

"It's a small town that needs to understand I'm not going to sit here twenty-four hours a day, staring at my phone and waiting to be called out."

"Back it up," Sam said, and then he chuckled. "That wasn't a criticism. I know Sean's back for a while, and Ryan's up and lord knows Rosie must be cooking up a storm."

"Yeah, she is."

"I was just trying to get a feel for what everybody's doing over the holiday weekend so when a call comes in, I have a rough idea of where everybody's staging from. I had the same conversation with the other guys, too. So I'm just wondering if you'll be spending most of the weekend there, that's all."

"Probably. During peak riding hours, I might hang around here, though." He couldn't spend *all* of his time at the campground because being around Laney that much would drive him crazy.

Sam shrugged. "As long as you're not drinking and have your phone on, it doesn't really matter if you're at the lodge. The access trail out of town goes almost all the way there, anyway, so technically starting from the Northern Star would shorten your response time to the main trail system."

That wasn't helping, but Ben didn't want to tell Sam he'd been fishing for a solid reason to *avoid* hanging out at the lodge. "Good point. I'll text you whenever I think I might be out there for any length of time, so you'll know. Otherwise, assume I'll be starting from here."

"Sounds good." The argument inside was escalating, and Sam looked over his shoulder. "I think we'll be washing and polishing the engine today. Those two need to spend some time in the fresh air."

"I'm going to get some fresh air myself. The guys are going out on a ride today after lunch and I might meet up with them out there."

"Good day for it. Things will start getting busy out there Friday night, once people have arrived and checked into their lodging. But they won't stray far the first night. Saturday and Sunday will be busy, and—oh crap."

Ben turned, frowning. "What's wrong?"

"I totally forgot about the library thing."

Hailey Barnett—town librarian and wife of Matt,

the game warden—was walking toward them pushing a stroller and with a black Lab and a half-dozen little kids with her.

Sam stepped through the open doors. “Field trip, boys. Look sharp!”

To buy them a few minutes to tuck in their shirts and make sure everything was reasonably well child-proofed, Ben wandered down the sidewalk toward them. “Good morning, everybody.”

The kids all shouted it back at him, and Hailey smiled. “How are you, Ben?”

“I’m good, thanks.” They’d met a couple of times, but he hadn’t met their little girl yet. She was in the stroller, kicking her feet while her hand rested on the neck of the dog, who’d sat down next to her as soon as Hailey stopped.

“This is Amelia. She’s nine months old. And that’s Bear.” The dog’s tail thumped.

“Bear is the dog,” one of the boys offered, apparently thinking Ben might be confused.

“Oh, that makes sense. Bear would be a funny name for a pretty little girl.”

“I saw Sam run away, so I guess it’s safe to assume he forgot the fire station is on our list of free field trips for the summer reading program?”

Ben laughed. “I think he just wanted to spit shine the old bell on the engine so it would be shiny for the kids. You guys want to ring the bell, right?”

His question was met with the kind of enthusiasm fire engines tended to bring out in the elementary age, and he smiled. “You know what’s even cooler than a truck with lights and a siren? An ATV with lights and a siren.”

Judging by the *ooh* sound from the kids, it was going to be a fun morning. Not a bad way to pass the time, he thought.

NINE

Emma

SITTING AROUND THE pool didn't have quite the same effect when it was an inflatable pool filled with a few inches of water. But the little kids were happily splashing in it and the women were relaxing in chairs set in a circle. The older kids were inside the fence, in the big pool. The men had all gone out on one of their guys-only rides, which meant they'd come home filthy and starving and hopefully not *too* battered, so they were enjoying the peace and quiet while it lasted.

"Seeing the kids all together like this sure does the heart good," Mary said. "The little kids *and* the big kids."

"I haven't seen Sean this happy in a long time," Emma said. "He loves it here."

Rosie smiled at her. "I can't even tell you how happy that makes me. I wasn't sure he'd ever come back, to be honest. He never liked it growing up, but I hoped when he left the army, he'd come back to Whitford. To the lodge. But he said he was going to spend some time in New Hampshire first, and then he met you, Emma. It was for the best, of course, because I can't imagine him without you, but seeing him here makes me feel whole again somehow."

Emma knew that Sean had visited New Hampshire

after his discharge because he didn't know what he wanted to do and he was afraid if he went back to the lodge, he'd get sucked into the family business. He'd never been comfortable growing up in a house he shared with strangers and he wanted no part of running it.

When push came to shove, though, he'd joined with his brothers to keep from losing it. And, whether it was simply letting go of his childhood or the fact it had brought the Kowalski kids back together again, Sean had even come to love the place.

"What's wrong, Emma?" Rosie asked, her voice low with concern.

"Nothing." She forced herself to smile. "I think I mentally wandered off for a minute, that's all."

"I hope I didn't make it sound like I'd rather Sean had come home instead of going to New Hampshire before. I wouldn't change anything, you know, because I love you and Johnny."

I'd rather Sean had come home... Because Whitford—or the Northern Star Lodge, to be precise—would always be Sean's home in everybody's mind. Maybe even Sean's. "I know that. That wasn't it, I promise."

"Are you feeling okay?" Mary asked.

"Yes. Tired, I guess. Getting Johnny to settle in the camper is a little challenging. Bedtime isn't too bad, because he's wiped out by then, but he's been waking up earlier than usual and I'm thinking about leaving the two of them in the RV and moving myself into the lodge."

"I'll drink to that," Beth said from the other side of the chain link fence. Because Brianna and Lily wanted to swim in the big pool, some of the women were inside the fence and some were outside, with the kiddie pool. "I'll drink a *lot* to that. Lily isn't bad, but Gabe doesn't handle us all being in the same room very well. He has his own little air mattress with a sleeping bag he got to pick out, but likes to roam around. He'll crawl in with Lily, but that wakes her up and she's cranky, so then he gets in with us. And as soon as it's light enough for him to see, he's ready to go again."

"That sounds like Johnny," Emma said.

"I asked Andy if he could paint windows black, and he laughed," Beth continued. "I guess he thought I was joking."

"We hung a princess curtain around the bottom bunk in our cabin," Keri said. She was inside the fence, with Beth. "That way, she has her own private room and she pretends it's a fancy bed like princesses have. But mostly it keeps the sun from waking her up in the morning."

"I'd steal it, but Lily could sleep through the zombie apocalypse. Gabe's the problem, and I don't think he even has to see the sun. He just *knows*."

Emma watched Johnny trying to show Gabe how to put his face in the water and blow bubbles, which led to Gabe sputtering, coughing and then laughing every time. Then Jackson, who was just sitting in the pool, slapping the surface of the water with his hands, would laugh. It was soothing, she thought, watching babies enjoy the smallest things in life.

"What do you think, Emma?"

"Huh?" She looked at Liz, who'd spoken to her. "I'm sorry. I was watching my son teach his cousin how to inhale pool water."

Beth snorted. “He’s kind of hopeless in the water. He’ll probably still be in the kiddie pool when the others go off to college.”

“He’ll get it,” Mary said. “I haven’t met a Kowalski yet who can’t swim.”

“Well, he’s got my DNA, too, and I know a few Hansens who sink like rocks.”

“What do I think about what?” Emma asked before the conversation derailed to the point nobody remembered what the original question had been.

“Oh, Laney,” Liz said. “Laney and Ben.”

“What about them?”

“Do you think they’re a thing?”

Emma was surprised by the question, and she wasn’t really sure what she should say. Sean had told her he thought Ben had a thing for Laney, but that as far as he knew, nothing had happened between them. But talk between two old friends that was shared with a wife in private didn’t make it family gossip. And she didn’t think Rosie had some kind of rule governing fraternization between Laney and guests, and technically he *wasn’t* a guest. But he was the guest of a guest…and an old friend of the family.

“I don’t know,” she said, before she could confuse herself to the point she couldn’t get any words out. “Why do you ask?”

“I think they’d be a perfect couple,” Rosie said.

Mary nodded. “I agree.”

“Well,” Liz said, “they’re pretty well doomed.”

They all laughed, but Emma knew Liz wasn’t kidding. Laney and Ben being attracted to each other plus Rosie and Mary deciding they belonged together would only equal one of two things—a happily-ever-after, or some kind of moment so awkward Ben would probably never return to the lodge again.

LANEY HAD SEEN the guys return from their big ride, and she was dreading what the bathhouse would look like. The machines had been caked with mud, and the men themselves were so dirty, she had a hard time telling them apart.

Even though they'd taken turns at the wash station, spraying each other and their ATVs with the hose, she had a feeling a whole lot of that dirt was going to be on the bathroom floors. And when steam from the showers and water splashed around mixed with it, she'd learned that muddy bathrooms were actually a thing that existed in campgrounds.

She'd taken the time the women were relaxing around the pool to do a thorough cleaning of the lodge and restock the bathrooms. Then after the men rolled back in, she'd taken her break and retreated to her camper. She made herself a grilled cheese sandwich because she'd loved them as a child but never eaten them again once she met Patrick. But she'd seen Beth making some for the kids on a griddle attachment for the grill, and fallen in love with them all over. That and a couple chapters from the book she was reading should have cleared her mind.

But even a good book couldn't distract her from the fact Ben had ridden in with the rest of the guys. He must have run into them out on the trail system and, since they all looked happy and relaxed—if really filthy—she assumed they hadn't dragged him out there for a 911 call.

The knowledge Ben was in the campground was

like a low electrical humming she couldn't ignore. She could eat her dinner and even read the words on the page, but part of her was always tuned in to that hum.

But she was determined to stick to her plan to give the Kowalski family some space and give herself some alone time. Once everybody seemed to have cleaned up and the grills were being lit, she would go clean the bathhouse and make sure they had everything they needed, and then retreat back to her camper. A good movie turned up enough to drown out the sound of his laughter should it drift all the way to her camper was just the thing.

Maybe a movie without kissing, though. Or sex. Or romance. A thriller, maybe, though thrillers without a love interest weren't easy to find. A horror flick was probably safe, but the last time she'd watched a horror movie and then done a late lap through the campground to make sure everything was good for the night, a guest stepping out from behind the tree he'd been peeing on had almost given her a heart attack. The feeling had apparently been mutual and as she walked away, she'd heard him trying to explain to his wife why he'd screamed.

No, probably not a horror movie.

But before she scrolled through the streaming options, looking for something devoid of anything that might make her think about the fact Ben wasn't that far away, she wanted to get the bathhouse clean.

It wasn't as bad as she'd feared, maybe because the men had all been raised by two women with high expectations they demanded be met. And partly because she knew from a conversation she'd overheard that the guys would strip to their boxer briefs outside the bathroom door if they were really muddy and Lily and Brianna weren't around.

She went through each bathroom, sweeping up the dirt. Then she sprayed down the showers and gave each toilet and sink a quick scrubbing. The toilet paper dispensers were fine, but all the bathrooms needed the paper towel dispensers filled and the trash cans emptied, probably because they'd all tried to clean up after themselves. Because the guests were all family and were staying so long, they were leaving shampoos and soaps in the bathroom, along with some other toiletries, so she left them alone.

It took her about an hour, since she wasn't hurrying. Once she'd put the cleaning supplies back in the storage closet, she washed her hands and called it good.

It looked like the family was cleaning up after dinner, which meant her timing had been perfect. She could hear a four-wheeler running, though, which seemed odd. When she walked around the back of the bathhouse, she could see it, driving around out in the field. It was Sean, she realized, with Johnny sitting in front of him on the seat. The helmet looked huge on the little boy, and he had his hands on the handlebars, as if he was steering. Sean had control of the grips and the throttle, though, and she knew he was safe.

She wondered how old Johnny would have to be before he got to ride his own, smaller ATV. She knew they made little ones because she'd seen Lily and Brianna taking turns riding a little pink one in the field, with adult supervision.

Too late, she realized the guy leaning against a pickup truck parked at the edge of the field wasn't one of Sean's brothers or cousins. It was Ben and, when he saw her, he smiled.

He was dirty. Even from a distance she could see that he hadn't cleaned up yet. There were even smudges on his face, and she wondered what it would be like to be riding behind him, her arms wrapped around his waist, while he splashed through mud.

Then he raised his hand and made a *come over here* gesture. She shook her head, but he only laughed. She could barely hear it, but she could see it, and then he waved her over.

And because she couldn't—or didn't want to—say no to Ben when he grinned like that, she went.

BEN HAD WAVED Laney over without thinking about it, but as she walked toward him, he didn't regret it. She was beautiful and nothing short of a real emergency could have torn his attention from her as she walked.

She'd been spending so much time outside, her skin had taken on a sun-kissed glow. Her hair had even lightened a little, and it was hanging loose past her shoulders. And she was wearing denim cutoff shorts and a Northern Star ATV Club T-shirt, which amused him considering what he was going to try to get her to do.

"You have some dirt on your face, right there," she said when she was close enough, pointing to his cheek. Then she opened her hand and made a big gesture like washing a window. "And pretty much all over...there."

Laughing, he pulled up the hem of his T-shirt and wiped at his face, knowing it wouldn't do much good. There was a smear of trail dust left behind on the fabric, but nothing short of a shower was going to get him clean.

But when he looked at her over the T-shirt still bunched in his hands, intending to ask her if that was better, she was staring at his bared stomach. He might not be twenty years old anymore and she couldn't count his ab muscles, but good genes and physical activity meant he didn't reflexively suck in his gut as she looked.

When he dropped the T-shirt, her gaze lifted and he did his best not to show any reaction to the light flush across her cheeks and the skin exposed by the V-neck of her shirt. "Did I get it all?"

That made her laugh. "No. Unless you want me to get a hose, I think it's a lost cause."

"I'll pass." Not that being blasted by cold water would be unwelcome after the way she'd just been looking at him. "You ready for a lesson?"

Her eyes widened. "A lesson?"

He pointed off to his right, where a couple of ATVs sat. One of them was Beth's, which was a lighter machine with a smaller engine, and it had the keys in it. "You want to learn how to ride?"

"Right now?"

While she looked hesitant, he hadn't missed the way her eyes lit up when she first looked at the four-wheeler. "Sure. You can just drive around the field a little, like Sean."

Not exactly like Sean, he hoped. While it might be smarter for him to be on the machine behind her, her butt between his thighs, he was hoping she'd take to it well enough so he could keep his feet on the ground.

"But it's okay if you don't want to," he added.

"Not everybody likes it. Hell, even Rosie doesn't ride, though she'll go out on the snowmobile with Andy if it's not too cold and he promises not to go too fast."

"I think I want to." She bit at her bottom lip for a few seconds and he noticed her hands balled into fists at her side. Then she gave a sharp nod. "I want to."

He grinned. "Then let's do it."

Operating the thing was fairly simple. Turn the key on and hit the start button. It had Park, Reverse, Neutral, Drive and Low. The thumb throttle was on the right grip and there were squeeze brakes, like on a ten-speed bicycle. There was also a foot brake on the right side foot well, but she wouldn't need that.

"Okay," she said when he'd explained it all to her.

"Just sit on it for right now. See how it feels."

She stepped into the foot well and threw her leg over the seat. Then she put her hands on the rubber grip and looked it over. When she turned her gaze to him, he could see the excitement in her eyes even before she smiled. "It doesn't feel as big when you're sitting on it as it looks when you're standing next to it."

"Go ahead and start it." He deliberately didn't tell her how again. He wanted to know how much of the information she'd retained. When she double-checked that it was in Park before turning the key to the on position, he smiled. Then she hit the run button and the engine fired. "Okay, now leave it in Park and give it just a little gas. Get a feel for the throttle and how the pressure you put on it makes the engine rev up."

A few minutes later, there was nothing else she could learn sitting still, so he handed her Beth's helmet, which had been sitting on the front rack, and helped her buckle it. With Sean and his little guy out in the field, Ben wasn't comfortable just letting her take off on her own. Sean was aware of what they were doing and he'd watch for her, but Ben wasn't taking chances with a three-year-old out there.

"I'm going to sit on the back for a few minutes, until you've got the hang of it." But he didn't want to distract her from what she was doing—or torture himself—so he didn't straddle the seat behind her.

Instead he stepped onto the foot well and sat sideways on the back rack. The metal tubes weren't exactly comfortable, but he knew he wouldn't be there long. He held on to the rack with his left hand, leaving his right hand free to yank her thumb off the throttle or grab the bar.

"Okay. Hold the brake and put it in Drive. Then let go of the brake and give it a little gas. Nice and easy."

He didn't think she'd mash the throttle and wheelie him off the back, but he tightened his fingers around the rack just in case.

But Laney was smooth on the throttle and she drove across the grass without a problem. Then, before he could prompt her, she squeezed the brakes and brought the ATV to a stop. She repeated the process a few more times, and Ben liked the fact she got a little more adventurous each time. Going a little bit faster. Braking a little more aggressively. Getting a feel for its turning radius.

"Okay, stop for a second," he told her. Once she had, he hopped off. "Go ahead and drive around for a while."

"By myself? Are you sure I'm ready?"

"Absolutely." Plus, his hip couldn't take sitting sideways on the metal rack anymore.

She drove around the field for about ten minutes. Once Sean saw that she had a good handle on what she was doing, he and Johnny played four-wheeler follow the leader with her. Sometimes she was in front and sometimes Sean pulled around her and led. It made Johnny happy and, judging by the smiles she sent his way, it made Laney happy, too.

Then Sean led her toward the woods and she stopped at the edge, looking at Ben. He waved for her to go and, after a few more seconds of hesitation, she followed Sean onto the trail and out of his sight.

Ben wasn't worried about her. He knew Sean wouldn't take her very far, especially since he had Johnny with him, and riding around in a grass field wasn't the same as being out on the trail. He did wish he was the one taking her out in the woods, though. Seeing her embrace something new that she clearly enjoyed made him happy and he was sad he'd be missing out on part of the experience.

But then again, maybe being alone with her out in the woods wouldn't be such a good idea, either. Sitting on a hard metal rack had caused him enough discomfort so he could handle sitting behind her on the ATV without his self-control slipping. But out in a clearing in the woods, with the machines shut off and nobody else around, he might forget he wasn't touching her again.

TEN

LANEY WAS A matter of mere paragraphs from the big *whodunnit* reveal in the mystery she was reading, since she hadn't been able to settle on a movie, when somebody knocked on the side of her camper. A moment later, Liz's face appeared on the other side of her screen door.

"Hey, Laney, what are you doing?"

"Just reading." She set the tablet down and went to the door. "What do you need?"

"We don't need anything. We want you to come play Scrabble with us."

That made Laney laugh, and Liz backed up so she could open the screen door and step out. "When did Scrabble become a campground game?"

"When it's girls' night out. Okay, maybe not *out* since we're already outside and we can't really go anywhere, but the men are in charge of the kids, and it's Dirty Scrabble."

"Dirty Scrabble?" With this crowd, Laney couldn't be sure if a game being called dirty meant it involved sex or mud.

"Come play and we'll explain it to you."

So much for her resolve to maintain some distance tonight. She'd already gotten talked into an ATV lesson by Ben. And then she'd ridden a couple of miles down the trail and back with Sean and Johnny. And she'd loved it, more than she'd thought she would, but then she'd found the strength to excuse herself so she could get back to her original plan.

And now this. She hadn't been very good at alone time since the Kowalski family showed up, but maybe she was overthinking. This summer was about learning to enjoy being by herself, but it was also about rediscovering what *she* liked. And she liked spending time with these people.

"Okay. Let me grab a sweatshirt."

Liz waited for her and when they got close to where the men—including Mike and Lisa's two teenagers—were helping the kids make s'mores, she leaned close to whisper. "Don't look at them. Do *not* make eye contact. Pretend they're invisible or they'll suck you into helping them."

Laney was tempted to laugh, but she suspected Liz was being serious. And through her peripheral vision, she saw all the men turn to look as they walked by.

"It's okay, Jackson," she heard Drew saying to Liz's little boy. "Mommy's going to play a game, but we'll be fine. I'll try not to get melted marshmallow in your hair. Or smear chocolate all over the T-shirt you're wearing, which is her favorite."

Liz snorted and kept walking. "He's the chief of police. He can melt a marshmallow."

Laney heard the men laugh and then Andy's voice. "That was weak, son. Don't forget she was raised by Rosie, so if you were looking for sympathy, you've gotta try harder."

"You know what Terry says," Evan said. "If you're looking for sympathy, it's between shit and syphilis in the dictionary."

"Wow, the Kowalskis are tough."

That was Ben's voice, and Laney was proud of herself. She didn't stop and turn around, or trip over her own feet. Anybody watching her probably wouldn't have guessed that her pulse jacked up and her cheeks got hot when she heard him talk. The more time she spent thinking—or fantasizing—about him, the stronger her reaction to seeing or hearing him, so she really needed to stop thinking about him.

Like that was going to happen.

The women were all gathered behind Leo and Mary's big RV, which made sense. If the little ones could see their moms, it would be that much harder on the guys. And despite Drew's little display, Laney guessed they were having fun being in charge and giving their wives a break.

"You got her!" Katie waved and gestured to an empty chair next to her. "Come sit next to me."

Laney did, noticing that Katie was sitting in a straight-backed kitchen chair instead of a camp chair, as was Paige. "Do you want to switch chairs? That doesn't look very comfortable."

"We can't bend over the boards from those chairs," Paige said. "I can barely bend over the board from *this* chair, but at least my butt doesn't sink down into it."

Liz clapped her hands. "Okay, the rules are pretty simple. We use regular Scrabble scoring, but we have three boards going at a time because there are a bunch of us. You get a bonus double word score for any word you can't say in front of the kids. And if you can't even say the word out loud, you get a triple word score."

"Obviously you want to get those words early in the

game," Lisa said, "because the longer we drink, the more uninhibited our vocabulary gets."

"So a shy person has the advantage?" Laney asked.

"Somebody..." When Lisa paused, they all looked at Beth, "tried to cheat once by pretending she couldn't say any bad words, but she forgot we know her better than that."

"So now we have the Beth Rule," Keri said. "If there's any doubt about a word being a triple, we go around and if anybody besides the person who played the word balks at saying it out loud, it's a triple word score."

"Do you want something to drink?" Rosie asked. "We have these cute little wine boxes with tiny straws. They're like juice boxes for adults."

"Sure." Laney didn't think a little wine would hurt, and she'd pretty much given up on having any kind of professional boundaries with these people.

It went around the women a few times before they had enough of a word base to start having fun. And then it came time to lay her first dirty word, but Laney bought herself some time by staring at her row of tiles.

She didn't have to say it out loud, she reminded herself. In fact, it was better for her game if she couldn't. But even putting the tiles down on the board was something she couldn't imagine herself doing.

But not too long ago, she wouldn't have been able to imagine herself living in a camper in Maine, laughing and drinking wine out of a box and making dirty words with women she barely knew.

After taking a deep breath, she picked up the first letter tile and leaned forward to place it on the board, working backward from the existing letter Y.

S. S. U. P.

Then she clapped her hands over her eyes. Not only would she not say it out loud, but she couldn't believe she'd just written the word out on the board.

The other women laughed, so she uncovered her eyes and laughed with them. "I had a pretty strict upbringing, language-wise. And my ex-husband had a stick up his...butt."

That made them laugh harder, but they gave her the triple word score because Rosie and Mary both waved off saying it. Laney would have thought having them playing would give an advantage with regard to anybody balking, but they had no problem saying *blowjob* or *gang bang*, so there went that theory.

An argument broke out over whether *gang bang* was one word or two, which led to Lauren looking it up on her phone. Unfortunately, she didn't have any safe search filters on and there was a lot of squealing and laughing before she wiped her search history and they decided to let the word stand. Whether it was one word or two, it was a good one, and it was hard to side against the very pregnant Paige.

So much for avoiding anything to do with sex in her entertainment for the night, Laney thought. Between occasionally hearing Ben's laugh mixed in with the other men's, and all kinds of naughty words that kept her mind tripping over provocative thoughts of him all night, she'd be lucky if she slept at all tonight.

It was more likely she'd spend the night tossing and turning, imagining his touch. His taste. His voice saying to her some of the words she'd read on the board tonight. If she did sleep, she'd probably hear him in her dreams.

"Hey, Rosie, can you toss me another wine box?"

OUTSIDE OF HIS professional duties, Ben couldn't remember a more grueling night. On the outside he probably looked like a guy who was chilling around a campfire, telling stories and laughing. But on the inside, he felt as if his body was a compass needle and Laney was his north.

Every time she laughed, his body tightened in his response. He wanted to turn in his chair, toward the sound, even though he knew he couldn't see her. And he wanted to ask the others if they heard her the clearest, or if the laughter of the women they loved stood out to each of them.

Not that he loved Laney. It was too early for that. They'd kissed one time, and it would be stupid of him to fall in love with a woman who didn't want to fall in love with anybody, never mind with him.

And if he asked these guys a question like that, he'd never hear the end of it. As it was, Sean knew how he felt about her, even though he hadn't told him. And he couldn't be the only one who'd noticed Ben always found Laney in a crowd.

But they'd told him what the women were doing behind Leo and Mary's RV, and he'd never wanted to know anything as much as he wanted to know what dirty words Laney was spelling out with Scrabble tiles.

"Hey."

Ben felt something slap his shoulder and he looked up to see Joe holding out a soda. "Thanks."

He didn't need the sugar, but once the kids had been put to bed—or had fallen asleep curled up in their chairs, like Gabe and Jackson—the fire had been fed until it was almost too freaking hot to sit near it. And the act of drinking seemed to go along with campfires, which was why there were several small coolers of beer and ice placed around the circle. But he wasn't drinking beer tonight and Joe never did, so there was one cooler of sodas.

"I figured I'd distract you before you crept through the woods to see what Laney's doing."

"Funny," he muttered as the others laughed.

Joe grinned and walked back to his chair. "You should go for it."

"She doesn't want a relationship right now."

Mitch held up his beer can, as if it was some kind of talisman that made it his turn to talk. "Paige didn't, either."

A few of the other guys nodded, so Ben got the impression they were trying to tell him Laney might *think* she didn't want a relationship, but that he could change her mind. The problem with that was the *why* she didn't want one. If he nudged her and got her to change her mind, would she resent him for it? She'd made it pretty clear she was only doing what *she* wanted to do this summer.

It had to be her call.

But before he could try to figure out how to explain that to his less-than-sober friends, his phone vibrated in his pocket. *Shit.* It was late for a call.

"Gotta go," he said, standing as he typed a quick reply into his phone. A side-by-side rollover with two passengers, no helmets, and at least one possible head injury. He wasn't too far from the location they gave him.

About 200 yards past the turnoff to the old Dabney hunting camp.

And that was why the town of Whitford had scrounged up enough money to lure Ben back from the city. He was probably the only paramedic on the planet who could ride a four-wheeler *and* knew where to find the overgrown path that led out to a remote hunting cabin that had burned down in 1987. In the dark.

On my way. ETA 20 mins.

"What's going on?" Andy asked.

"Rolled a RZR."

"You want me to go with you?" Josh asked. He asked out of habit, but a second later, he looked down at the beer can in his hand. It wasn't his first. "Shit."

"I'll text you an update," he said.

He was almost to his four-wheeler when he thought of Laney. It didn't seem right to leave without saying goodbye to her. But walking into the group of laughing women to specifically say goodbye to her would only fan the flames of the Kowalski matchmaking fire. And he didn't really have time.

After buckling his helmet, he fired up the machine and, after plugging in his phone, put it in its mount. If somebody from dispatch or the cell phones programmed into a certain list reached out to him, a small red light on the side of the mount would flash. Going down the trail, it was easy to miss a vibrating phone in the pocket. He hit the switch for the flashing red light, mounted on a short pole behind him so it wouldn't interfere with his vision, and then headed for the tree line.

THE WOMEN ALL paused when they heard the four-wheeler start. There had been a lull in the laughter, so the engine sounded loud in the night.

"It's probably Ben heading home," Rosie said. "I

forgot he met up with them on the trail, so he's on his ATV."

Laney hoped the sinking feeling of disappointment she felt didn't show on her face. She knew it didn't make any sense. It wasn't as if they were going to hang out together when the women got bored with the Dirty Scrabble game—she'd noticed the scorekeeping went downhill over the course of the night and she wasn't sure how the game technically ended—or hook up after everybody else went to their campers. But just knowing he would be gone sucked some of the joy out of her night.

Then a red light started bouncing around the trees as the engine revved and she couldn't help standing up. After a few steps she could see around the RV well enough to watch him disappear down the trail. Even though he was out of sight, except for the occasional flash of red, she could still hear as he gave it more gas to increase his speed.

"Be careful," she whispered, her stomach clenching at the thought of him driving through the woods in the dark. He had lights. His ATV even had more lights than some of the others because his had aftermarket LED lights mounted on his front grill.

"He'll be fine," Liz said, resting her hand at the small of Laney's back.

She tensed, suddenly feeling ridiculous. And conspicuous. But there was no hiding now that she felt something for Ben, even if she didn't know what it was. Not from these women. "It must be so dark in the woods."

"It is. But Ben's been riding in these woods his entire life. He and Sean and my brothers—and Katie because she was a huge tomboy—used to ride dirt bikes and ATV through those woods so fast Rosie had *the Northern Star kids* added to the Whitford church's prayer list as a standard weekly feature."

"It's true," Rosie said.

"He lived in the city for years. Just because you did something as a teenager doesn't mean you can do it now."

"Laney." It was Rosie again, and she waited for Laney to turn and look at her before she continued. "The first thing Ben did when he got back was ride every mile of the trails with Andy. And again with Josh. And by himself. He studied maps and spent a lot of time reacquainting himself with the woods around Whitford. But he's also a smart guy, and he's not going to be reckless."

"It sounds like he was going so fast."

"You ride my machine and it's a lot smaller and a lot quieter," Beth told her. "His has a big engine and it's not only a lot louder, but it has a different tone when he gets on it a little bit. He wasn't going as fast as you think he was."

"I'm being a total idiot right now. Sorry." She laughed, but it sounded high-pitched and a little hollow. Then she sat back in her chair, hoping the heat in her cheeks didn't show in the dim light of the lanterns.

Liz sat down, too, but she wasn't done trying to make her feel better. "I hate when Drew gets called out at night, too. It's usually for an accident and around here, I don't worry too much about violence, but I worry about him speeding to the scene in the dark. You just have to trust that experience has taught him his limits and that he knows what he's doing."

Laney was uncomfortable with all the focus being on her. And she was *really* uncomfortable with the idea that she'd accidentally exposed feelings she preferred to keep secret because she didn't even want to be feeling them herself.

"We're just friends," she said quietly, anticipating them laughing at her and probably teasing her until she could escape without looking like she was running.

"And we worry about friends," Mary said, no laughter in her voice. "You probably would have been concerned no matter who left going fast with ATV lights flashing because you're not used to it. We've all been four-wheeling and riding snowmobiles for most of our lives, so it doesn't bother us as much."

Overwhelmed with gratitude for being gifted an explanation other than her having feelings for Ben, Laney smiled. "I'll probably get used to it in time. They seem so big and loud, but when I rode Beth's today, it wasn't scary at all. I actually enjoyed it."

"We'll sneak out for a ride at some point—just the women," Keri said. "You'll have to go with us."

"Maybe," she said, because she wasn't sure riding Beth's ATV for a few miles qualified her to go out on a ride with them. "Whose turn was it?"

With their attention turned back to the game, Laney felt herself relax. Or maybe it the mini box of wine somebody stuck in her hand. "How many of these things did you buy?"

"All of them," Rosie said.

They played for another hour, until there was more yawning than laughing. Then they picked up the games, but decided they'd leave the chairs for the men to drag back to their corresponding campsites the next morning.

"Thank you for tonight," Laney said. "I had a really good time."

"The more the merrier," Lisa said. "And you know a lot more dirty words than you thought you did, right?"

"I guess I do."

Rosie snorted. "And we also learned not to search for some words and phrases on the internet without some kind of porn filters on."

"Mom." Katie shook her head. "Please don't say porn again."

"She said *ball sac* earlier," Keri said. "I think that's worse."

"I don't see why ball sac got eliminated for being two words, but gang bang got to stay," Rosie grumbled.

"I thought the worst part about being pregnant was throwing up and peeing all the time, but having to be sober while playing Dirty Scrabble with your mom is the worst part."

When Laney walked around the RV, she saw that the fire had burned down quite a bit, though the guys were still sitting around it. They were talking quietly and in the dim light of the flames, she saw a little foot dangling from one of the chairs.

When the others went to collect their men and the children who were sleeping, Laney walked with them. She would say good-night to them there, and then make sure all the food was put away and the Dumpster secured before going to her own camper.

But she was mostly hoping they would tell them what was going on with Ben. Drew was the police chief, so surely he would know?

Finally, when it looked like they might just bank the fire and go inside, she couldn't take it anymore. "Have you heard anything about Ben?"

Drew nodded. "The driver broke his left arm, but he'll be okay. His wife hit her head and hadn't been conscious very long when Ben got there, so they're meeting a med flight for her."

"That's scary. I hope she'll be okay."

He nodded and then lifted a sleeping Jackson into his arms. Laney knew they were staying in the lodge tonight, since both he and Liz had been drinking. "Me too."

"Will he go on the med flight with her? Ben, I mean."

"Probably not. He'll ride back with Sam and the others, since they responded, too." He started to turn toward Liz, but then stopped. "So Ben's not alone out there now. He's with the others."

"Thank you," she said. "Mary said I'd get used to all of you running around in the woods on ATVs, but it's still a little hard on my nerves."

He smiled, and then there were good-nights all around. Laney did a final round of the campground and then walked back to her camper.

What a crazy night, she thought as she crawled into her bed. So much laughter and fun, but also worrying about Ben. She wondered if he was home yet, but she had no way of knowing since she didn't even know how far out into the woods he'd had to go.

Like she had every night for a while now, she fell asleep thinking about Ben.

ELEVEN

LANEY SLID INTO the booth opposite Nola and gave an exaggerated sigh of relief. "I didn't think I was ever going to get here."

"A little crazy, is it?"

"Just a little. And once everybody found out I was running into town to get some stuff for Rosie, the list just grew and grew. I'd start to leave and somebody would call me back to add just one more thing."

"How long is the list now?"

Laney sighed. "The fact my Camaro's back at the lodge and I'm driving Andy's pickup might answer that question."

"They know the market isn't exactly a major supermarket, right?"

"Yeah. They know I'll do the best I can and, since it charges to the lodge, the prices aren't my problem."

Paige was working, and they chatted with her for a few minutes before ordering the barbecue chicken wraps that were the lunch special. They'd both ordered sodas, too, because Laney thought she might need the extra sugar content to get her through the Kowalski family shopping list. *Of doom*, she thought, which made her giggle.

"What's so funny?"

"Oh, nothing. I was just thinking about the shopping list. So how are things with you?"

"Good. About the same." Nola used her straw to stir the ice around in her drink. "Your mom asked my mom about you. So my mom asked me how you're doing and stuff."

The words hit Laney about the same way Nola tossing the soda in her face would have, killing her good mood. "What did you say?"

"I told her you're incredibly happy and loving your job and that everybody in Whitford adores you."

Laney couldn't help smiling. "A little bit of an exaggeration, maybe, but thank you."

"Not the part about loving your job or everybody in Whitford who's met you adoring you. Maybe you're not *incredibly* happy, but you're happier than you've been in a very long time."

"That's true."

"I bet you'd be even happier if you slept with Ben Rivers."

Laney hissed at her, glancing around to see if anybody was close enough to overhear that. Luckily, it was a little late in the day for lunch and the only other customers were at the other end of the dining room. "Don't say that."

"You want to."

"Stop it." She did want to. And it *would* make her happy. For a while. Until it was time for her to start making decisions about what came next in her life and she found herself doubting whether she was making the decisions for herself, or for the man in her life. Not having a man in her life erased the doubt.

"Okay, then we'll go back to talking about your mom."

Laney groaned. "Punishing me for not talking about something we shouldn't be talking about in public?"

"Yes. How come your mom is asking my mom to ask me how you're doing instead of asking you?"

"You know we've had some issues in the last couple of years. We're not really close at the moment."

"You told me you weren't getting along during the divorce and everything, but that's all behind you now and your ex is in your rearview mirror."

Laney shrugged, thankful when Paige showed up with their plates so she had a minute to think about what she wanted to say because she knew no matter how good Nola's intentions were, there was a good chance whatever she said would get back to her mother through the family grapevine. She didn't want to make the situation worse than it was because she hoped her time here would help her feel strong enough to heal her relationship with her parents.

Once Paige had gone back into the kitchen, Laney salted her fries and resumed the conversation. "Just because the divorce is final doesn't mean I've forgotten they took Patrick's side through all of it. And before you say it, I know they felt like staying married was best for me, but they should have supported *me* and not their idea of what my life should be."

"Are you going to go back to Rhode Island in the fall?"

"I don't know what I'm going to do yet. I feel like worrying about my future plans now works against the entire reason I'm here. Even though it's not that far away, I think September-me will look at life a little differently than current-me does."

"It's not like you to not plan out your year in advance."

Laney grinned. "I know. Isn't it great?"

They moved on to other topics, like a television show Nola had recommended and Laney was catching up on. Movies they both wanted to see badly enough to make the long drive to a movie theater. Whether or not Laney wanted Nola to teach her how to knit. But once they were done eating, they couldn't linger because Nola had to get back to the town hall.

"You should take an actual night off sometime soon and come over so I can teach you how to knit."

"I might do that." She'd always been told knitting while watching television or listening to audiobooks was relaxing but the time she'd tried to teach herself how had been a disaster and pretty much the opposite of relaxing.

"Where did you park?" Nola asked when they left the diner.

Laney felt herself blush. "I parked at the market and walked over here."

"That's quite a walk."

"I don't have any trouble driving Andy's truck in a forward motion, but backing up? It's a little bigger than my Camaro. And there's zero chance of me ever parallel parking it, so taking it straight to the market was safest for everybody."

"I'm going the other direction, so I'll see you later. Good luck shopping."

Laney waved and set off in the direction of the market. She didn't hurry, not minding the warm sun today, since the humidity level was low. She had told Rosie she might try to see if Nola could take a later than usual lunch and been assured they were in no hurry for the groceries, so she could take her time in town.

Despite the beautiful weather and the nice lunch

she'd just shared with Nola, Laney couldn't fully enjoy the walk. She wished Nola hadn't mentioned her mother.

It did make her feel good to know her mother cared enough about how she was doing to reach out to Nola's mom, but she wasn't ready yet to let her parents back into her life. They'd encouraged her to stay with Patrick long past her realization she was unhappy, and they'd actively campaigned for reconciliation through the divorce process. In this case, reconciliation didn't mean communication and compromise. It meant Laney giving up on whatever midlife crisis they imagined she was having and stepping back into the same life she'd been living for ten years. And she was having a hard time forgiving them for that.

She happened to glance over when a couple of kids shouted to each other, and she realized she was across from the fire station. The big, double garage door was open and a couple of men were standing outside talking. They were next to a four-wheeler, which was easily recognizable as Ben's—and as she stopped walking, Ben stood up behind it. He must have been bent over at first, checking something on the machine.

Just the sight of him cheered her up and, before she could talk herself out of it, she looked both ways and then crossed the street to say hello to him.

BEN COULDN'T THINK of a more welcome sight after a long, mostly sleepless night than Laney smiling at him. Except maybe a smiling Laney crossing the street to talk to him.

"Hey, you escaped for a while," he said, noticing the other guys moved away to give them a semblance of privacy, though it wasn't actually privacy since they made sure they were still in earshot.

"I'm doing errands for Rosie." She looked at his ATV. "I was worried about you last night. It sounded like you were going so fast in the woods. But Drew told me later that everybody was okay and that you were with the other guys from the fire department."

She'd worried about him. For some reason, that made him incredibly happy. "I never go faster than I should be. But I'm sorry you were worried."

"Were the people in the accident okay?"

He shrugged. "I hope so. It made the news this morning and it sounded like she was expected to make a full recovery."

"If you call the hospital, do they tell you how they're doing? Since they started as your patients, it seems like something you'd be allowed to do."

"No, I don't call." He wasn't sure he could explain it to her. "It's a little different here, but I spent most of my career in the city. There are so many calls. So many accidents and overdoses and injuries. I treat them the best I can and then turn them over to the doctors. My job ends there and I have to let them go. I think if I tried to do more, I wouldn't be able to keep doing it."

Her brow furrowed for a moment. "I guess I can understand that. But I'm glad you're safe."

"Always." But he knocked on the wooden frame of the door behind him, just in case.

She looked at the machine again. "Josh told me the ATV trails closed when it snows and they switch over to snowmobile season. Do you have a rescue snowmobile, too?"

"No, I don't. I mean, there is such a thing, and they

make a sled that can be towed behind them. But I can ride my four-wheeler on the trails because they groom the snow, so it's packed down hard."

"You're the exception to the rules, then."

"Whenever I can get away with it." That made her laugh, and his day got even better. He loved her laugh all the time, but he loved it even more when he was the one who brought it out. "So what kind of errands do you have to run?"

"I met Nola for lunch, but now I have to go to the market. Fran's going to be happy because everybody found out I was going and it's not a short list."

"Want some company?" The words popped out before he really gave them any thought, but it didn't sound like a bad idea to him.

"I...don't know. Aren't you working?"

"It's kind of a weird situation because, technically, I'm *always* working. They call, I go. When there are no calls, I just wander around looking for things to do. So—fair warning, I guess—but I could have to abandon you in the potato chip aisle at a moment's notice."

She made a thoughtful face for a moment, and then shrugged. "If you're going to be abandoned, what better place than the potato chip aisle?"

"I could grab a few things myself, since I haven't been shopping in a while. I'm down to a few microwave meals with questionable expiration dates and a bottle of ketchup."

"Shopping isn't as much fun alone." She smiled, but then gave him a skeptical look. "Unless this is some scam you first responders do where you fill up your cart, but then a call comes in and you have to abandon me. But I'm a nice lady, so I'll get your groceries and even deliver them for you."

He laughed hard enough so the other guys stopped pretending they weren't watching and frowned at him. "No, I'm not trying to scam groceries out of you. If I have to leave, Fran puts my basket aside, except for cold items. Those she puts in a bag in the walk-in, so when I get back there, I can pick up shopping where I left off."

"That's nice of her."

He shrugged. "It's a nice town."

"Yeah, it is."

"So you like it here?"

She nodded. "I do. I mean, there are a lot of things I'm used to that Whitford doesn't have, which is challenging. There's no takeout, for one thing. And from what I understand, going to a movie theater is literally a road trip."

"That's true. Although, there's kind of takeout. If you called in an order to the diner, they'd probably find someone going out by the lodge who'd drop it off. You might have to reheat it by the time it gets there, but technically you *could* have food delivered right to your camper."

She laughed again, and then turned toward the market. "So how are we doing to do this? I have Andy's truck, which is already parked in the parking lot there."

"Little harder to parallel park than your Camaro, is it?" He nudged her with his elbow when she blushed.

"Yes," she confessed. "Maybe I should ride a four-wheeler into town, pulling the little wagon behind it, like Andy does when he's doing yard work."

"If you do, let me know ahead of time, so I can watch you trying to back a trailer up. But for now,

I'll walk down with you and we can get the stuff on the list. Then you can run me home and I'll throw my groceries inside and you can drop me back off here."

"Okay." She did that biting her bottom lip thing again, that meant she was anxious about something. "What if you get a call while we're out in Andy's truck?"

"Then we're going to switch places and I'll drive back to the station and you can take my groceries to the lodge with you. I'll pick them up there later." He smiled. "Let me put the machine inside and then we'll go. I can't leave it out here."

"You heading out?" Sam asked, after he'd backed the ATV into its spot.

"Yeah, I'm going to go to the market with Laney and see Fran. Maybe get some food so I don't have to beg off my mom."

"That's sad." Sam shook his head. "Not the begging meals from mom because I would totally do that if my mom lived around here. But you're taking her grocery shopping?"

"It's not a date."

"I sure hope the hell not. Although it would explain why you're still single."

"Funny. Why are *you* single, smart-ass?"

"Because my wife banged the meteorologist from our local news channel, so I divorced her and then had to move to a different state so I didn't have to see his smiling face on my television every fucking day."

"Oh." He hadn't known Sam was divorced. The man rarely talked about himself. "That explains your irrational anger toward meteorologists, then. I thought you just really hated weather forecasts."

"I can look out my window if I need to know the weather."

"But you can't look out your window and find out the weather for Tuesday."

"I can wait until Tuesday and then look out the window."

"Okay. Fun talk."

Sam laughed. "Have fun shopping. Maybe buy your girl a nice can of peas or something."

Ben flipped him off before walking back outside. Laney was watching the cars go by, and she smiled when he touched her arm. "You ready?"

She nodded and they started walking toward the market. He wanted to hold her hand in the worst way, but he'd promised nothing was going to happen between them that she didn't initiate. Maybe hand holding wasn't the most outrageous thing, but it was intimate. It implied there was hope for a kiss. Maybe even more.

So Ben shoved his hands in his pockets and was content to listen to her talk about the shopping list of doom, which sounded ominous. He didn't care. The longer the list, the more time he got to spend with Laney.

"YOU DIDN'T SAY anything about carrying groceries up a flight of stairs." When Ben turned back to scowl at her, Laney laughed. "When I asked if you wanted a hand bringing the bags in, you didn't mention that part."

"I told you I live in an apartment over my parents' garage. There aren't too many underground garages in this part of Maine, so the stairs were implied. But I can grab them if you'd rather wait in the truck."

She was teasing him and he knew it, so she started up the stairs after him. Now that she was here, she wasn't leaving without seeing where he lived. And Andy had tossed a couple of big coolers in the back of the truck for her, so the few cold items Rosie had asked for were on ice. She had a little bit of time.

When he opened the door at the top of the stairs, he paused and then looked down at her. "I think it's reasonably clean, but it's kind of small, so it probably looks more cluttered than you're used to."

"You're kidding, right? I live in a camper. A camper with no bump-outs, even."

The apartment was cleaner than she'd expected, actually. Maybe she'd seen too many sitcoms with single men being total slobs without women to pick up after them. But Ben seemed like he kept things neat. There was the requisite couch and what looked to her like a giant television. It was probably normal, of course, but she watched everything on a tablet, so it looked huge.

There was also a coffee table to hold the remote control for the big TV and a few books. She tilted her head to read the spines. Horror. She was surprised at first, because he'd mentioned in passing during one of their conversations that he liked reading military thrillers, but then she realized they were all by the same author. Joseph Kowalski.

And because it was a studio apartment, she also got to see his bed. It was big—probably a king—and it had blue sheets and a taupe comforter, all of which were bunched up because Ben hadn't made his bed.

She wondered what he would do if she crawled between the messy sheets and asked him to join her.

Ben closed the refrigerator door after putting his groceries away and turned, but she was having a hard time looking away from the bed. The sheets looked soft, and a ceiling fan over the bed made slow circles.

"Yeah, I don't make my bed," he said, sounding embarrassed. "Sometimes I do, but most mornings I don't. It seems like the ultimate waste of time to me. Plus I don't like them being tucked in, so if I make the bed properly, I have to toss and turn until the sheets are just the way I like them again."

It was surreal, she thought. Standing in Ben's apartment, listening to him talk about how he liked his bedsheets while actually staring at his bed. And words came out of her mouth before she could stop them. "I was really worried about you last night."

"I'm sorry." He moved closer to her. "I wanted to tell you I was leaving, but that would have seemed really conspicuous and… I didn't want to subject you to teasing and speculation, if you know what I mean. They're good people, but they do love trying to hook people up."

"I probably took care of the speculation when I jumped up out of my chair and told you to be careful even though you couldn't hear me." He nodded, but she noticed he shoved his hands in his pockets. And he wasn't smiling. "So, I'm sorry if you get any teasing or anything."

"Don't be. It's nice to have somebody worry about me, even if I feel bad that you *were* worried."

"You don't look like you're very happy right now."

"I am. I just…" He sighed and took his hands out of his pockets. "After I kissed you, we decided it wasn't a good idea. I know you don't want to date anybody and I know why. So I told myself I couldn't touch you or kiss you again unless you made the first move."

"But you do want to."

"Yeah, I do. I wanted to hold your hand walking to the market, too."

She'd wanted that, too. She'd imagined their hands brushing and then his fingers lacing through hers. But then he'd put his hands in his pockets and left them there until he held the door open for her at the market. They'd laughed the entire time they shopped, especially when he cracked a joke while she was trying to pick a ripe cucumber and Fran cleared her throat in a *very* obvious way. In the truck, though, he hadn't even put his arm on the center console. He'd made sure he stayed in his own space.

Because he was a nice guy who didn't want to make her feel pressured.

Without giving herself time to overthink and talk herself out of it, Laney wrapped her fingers in the front of his T-shirt and pulled him close. She had to stand on her tiptoes to kiss him, but cupping her other hand behind his neck helped.

When Ben groaned against her lips, her fingers tightened in his shirt. His mouth devoured hers and she surrendered to him, letting him take control as his hand clenched her hair and his tongue moved over hers. Her knees felt weak and she was breathless by the time he broke off the kiss.

"You sure know how to make a first move," he said, and the fact his voice was slightly hoarse told her he was probably feeling the same thing she was, which was an overwhelming need to move across the room to that bed.

"It's still a bad idea," she said, feeling a need to

make that clear. "But I can't stop thinking about you. About this."

"I'll give you whatever you want," he said, looking her in the eye. "And only what you want."

"I want you. In that bed."

He kissed her again, harder this time. Having given herself permission to do this—to finally enjoy what she'd been denying them both—Laney moaned against his lips and pulled the hem of his T-shirt free of his pants so she could slide her hands underneath. The smooth muscles of his back tightened under her fingertips.

She wanted to touch him. She wanted to know what he felt like and how he liked to be touched. And when he broke off the kiss and looked into her eyes, she realized she wanted to know what he looked like when he was totally sated and relaxed.

"We should probably be quick, though, because of the groceries." As soon as she realized she'd said the words aloud, she groaned and dropped her head to his chest. "That…is not what I meant to say."

She felt his chuckle like a low rumble. "There was plenty of ice in the coolers, but we can fast forward through the getting naked part if it helps."

Rather than say something else that might come out wrong, she pulled her T-shirt over her head and tossed it aside. It had been so long since she'd been naked for the first time with a man, and stripping quickly was like ripping off a bandage. She didn't really have time to feel self-conscious before his hands were on her skin and she couldn't miss the heat that flared in his eyes.

When she climbed onto his bed, he moved with her, so she was spared the vulnerability of having him standing over her, staring at her. He was sweet, she thought, wrapping her arms around his neck. Sweet, but in an incredibly hot and sexy way.

"Tell me what you like, Laney."

His words weren't a glass of ice water in the face, exactly, but she felt some of the urgency slipping away. She wasn't sure she even remembered how she liked to be touched anymore, and that thought didn't really make her feel like a sexy, confident woman.

"Hey." Ben tipped her chin up so she was looking into his eyes. "New plan. You told me you've been thinking about this. Just show me what you saw when you closed your eyes and imagined us together."

It was easier to close her eyes now, and she ran her hands over his shoulders. Down his arms. Then she touched his chest, skimming her fingers through the dusting of hair across his skin. Her thumbs brushed over his nipples and he sucked in a sharp breath, so she opened her eyes. She wanted to see his face.

His skin was slightly flushed, like the tips of his ears, and he looked like a man who was fighting for self-control. It emboldened her and she slid her hands down his abs until her fingers felt the crinkle of hair again. Then she ran her palms over his hips and around to cup his butt.

Ben was trembling slightly, but he only watched her as she explored his body. His back muscles twitched under her touch, and she loved the way he sucked in his breath any time her hands slid below his waist.

"You feel amazing," she whispered. "And I thought about you touching *me*, too."

With a groan, he dropped his mouth to hers as he cupped her breast in one hand. He kissed her, his tongue dipping between her lips as she opened her mouth to him. Then he explored her body as thoroughly as she'd explored his, touching her everywhere and finding the spots that made her tremble. Behind her knees. The small of her back.

But like her, he deliberately avoided the one spot that ached for him.

When she couldn't take it anymore, she reached down and closed her hand around his erection. Ben's breath left him in a long, shuddering sigh as he went totally still. She stroked the hard length of him and watched his jaw clenching and unclenching.

"Maybe we should talk about the groceries some more or this is going to be over soon," he said, his voice tight.

She'd never been with a man who had a sense of humor during sex, and it just made her want him more. And because he made her feel sexy, she wasn't shy about telling him so. "I want you now, Ben. Please."

When he moved away for a moment, she felt a pang of doubt, until she realized he was getting a condom from his nightstand. She watched him put it on before realizing that might make him feel self-conscious, but he gave her a sizzling look before covering her body with his own.

She opened her thighs, raising her hips as he guided himself into her. Slowly, almost gently at first, until the delicious sensation of being filled wrung a sigh that was almost a moan from her. His mouth stifled the startled cry of pleasure when he pushed fully into her, and she buried her fingers in his hair to hold him close.

He kissed her as he moved his hips, slowly at first, but with increasing urgency. Then he lifted his head and looked into her eyes. “I wanted to take my time with you. I wanted to touch you more. Taste you. But I can’t…you feel so good, Laney.”

She didn’t want to think about a next time—she wasn’t even sure there would *be* a next time—so she wrapped her legs around his hips and urged him to move faster.

When he obliged, thrusting into her hard enough to make the bed rock, she felt the orgasm building and she put her hands on his shoulders. Her fingers pressed into the firm muscles and she moaned as she surrendered to the waves of pleasure.

Ben’s hips moved faster and then his body shuddered under her touch as his orgasm hit. He groaned and kissed her hard on the mouth before slowly lowering himself on top of her.

Laney trailed her fingertips lightly over his back, and he twitched before making a satisfied moaning sound against her chest. She wasn’t sure how long they lay there, but slowly their breathing returned to normal and she felt the relaxation that came from being utterly satisfied seeping in.

He rolled to his side, probably to dispose of the condom, and then he wrapped his body around hers, kissing her shoulder. “I could stay here all day.”

“Me, too.” But she couldn’t and she felt anxious suddenly, unsure of how to go about the leaving part. “But I really should go.”

“Mmm.” He nuzzled her neck. “Five more minutes.”

“I have groceries in the back of the truck. I have *Rosie’s* groceries in the back of the truck, which is even worse.”

“Yeah, we should probably get dressed.”

It felt awkward, putting her clothes back on in front of him in the light of the afternoon, even though it hadn't felt weird at all taking them off.

It wasn't until they were climbing into Andy's truck that she realized the house next to the garage belonged to his parents. And there was a car in the driveway. Her cheeks felt hot and Ben must have figured out why because he chuckled.

"They're not home right now. They were driving into the city to visit some friends of theirs."

It was silly, since they were both adults, but she was relieved. She knew that Rosie knew Ben's parents—which wasn't a surprise in Whitford—and the last she needed was his mom calling the lodge to gossip about her.

It wasn't long before she was pulling up to the fire station. By some miracle, there were three empty spaces in a row, so she just pulled the truck in and put it in Park.

Ben hesitated before getting out. "I feel like I should have asked this a long time ago, but can I have your number?"

"Wow, my number? Next thing you know, you'll be asking me out on a date."

"Hey, I went grocery shopping with you. It's not an awesome date, but..."

"It was the most fun I've ever had in a food store, so I guess it counts." When he handed her his phone, open to a new contact page, she typed in her cell phone number.

"Thanks," he said. "There are times I can't show up for things when I say I will, if I show up at all, so being able to call you or just shoot you a quick text message would be nice. And I'll text you my number in a bit, so you'll have it."

"Sounds good." It was tempting to kiss him again, but she was afraid if she did, it would lead to making out in the cab of Andy's truck. One, it was Andy's truck and, two, they were in public. And she wasn't sure how long ice lasted in a cooler in the back of a pickup in July. "I'll see you soon."

"I hope so."

After he got out and walked around the front of the truck, she gave him a wave and then put the truck in gear. It wasn't until she'd gotten through town and was on the road back to the lodge that she allowed herself to really think about what she'd done.

She didn't regret the sex. It had been amazing and she wasn't going to let herself be sorry it happened. But the cell phone number exchange. The hope to see her soon. That was going to cost her some sleep.

Ben wanted more than she could give him. He'd made it sound otherwise—that he'd only give her what she wanted—but she knew he wanted a family. A wife. Laney had wanted to surrender to some pleasure with the man she couldn't stop thinking about. But the last thing she wanted right now was a husband. Or to hurt him.

TWELVE

Sean

SEAN HAPPENED TO be sitting in a rocker on the front porch of the lodge late Friday afternoon, talking to Andy about old tractors, when a car with New Hampshire plates pulled up the driveway.

"That'll be the kids," he said, pushing himself to his feet. Andy stood, too, and they walked down to where the car rolled to a stop. They hadn't even reached the edge of the drive when a car with Massachusetts plates pulled up behind it.

Nick, Lauren's son and Sean's step-nephew—not that they added that step as a rule—got out of the second car. "Hey, how's that for timing?"

Sean laughed. "There's no way you left from Mass and these guys from New Hampshire and got here at the same time."

"I was at my dad's and they sent me a text when they were almost to town. That would have been cool, though. We could have used the GPS apps to try to time it exactly."

"Maybe next time." Sean leaned down to look in the passenger window of the first car. Stephanie, Terry and Evan's daughter, was riding shotgun. Joey, Mike and Lisa's oldest was driving and his brother, Danny, was in the backseat. "How was the trip?"

"Good," Stephanie said. "We solved a bunch of Danny's plot problems for him."

Danny was working on his novel while attending college, since he was destined to be a writer like his uncle Joe. Sean peered into the backseat. "Maybe you should go on road trips more often."

Danny rolled his eyes. "Aliens kidnapping my protagonist and giving him an anal probe didn't really solve any of my plot problems."

"Oh, you write science fiction?"

"No."

Joey and Stephanie were laughing, so Sean just chuckled and slapped the side of the car door. "You can drive out back to unload your stuff, but not very far. And don't run over any of the kids. Then you'll have to bring your cars back out here and park them on the lawn somewhere."

They waved to Andy and then Joey put the car in gear and drove toward the camping area. Nick got back in his car and followed. His dad, stepmother and younger siblings lived in Whitford, though he'd moved to Brookline with his mom and Ryan. He spent a lot of time driving back and forth between the states, plus he made a few trips to New Hampshire each summer to visit that half of the family since he'd developed friendships with those kids. And he'd chosen to camp out at the lodge instead of making the short drive back to his dad's each night.

"I'll go let Rosie know they're here," Andy said. "She was rocking Jackson last I knew, trying to get him to nap for a little while. Last time she did that, she fell asleep and Jackson sat quietly on her lap and unraveled the entire scarf she'd been knitting. I swear, that woman has the patience of a saint. She just wound it all back into a ball and started over."

"She had a lot of practice being patient with brats," Sean said, chuckling. "I'm going to go out back and watch them try to put up their tents. Should be funny."

By the time he reached the camping area, the kids were done running the gauntlet of hello hugs and kisses and were emptying the contents of their trunks onto the area of grass Rosie had saved for the tents.

"Wouldn't it make more sense to put the tents up first and then unload from the cars into the tents?" Sean asked. "That way you're only moving the stuff once?"

"We put the tents in first, so they're on the bottom," Joey said, and judging by the look he gave his brother, Danny had been the one who packed the trunk.

"Steph!"

Sean turned to see his son running as fast as he could toward his cousin. Johnny loved Stephanie and the feeling was mutual. Even when Sean and Emma weren't paying her to babysit, she'd drive out to their place just to hang out with him. Her visits were a little more scarce now that she was working and going to college, which just made the times Johnny did get to spend with her all the more special.

Steph caught him when he launched himself at her, and then grimaced. He was getting heavy. "Hey, squirt. Did you save me any s'mores?"

"Nope." He held out his hands. "We ate them all!"

Sean laughed at Steph's expression. "We did save you some marshmallows, chocolate bars and graham crackers, kid."

"Okay, let's do this," Nick said, looking at the three

tent packages on the ground. They still had the tags on them.

"Do any of you even know how to set up a tent?"

"I watched some YouTube videos," Steph said. "The ones they had didn't look exactly like these, but it's just poles and…whatever tents are made of."

"I hope the directions explain why we have two roofs," Danny said, scowling at the picture on the packaging of one of them.

Sean didn't bother to tell him what the fly was for. He'd figure it out. The two brothers had a bigger, slightly fancier tent, while Nick and Stephanie had each opted for the basic pop-up dome tent. The rest of their supplies seemed to consist mainly of blankets, pillows and extension cords.

"Hey, new arrivals."

Sean turned at the sound of Laney's voice and found her looking at the piles of belongings. "Hey, Laney. This is Joey, Danny, Stephanie and Nick. Guys, this is Laney and she's the boss."

He pointed to each of them as he named them, and she gave them a group wave. "I'm more like an underboss. Everybody answers to Rosie."

"Do you know how to put up tents?" Danny asked her.

Sean shook his head and she must have caught it out of the corner of her eye, because she shrugged. "Nope. Sorry. I bet you'll figure it out, though."

When she moved over to where he was standing, Sean leaned close so he could keep his voice low. "Watching them put up tents is going to be the best entertainment we've had all week. We might have to make some popcorn."

"What do you think the chances are they'll give up and beg rooms from Rosie?"

"I think if they end up in rooms, it'll be because they're uncomfortable in the tents. But they're all stubborn enough so they'll get them up. Especially if we're heckling them."

"It's good that they were all able to get the long weekend off and come over."

Sean laughed. "What Mary and Rosie want to happen usually happens. But, yeah, they all work for good people. They can't have the entire two weeks off, but one weekend with everybody together is good enough."

"Tomorrow will be crazy," she said.

"That it will." Tomorrow they'd be having the *big* barbecue with not only the entire family, but there had been an open invitation to friends. Once it was dark, they'd be having a small fireworks show for the kids, and then it would be campfire time.

"You are not even going to believe how much food will be cooked tomorrow," he added. When she smiled, but didn't say anything, he realized that no matter how often they dragged Laney over to eat with them, she wasn't the kind of person to assume she was always invited. "You know you're joining us, right?"

She laughed. "I am?"

"You don't have to, of course, but I think you already know what'll happen if Rosie or Aunt Mary finds out you're not eating with us."

"I spent some time with Rosie and Mary making lists and figuring out who was making or bringing what. Rosie might have mentioned that I'll be joining in on the food and fun, not just helping out."

Sean spotted Emma walking toward them and he

lifted his arm so she could slide up next to him and loop her arm around his waist. He squeezed her shoulders. "Did you come to watch the tent debacle?"

"Don't you think you should distract Johnny so he'll leave Steph alone for two minutes?"

"Nope." He laughed. "It's more fun watching him help her."

When Johnny took the instruction pamphlet for Steph's tent and ran off toward the campers, Sean laughed. But Steph was getting frazzled, so he took pity on his young cousin and went after his son.

"Run faster," Emma called after him. "He likes to flush papers down toilets."

LANEY WASN'T SURE they could fit any more people on the Northern Star property if they had to. It seemed as if everybody in town was there, including a lot of people she hadn't met. When Rosie had told her it would be a *big* barbecue, she hadn't been exaggerating.

But there were enough people she did know so that there was always somebody nearby to talk to, including Nola, who was wandering around somewhere. The only people notably missing were Ben, Drew and Matt. She'd seen Matt's wife, Hailey, with their daughter and Bear, and obviously Liz and Jackson were there. The paramedic, police chief, and game warden all being gone meant there was a problem somewhere.

"You look worried," Josh said, and Laney turned. She hadn't even known he was standing there.

"Not worried. I was just noticing the three people I expected to be here and aren't are people who respond to emergencies."

"Yeah, they are. A woman rolled her four-wheeler on

a rocky hill and they think her hip is broken. And she couldn't have been any further from a decent extraction point if she'd tried on purpose. It's a slow, painful ride out in the basket for her. Last I knew, they were bringing an ambulance in as close as they could get, which is about four or five miles, and then the ambulance would get her to a helicopter."

"I..." She stopped, not sure what she could say. "That sounds awful."

"It is. Accidents happen, unfortunately. But she was wearing a helmet, so at least they can fix her up. And because we have Ben, she doesn't have to make that trip out without something to help with the worst of the pain." She must not have looked convinced because after a short pause, he kept talking. "Everything we do in life has risks. Driving a car. You can go sledding in the backyard and run into a tree. With four-wheelers and snowmobiles, you need to be taught well, wear safety gear and know your limits. I think because you and Ben are friends or whatever, you're focused more on the few accidents and not the thousands of people safely enjoying the sport."

Friends or whatever. "Maybe you're right. I've gotten to know your family pretty well, and I know they wouldn't take their kids out on them if they weren't pretty sure they'd be safe."

"As sure as it's possible to be." He handed her a brownie, which she took even though she'd just eaten more deviled eggs than she cared to think about. "That has walnuts in it, so if you have a nut allergy, don't eat it. Dave and Ben are both out in the woods somewhere."

She laughed. "No allergies. And thanks."

"No problem. I need to get this one to Katie. She's having a chocolate craving."

Once he'd walked away, Laney ate her brownie and tried not to think about Ben. It had been two days since she'd dropped him off at the fire station. He'd texted her later that evening so she'd have his number, and they'd exchanged a few text messages since, but she hadn't really talked to him since she'd left his bed. And the longer it went, the more she worried about seeing him again.

Once the brownie was gone, she realized she'd need a drink, so she went to the long folding table that held three big drink dispensers. Two of them had lemonade and the other was iced tea. After considering the amount of sugar she'd just consumed, she opted for the iced tea.

"The only way you could keep up with me on the trails is if you were on the end of a tow strap hooked to my back bumper," she heard Stephanie say.

When she turned, Laney saw that she was talking to Bobby, Mike and Lisa's youngest son. He was getting ready to turn fourteen soon, according to his mother. Brian, who was sixteen, was just watching them while eating from a pile of potato chips in his hand.

"I could drive in Reverse and go faster than you," Bobby told his cousin.

"Any time you want to race, brat. But have a tissue in your pocket for when you cry in the losers circle."

"Like I'm going to get beat by a girl."

"Hey! The only thing a man can do that a woman can't do is piss in his own face."

"Stephanie!"

The young woman rolled her eyes at her mother's tone. "Language. Sorry. But it's true."

Laney couldn't hold back her smile, so she turned a little, hoping Terry wouldn't see it. But she couldn't help admiring the girl's attitude. Maybe her statement wasn't *exactly* true, but she was willing to bet Stephanie would never stay too long in a bad relationship because it seemed easier than being on her own.

"That's enough with you two," Terry said. "You're not racing, so there's no sense in bickering with each other all day."

Laney's phone vibrated in her pocket and she felt her pulse quicken. She pulled it out and read the text message from Ben..

I'll be there in about an hour. I hope there's food left.

She'd see him again in about an hour. That meant she had less than an hour to worry about how that first face-to-face was going to go. They just fired the grills, so you'll be just in time.

Awesome. See you then.

She slipped the phone back in her pocket and blew out a breath. Then she topped off her iced tea and went in search of her cousin.

Nola was talking to some people Laney didn't know, but she said something and then separated from them when she saw her coming. "Are you having a good time?"

"Yeah." Laney looked at all the people milling around and jerked her head toward the front of the camper. "Want to go have some quiet for a few minutes?"

Nobody stopped them as they walked to Laney's camper. Once they were seated in the pink chairs, Nola looked at her and frowned. "What's going on?"

"So, I slept with Ben."

"Huh. I really thought you'd look happier about that."

Laney laughed. "I was *very* happy, trust me. But I haven't seen him since then and he'll be here in an hour and I don't know how I feel about it."

"Wait, since when? I saw you two days ago and you wanted nothing to do with a conversation about sex with him."

"I wanted nothing to do with that conversation *in the diner*, which is basically the home base of gossip in every small town."

"That's actually the market in Whitford because Fran's so dedicated to it, but the diner would be second, I guess."

"Okay, fine. I didn't want to have that conversation in the gossip central runner-up. But it was after that. After lunch, when I was walking back to the market and he was outside the fire station."

Nola leaned back in her seat, and then she laughed. "You're going to have to start giving up some details because you and him both being on the main street at the same time isn't helping me understand how sex got involved."

"He offered to go shopping with me and he got some groceries, so we drove to his place. I carried some groceries up and his bed was right there and...we had sex and then I drove him back to the fire station and luckily got Rosie's groceries to her before the ice melted."

"That's pretty much the least romantic first time story I've ever heard."

"No, it was good. It was better than good. It was… perfect."

"I'm still hung up on the fact he offered to go grocery shopping with you. That part's kind of romantic."

"You're not helping." She took a long sip of iced tea, hoping to calm her nerves.

"Okay, so you haven't talked to him since?"

"A few text messages, but no, not really."

"I'm not really the best at relationship advice under the best of circumstances, but I'm trying," Nola said. "And I think I'd have a better idea of what to say if I knew what the problem was. Are you afraid he's going to show up thinking you're his girlfriend now, or are you afraid he won't?"

"I don't want a boyfriend," Laney said, but she wasn't sure if she meant it or if it was a reflex. "What good was coming to Maine and living in a camper for the summer to learn how to be myself without a man in my life if I let a man into my life?"

"You came here to find your joy. I think if something—or somebody—makes you happy, you should be open to it because maybe that's part of the joy."

She thought she understood what Nola was trying to say, but she couldn't let go of the fear. Fear that if she wasn't strong enough yet to live her life the way *she* wanted to before letting somebody else share it with her, she would fade away again.

"You don't know how he feels about it?" her cousin asked.

"About me? Not really, other than he's attracted to me and we seem to be good friends. But I do know he wants to settle down and start a family as soon as possible. We're in very different places in that respect. But he knows that."

"You might be thinking *too* much about it. If he knows you're not at that place, then he might not have any expectations. You won't know how it is until you see him, so you're winding yourself up for nothing."

That was easy for Nola to say. She wasn't about to have a potentially awkward moment in front of essentially the entire town.

Emma

SHE LOVED HER in-laws like crazy, but right now Emma wished her grandmother was there with her. Sean was surrounded by his family and old friends and people who'd known him his entire life, and it just drove home to her how much he was from this place.

To give herself a break, she took Johnny into the camper for some quiet time. She knew he needed it because he didn't put up a struggle. Instead, with the air conditioner cooling him off and offering the low hum of white noise, he'd curled up on the big bed with a couple of stuffed animals. He'd be asleep within five minutes as long as nobody interrupted them.

And she felt better just being inside what was now her grandmother's home, even if it was on wheels. It was a comfort, and she smiled when she looked at the framed picture of Cat and Russell that was screwed to one of the kitchen cabinets.

Then she saw the sticky note on the next cabinet

over. The small yellow square was filled with Sean's handwriting, and her eyes were already filling up with tears as she peeled it off.

No matter what I'm doing right now, I'm thinking about you because I love you.

She sighed and wiped at her eyes before she could drip tears on his note. Random sticky notes from her husband weren't a surprise. He'd gotten in the habit of leaving sticky notes on the mirror in the bathroom they shared back when they were trying to fool her grandmother into thinking they were engaged and they weren't always free to talk to each other in the house. And he'd continued leaving them after their pretend romance became a very real one, though they'd become more about loving her and less about hating certain green vegetables.

What surprised her was how often the sticky notes appeared when she needed them the most. They lifted her mood or soothed her anxieties and, no matter what was going in life, reminded her she was loved. And now, when she was taking refuge in the RV and hadn't even known he'd packed sticky notes and a Sharpie. Or scavenged them from Josh's office. But instead of peace, today's note just made the turmoil churn harder in her mind.

What would she do if he brought up the possibility of moving to Whitford?

Before they'd arrived here, the thought would never have crossed her mind. She wasn't totally sure it would have occurred to Sean, either. But it was crossing her mind now. Every time she saw Sean or Johnny with Rosie and was struck by the strength of that bond. When she saw him with his brothers, all of them looking younger and happier just because they were together and enjoying it so much.

And she didn't want to lean on practical considerations. Yes, she'd spent years building her landscaping business and there wasn't much call for her specialty in this part of Maine. Sean, too, had built a reputation just in the years he'd been working in the area. But when push came to shove, they were jobs. They could probably find work in the area. And the house was paid for, but it could be sold.

She ignored the jolt of pain that thought caused her for now. It was a house. And her grandmother and Russell could drive their RV to Maine just as easily and often as they drove it to New Hampshire. She wanted Sean to be happy and he was certainly happy here.

But she wasn't sure she would be, and it just started the loop of *what if* over in her head. Rather than drive herself into a real crying jag, she ran her fingertip over the words Sean had written on the sticky note and then tucked it into her purse. She had a wooden trunk in her closet where she kept them all and she'd add this one when they got home.

Home. Sighing, she went to tuck a light blanket over her sleeping son in case the AC was blowing too much on him. Then she carefully stretched out beside him and closed her eyes, trying to let her tension ease away as she listened to Johnny's soft breathing.

THIRTEEN

WHEN BEN FINALLY pulled into the clearing behind the Northern Star, he was exhausted. The calls had started shortly after Laney dropped him back at the station, and except for late-night and early-morning hours when people weren't supposed to be riding, he'd pretty much been on the run.

Luckily, most of them had been overreactions or minor injuries, but the last call had flipped the switch from tired to utterly drained. Jordan, the fire department's youngest volunteer, had ridden Ben's ATV behind the side-by-side so Ben could ride with the patient. She'd been in excruciating pain and he'd been afraid to give her too much for the broken hip because she'd seemed mentally altered, too. Mildly, but even with her helmet on, she might have suffered a concussion and he needed to be able to monitor that, as well. Her crying had been heartbreaking and it had taken a toll on all of them.

But as he'd done for years, he did his best to take the incident and mentally file it away as he parked his four-wheeler alongside the others. He needed food and some laughs, and he needed to see Laney's face.

It would have been easier to find her face if Rosie hadn't invited the entire town, he thought. He wandered around the crowd, saying hello and making small talk. He deflected all the questions about the calls he'd been on, preferring to focus on the happy vibe running through the gathering.

He finally found her near the food tables, where she was helping set up the condiments. Her face lit up when she saw him, and it felt like a weight tumbled off his shoulders. "Hi, Laney."

"You look exhausted," she said, frowning as she moved closer to him. "Are you okay?"

"Yeah. It's been busy, so I'm hoping to get enough downtime to eat some of this food before my phone goes off."

"Do you think it will?"

"I hope not. I'm going to tell myself all the riders are back at wherever they're staying, barbecuing." He shrugged. "It's a holiday weekend and that's how they go. Are you having fun?"

"Yeah. It's getting a little hectic now that it's time to set up the food, but it's been fun so far. Are Drew and Matt here, too?"

"They will be. Matt needed to take some pictures and make sure the ATV is taken care of and Drew went back into town to deal with somebody setting off fireworks in their backyard, and then he's driving over."

"That's good. Can I get you anything?"

"No, I'll go grab some lemonade and wait my turn for food."

When she smiled and went back to the table she'd been setting up, he tried to tell himself she was just busy, but that wasn't the vibe he'd gotten from her.

Laney was holding back. He wasn't sure if she was upset about something specific or she was trying to put some distance between them after they'd made love in his apartment, but she was definitely trying to keep him at arm's length. He hadn't expected her to kiss him in front of everybody, but she hadn't so much as touched his arm.

And he'd go along with it. For now. The sex had been incredible and maybe that, combined with the fact they'd grown close enough so she'd been worried about it, had been too much for her. He knew she was still trying to regain her footing after being married a long time and an ugly divorce, and that would take time.

Right now he would just remember the way she'd smiled so brightly in the instant she first saw him. Before she put her guard up, for whatever reason.

Once the food started coming off the grills—steak, burgers, chicken and hot dogs—to be set out with the most astonishing array of potluck dishes he'd ever seen, Ben filled his plate and found an open spot at a picnic table. Conversation went on around him, mostly about sports, but he focused on eating. He needed the sustenance.

Once he'd cleaned his plate, he realized he should get up and move around or there was a very real possibility he'd go to sleep sitting there on the picnic table bench. He tossed his plate and went to refill his cup with lemonade. Maybe a little sugar would help.

Rosie had just finished dumping more iced tea in a dispenser when he got to the beverage table, and she gave him a long look. "You know you can go find yourself an empty bed in the lodge and get some rest. Somebody will make sure you wake up if there's an emergency."

"Thanks, but I keep telling myself if I hold out a few more hours, everybody should be off the trails for the night and I can actually sleep."

"You know you're welcome to sleep here. The older kids didn't move into the lodge like I expected them to, so there are beds already made up and everything."

What he really wanted to do was crawl into Laney's bed, hold her close and fall asleep breathing in the scent of her shampoo. "You know, I might take you up on that, Rosie. I'm pretty beat."

Her eyes widened. "You must be if you're admitting it."

He chuckled and leaned over the table to refill his cup. "I'm not as stubborn as some of the men you know."

She rolled her eyes. "And thank the heavens for that."

A half hour later, he was reconsidering her offer of a place to nap when Laney turned up next to him. She was close, so she could keep her voice low. "Can you walk with me for a minute?"

"Of course." He tossed his empty cup in the garbage and followed her. She didn't walk toward her camper, but toward the field instead.

"I've had so much anxiety about seeing you again," she said. "I wasn't sure what to expect."

"I wasn't either, to be honest."

"And now it's awkward, which is the last thing I wanted. And I'm not really sure how to fix it."

It wasn't helped by the fact he could see she was keeping them within view of the lodge's guests, which automatically kept some distance between them. "I don't think anything needs fixing, Laney. Neither of us really knows where we stand because we haven't talked about it, and I'm really tired right now, but I don't think everything has to change."

She stopped walking and turned to face him, though she remained just out of arm's reach. "You said you'd give me only what I want."

"And I meant it."

She nodded, her eyes sad. "I just… I don't *know* what I want right now. I did in that moment. And I know I don't want to not see you again. But other than that, I'm just not sure."

"I'm not going anywhere, Laney. I know you're trying to figure things out in your life, and I'm not trying to put any pressure on you. We'll just hang out and take it day by day."

"I feel like that's not fair to you."

He shrugged, trying for a nonchalance he didn't feel. "I'm not going to run out and find a wife who'll put up with me thinking about you twenty-four seven, so for right now, I guess I don't know exactly what I want, either."

"So we're okay, even if I hit the brakes a little?"

"We're okay." As long as he knew where he stood, he could manage his expectations. He just needed to be careful not to let his heart get involved.

Then his phone vibrated and he dropped his chin to his chest for a second before pulling it out and reading the screen.

"Oh, no." Laney did step closer, then, and put her hand on his forearm. "You can't go back out. You're exhausted. Let somebody else go."

"It's bad. I have to go. And I probably won't be back tonight, but I'll call you tomorrow, okay?"

She nodded, and he gave her a quick smile before heading for his ATV. Then he put her out of his mind because the text was from Matt, who'd come upon an accident on his way back, and it didn't look good.

As soon as he had his helmet on and revved the engine, he felt the adrenaline starting to build. He'd get his second wind and get the job done. Hellish schedules were part of the job sometimes, and he might suck at relationships, but this he knew how to do.

Sean

SEAN LIFTED THE blanket and slid back into bed, smiling when Emma groaned and tried to pull the cover up over her head. It was definitely early, but they were also alone for a little while.

Johnny, who seemed to think sunrise was the best part of being on vacation, much to his parents' dismay, had been looking out the window when he saw Laney coming out of the bathhouse. He'd been excited and, before Sean could pull on a pair of sweats, had opened the door and gone to see her.

He must have looked rough, because Laney took pity on him. She was on her way into the lodge to steal some muffins and have coffee with Rosie, and she offered to take Johnny with her if Sean wanted to go back to bed for a while.

Hell yeah, he wanted to go back to bed.

But now that the door was locked and he was between the sheets with his warm—if slightly grumpy—wife, he wasn't sure he wanted to go back to sleep. He kissed the spot behind her ear. "We're alone right now."

She opened her eyes and sat up. "Where is Johnny?"

"Relax." He pulled her back down, tucking his arm under her. "He's with Laney. They're going to have coffee and muffins with Rosie. Well, Laney is. I'm hoping they don't give Johnny coffee."

"It's too early for that kind of visual. It's too early for everything."

"Everything?" He skimmed his hand down her stomach, looking for the hem of her pajama top. "Are you sure about that?"

"I'm sure that no matter how long we're married, morning breath will not be sexy."

"Then I won't kiss you." He pushed her top up so he could kiss her stomach. "Not your mouth, anyway."

"We're in a camper, Sean."

Maybe the words were meant to put him off, but her fingers skimming up his spine until she buried them in his hair were an invitation. "You'll have to be quiet."

"And fast," she said. "You know we're not going to be left alone very long."

"I can do fast," he replied, closing his mouth over her nipple through the fabric of her top and taking his hands off of her only long enough to get rid of his sweatpants.

She hissed before threading her fingers through his hair. "I can try to do quiet."

Sean tugged at the cute little sleep shorts she wore until they slid free and he could toss them aside. Then he stroked between her legs until she relaxed her thighs and lifted her hips off the mattress.

One of the best parts of being married was knowing his wife's body so intimately. He knew how to touch her if he wanted to torment her for a while, and he also knew how to send her straight over the edge.

After swirling his tongue over her nipple because, damn, he loved her breasts, he moved to her throat. Her hips lifted as he buried two fingers deep inside of her, while he gathered her hair in his other hand. Tugging, he pulled her head back so he could run his tongue over the hollow at the base of her throat.

Emma hissed, her fingernails digging into his ass almost painfully, and he grinned against her neck. "What's the matter, sweetheart?"

"Now," she demanded. "And do *not* make me scream, dammit."

Sean pushed his fingers deeper inside of her for a moment, pressing the heel of his hand hard against her clit while biting that soft spot at her neck, until she growled and pounded her fist against his shoulder.

Without letting go of her hair, he shifted on top of her and replaced his fingers with his dick. He wasn't gentle about it and she gasped again, turning her head until she met the resistance of his hand still clutching her hair.

He thrust hard into her, over and over, and he didn't give a shit if the camper rocked. All he knew was his wife and the heat of her body and the way her lips parted on a small cry as she raised her hips to meet him.

When she closed her eyes, her breath shortening, he tightened his fist in her hair and covered her mouth with his to keep her from crying out his name or any other words that would embarrass her later.

Her body clenched and she moaned against his lips while he struggled to hold on until the last tremor of pleasure racked her body. Then he let go and emptied himself into her with a deep groan. Then she wrapped her arms around him as he collapsed on top of her, welcoming his weight.

"I wasn't supposed to kiss you," he said as his body relaxed. "Unsexy morning breath and all that."

Her laughter shook both of them. "I didn't even notice."

Sean rested his hand on her stomach and kissed the side of her neck. "Wouldn't it be amazing if this was the time?"

"The time?"

"If we conceived a little brother or sister for Johnny here at the Northern Star."

He thought she'd laugh, but she just nodded. "That would be great."

Something was bugging her. She'd been slightly off for days, but he couldn't figure it out. She'd even left the barbecue for a while the previous afternoon, claiming Johnny needed a nap. And she'd probably been right, since he'd found them both sound asleep when he went looking for her, but that wasn't the only reason she'd gone in.

Maybe it was the baby thing, which would explain her lukewarm reaction just now. It had been weighing on her—on both of them, really—for a while, and he'd been thinking about how to broach the fact they might need to get their doctors involved.

But he didn't want to have that conversation now, so he went for something fun. "Speaking of children, Mitch and Josh and I were talking about how cool it would be to have a tree house for the kids, like we used to have. It's long gone now, but we loved that thing. But Josh said that would be a problem because of the guests. Insurance liability and all that. He said he's been looking at play structure kits, though. Like for playgrounds? He said they make one that looks like a big pirate ship. Johnny would love that."

"Yeah, he would."

Something in her voice sounded wrong, so he rolled up onto his elbow so he could look down at her face. "What's the matter?"

"Nothing." She smiled, but it was forced. He loved this woman more than life itself, and her many expressions were etched in his mind.

"You don't like pirate ships? They have a castle, too. Maybe the castle would be better for boys *and* girls."

She slapped his shoulder. "Girls can be pirates, too."

"Oh, I see how it is. You want both structures and then the girls can be pirates and make the boys clean their castle."

This time her smile reached her eyes. "I bet I could get Katie to talk Josh into buying both."

"They're pretty expensive, so I'll only vote for one." He thought about it. "I think the pirate ship would be more fun. I can picture Johnny with a fake eye patch and a foam sword. And if he had a little brother or sister, Johnny can be the captain and boss the little one around."

"This pirate ship doesn't have a plank to walk, does it?"

"I don't know, but that would be a serious hazard. I'll make a note to ask him."

"Are you going to leave him a sticky note?"

"Of course not." He kissed the tip of her nose. "Those are only for you."

She sighed and turned her head to look at the clock. "I hear people moving around out there. It won't be long before Johnny comes looking for us."

"The door's locked."

She laughed and pushed him away. "He's three. Put some pants on and let's go visit whoever's already made coffee."

THE SCREAMING HAD drawn Laney to the pool. She thought it was playful screaming and not panic, but she felt like she had to check.

She hadn't expected to find half the men in the pool with the kids, playing what looked like a cross between volleyball and rugby with an inflatable beach ball. After probably fifteen minutes, she still couldn't figure out the rules of the game and she was starting to suspect the game didn't actually have any.

"You might not want to watch this."

Laney turned to see Mary walking toward her. "If I had a whistle, I'd probably be out of air already from blowing it."

"Your nerves just haven't had a chance to build up a resistance yet."

"Resistance to the noise? Or to the potential for drowning?"

"Resistance to doom." Mary smiled and leaned on the fence to watch the chaos. "Everything's doom with this bunch. Camping trip of doom. Or, in this case, water ball of doom."

"I've experienced the shopping list of doom." Laney laughed. "For this one, though, I might need a margarita of doom."

"Those don't hurt." She held up her purple insulated tumbler. "This *might* be wine. But they swim like fish and, even though it doesn't look like it, they watch out for each other."

"You have a wonderful family, Mary. I envy you, really." She realized that probably sounded weird and felt herself blush. "I mean, I wish my family were more like this. They're a little stuffy."

That wasn't all of it. She knew the odds she'd ever stand by a pool and watch with amused affection as her grandchildren tried to kill each other with a blow-up ball grew slimmer every year. But she wasn't sure how to explain that without sounding like she'd given up, and then she'd get the obligatory pep talk about how she was still young. And Ben's name would probably be mentioned.

At least he'd texted her, as promised. I'm home and going to sleep for as long as I can. Just wanted to let you know I'm off the trails.

Laney had wished him sweet dreams, not seeing until a few hours later on the news channel's Facebook page that there had been a fatal ATV accident late last night. She didn't know if she should say something to him and, if so, what she should say. But she did know that the best thing she could do until she heard from him was assume he was sleeping and let him be.

"Laney! There you are."

Usually when a guest was looking for her, a toilet was clogged or they'd just blown a fuse in their camper. But when this family came looking, she was about to have an adventure.

"We're going for a ride. Just us girls, so let's go."

"A ride. You mean on the four-wheelers?"

"My helmet should fit you," Mary said. "I'm going to stay here, so you can wear it."

"And you can ride Bobby's machine. It's the same as Beth's, so you already know how to drive it."

Laney was still trying to wrap her head around it—especially considering the news still fresh in her mind—but Emma was practically dragging her toward the other women, who were gathering their riding gear and putting bottles of water in the machines that had cargo boxes on them.

"I don't know if I want to do this."

"You're going to do fine, I promise," Emma said, even though Laney wasn't sure how she could promise that since she'd never seen her ride.

"I've only ridden out on the trails a couple of times. I'm not very good at it yet."

"This is how you *get* good at it. You just do it."

Laney still wasn't convinced. "I'm sure you all ride a lot faster. I'll just slow everybody down."

"Nope. We ride at all different speeds. And those of us who ride a little faster will stop and wait at intersections for those who prefer to take their time. Or if there's a rough bit of trail, we'll wait to make sure everybody gets through. You'll be with Lauren and Beth, mostly. And Mary's only been riding alone for a couple of years. She always rode behind Leo, but we finally talked her into trying it herself and she loves it."

"Really?"

Emma grinned. "Don't make me bust out the *if Mary can do it, so can you* line."

"Mary keeps this family in line. I'm pretty sure there's nothing she can't do," Laney said. "But I would like to go, if you're sure I won't be holding anybody back."

"You won't. And if it helps, I've already been told you're a natural."

Fifteen minutes later, she was actually driving an

ATV, following her friends out of the campground and into the woods. She was tense at first, but Beth was in front of her and Lauren behind her, so she just kept pace with them and tried to follow where Beth went.

When she splashed through a big, muddy puddle and soaked herself, she actually laughed out loud. And then she saw Liz standing in the trees, taking pictures of them as they went by. Imagining her mother's reaction if she sent her that picture amused her almost as much as the splash had, and she realized that even though it was still a little scary to her, being out here with these women and getting dirty, just might be part of finding her joy.

FOURTEEN

BEN WAS IN the process of reaching over to hit snooze on his phone for the fourth or fifth time when he realized it wasn't the alarm. The phone was ringing and his mom's face was on the screen.

He pulled the charger cord free before he answered so he could roll onto his back. "Hey, Mom."

"Good morning. Did I wake you up?"

"Nope. I was awake." Somewhat. He'd been awake a few times already, but he kept falling back to sleep. "What's up?"

"I'm making Swedish meatballs in the slow cooker for supper, and they're Jimmy's favorite. And you've been so busy this past week, we've barely seen you at all, so I thought a family dinner might be nice."

"A family dinner on a Tuesday?" He didn't realize he'd said it out loud for a few seconds and, when he did, he hoped it hadn't come out too harshly.

"You told me Tuesdays and Wednesdays are your least busy days, and I know your father and brother's schedule, so this is a night when everybody's free. Plus, like I said, it's his favorite meal and I always make too much when I use the slow cooker. You know that."

Since he still had too many plastic containers of chili and beef stew in his freezer to count, he definitely knew that. "Swedish meatballs sound good, Mom. I'll be there."

"Only if you don't have any other plans, of course."

Of course she waited until after he'd committed to give a token way out. Or she'd heard something around town and was fishing for details. "I don't have other plans. And they might be Jimmy's favorite, but you know I love your Swedish meatballs, too."

"I'll see you for supper, then."

Once he'd hung up, Ben threw his arm over his eyes and thought about going back to sleep. The holiday weekend had been brutal and he'd made it clear that unless a situation came up that was literally life or death, his ass was not getting on a four-wheeler today.

But he was awake now, so he hit the button to make coffee happen and jumped in the shower. Then, mug in hand, he turned on the morning news and sat at his small table to open his laptop. He made the usual rounds—his calendar, the weather forecast, the Facebook account he mostly ignored other than using it as a way to keep track of birthdays—and then, once the caffeine started kicking in, he checked his email. He was waiting for information about the continuing education hours he needed for his license renewal, which still wasn't in his inbox. Clicking over to his to-do app, he added following up on that. Changing his ATV's oil and cleaning the air filter were still unchecked and he made a mental note to get to those this week. Or maybe today if he got bored, since it was a long time until supper.

Then he clicked back over to Facebook, since he'd accidentally mentioned it while talking to the teenagers and he'd gotten friend requests from several of the Kowalskis in the last couple of days. And they liked to post pictures, so he clicked through those. There were a lot of photos of the kids, which was to be expected. And a lot taken out on the trail.

Then he came across some from the big barbecue on Saturday. Those he scrolled through more slowly, until he came to one of him and Laney. They were away from the others, facing each other as they spoke. It was a nice picture of them, except he knew that at that moment, she was telling him she wanted to hit the brakes on what was happening between them.

And then he'd had to leave and he hadn't seen her since then. He'd been too busy and, when he wasn't busy, too exhausted. They'd exchanged a few text messages, so he knew their friendship was still intact.

But he wasn't so sure about the more-than-friends they'd become.

Rather than mope over the picture, he closed the laptop and scrambled up a few eggs for breakfast. After laying some cheese slices over the eggs to melt, he popped an English muffin in the toaster and, when that was done, he ate standing up at the counter.

He was about to give up on being lazy and go do the maintenance on his four-wheeler when his phone chimed. It was Laney.

Are you busy right now?

Just finished breakfast. What's up?

He stared at the little bubble that showed her typing for what seemed like forever before her response came through. Not much. I haven't seen you, so I thought I'd see if you're recovered from the holiday weekend.

I'm glad it's over. What are you up to today?

I have the day off, more or less, because they all went on a big family ride with a picnic lunch and Rosie and Andy are watching the kids. I'll probably sit in my pink chair and do nothing.

He should tell her to enjoy her day off and leave it at that. She wanted to hit the brakes, and he had to respect that. But she'd reached out to him, so maybe she didn't want to stop their relationship in its tracks, but just slow it down a little.

You have two chairs, he typed into his phone. Want some company?

He figured if she really wanted to slow everything down, she'd tell him she was planning to read or something, and maybe another time.

Sure. I don't have much for lunch stuff, so you can bring something or we can raid Rosie's kitchen.

Turkey sandwich from the diner?

My favorite. Then there was a happy face. See you soon.

He sent back a happy face, knowing if he got up and looked in the mirror, he'd see the same expression looking back at him.

When his phone chimed again, he held it up, expecting to see another text message from Laney.

Please help your dad figure out why the lawnmower won't start before he sets it on fire in the driveway.

At least he'd have a way to pass the time until he could head for the diner, and then out to the lodge. He never would have guessed he'd come to love pink chairs so much.

On my way, Mom.

"I CAN'T BELIEVE you've never seen *Armageddon*. How is that even possible?"

Laney laughed and balanced her takeout box on the arm of her chair. "That's a space movie, isn't it?"

"Yes, but it's *way* more than a space movie. It's an action movie and a drama and a comedy and a romance. You're on the edge of your seat and it makes you laugh and then cry." Ben stopped, frowning. "I didn't cry. But you probably would."

"Because I'm a girl?" She arched an eyebrow, thinking maybe he'd squirm a little and she'd enjoy that.

"Because you just told me the book you're reading made you cry. If books make you cry, then movies do, too. And *Armageddon* definitely will."

"I'll have to watch it, then, and see for myself."

"I own it. You can come over some night and watch it with me. I'll put tissues on my grocery list."

She wasn't sure if that was an actual invitation—like a date night—or a throwaway comment, so she just smiled and ate another fry from the box. She'd already eaten her sandwich, which had been delicious, as usual. And Ben had remembered it was her favorite lunch offering from the Trailside Diner. He either had an exceptional memory for random things or he cared enough to remember her likes and dislikes.

The possibility it was the latter both pleased her and

jacked up her anxiety level. She liked Ben, and she knew he liked her. It worried her that she was happy and couldn't tell if she was accomplishing her summer goal of rediscovering herself, or if being with Ben made her happy. Patrick had made her happy once upon a time, too, until she'd gotten so caught up in making *him* happy, she'd lost sight of what she wanted.

"Wow, that is one serious expression," Ben said, jerking her back to the present. "I can just lend you my copy of the movie if that's what's making you frown like that."

"No, I was thinking about something else." A man she didn't want to think about anymore. "I'd love to watch it with you sometime, and I can bring my own tissues, although now I feel like I have to *not* cry just to prove you wrong."

"A challenge," he said, grinning. "Trust me, you'll cry."

"Have you ever cried during a movie?" She was watching his face, so she saw the truth even though he shook his head. "Come on. Tell me. Was it for the volleyball in that Tom Hanks movie? Everybody cried for Wilson. There's no shame in that."

"I didn't cry for the volleyball."

"Tell me."

"I'll tell you if you go for a walk with me. There's a nice breeze today and we can walk off those fries." He stood and picked up their empty takeout boxes. "A short walk, anyway. I don't like to be too far from my vehicle, just in case."

"You take your job pretty seriously," she said, walking beside him to the Dumpster so he could toss the trash.

"It's a pretty serious job." He started walking toward the tree line. "And Dave and the other guys from the fire department have been doing a great job for years but now that I'm here, I feel like I need to be ready. It's different than before, in the city, when there were other guys who could do the same job."

"Did you ever think about becoming a doctor?"

"Nope. That costs a lot of money and trying to work to support yourself *and* get through medical school never appealed to me. I like what I do. What about you? What do you do when you're not spending the summer working at a campground?"

Laney shrugged. "I got a business degree I never used, and I worked at a jewelry store before I got married. Then my job was being Mrs. Patrick Ballard for ten years. I much prefer working at a campground."

He laughed, and when his hand brushed against hers and then lingered, it felt totally natural to lace her fingers through his. "Have you thought about what you're going to do when the season ends?"

It was a question she couldn't really answer yet. "I've thought about it. I don't know yet. My dad wants me to work for him, but I can't imagine anything I want to do less."

"What does he do?"

"He sells insurance."

"I think you like being outside too much to be stuck in an office all day."

Laney squeezed his hand, smiling. "I think you're right. But I try not to think about it *too* much because then I'll feel like I need a plan, and then a plan to execute that plan. Before you know it, I'll be stressed out and planning instead of enjoying my time here."

"Cross that bridge when you come to it."

She'd figured out that he was simply walking the tree line around the field, rather than going into the woods, so they were about halfway through with their walk. He'd told her when he first arrived that he'd promised his mom he'd have dinner with them and they ate at five o'clock.

"It seems unnaturally quiet around here today," he said, looking at the empty campground.

"It wasn't earlier, when they had the kids outside, but Rosie decided today was a good day for cartoons and hanging around inside. Paige and Katie didn't go on the ride because they're pregnant, and I think Katie went to work. But I guess they traditionally do a big ride to someplace where they can have a picnic. You wouldn't believe the stuff they packed on their four-wheelers. Leo even had a small barbecue grill on his."

"They're a fun bunch, but you'll probably be a little relieved when they're gone."

She thought about that for a moment before shaking her head. "Not really. I like them a lot. I was worried before they got here, because they're the boss's family and all that, but they're so nice and they clean up after themselves, so it hasn't even seemed like work."

When they had made the circle around the field and back to her camper, she wasn't sure if he was going to tell her he was leaving, but he didn't. Instead he sat back down in the chair and took a sip of the lemonade she'd poured for him.

"Okay, I went for a walk," she said. "Now you tell me when you cried during a movie."

The tips of his ears turned pink. "I was hoping you'd forget."

She laughed. "Not a chance. Come on. A deal's a deal."

"One of my mom's favorite movies is *Hope Floats*, and there's this scene where the asshole ex is driving away and his little girl is chasing after the car, crying for him." He stopped and cleared his throat. "I might have had something in my eye, though."

Laney knew the movie well and she always cried during that scene. "That's definitely a multi-tissue movie for me."

"If I'm lucky enough to have kids, I couldn't imagine doing that."

She couldn't imagine him doing that, either. She'd seen him with the Kowalski kids, and she'd also seen him with people in general, and he was too good a guy to abandon somebody he loved. But she was also reminded that Ben did want kids, and the sooner, the better. He was a man who was past ready to settle down, and she just wasn't there yet.

For now, though, he seemed content to sit in the shade of her awning and talk to her. It was a relaxing way to spend an afternoon, and she found herself wishing it wouldn't end. But two lemonade refills later, they heard the distant rumble of ATV engines, and Ben stood.

"I should go before they get here," he said. "Otherwise I'll end up standing around, shooting the shit and listening to the stories and, before you know it, I'll be late for dinner."

"I'm glad you came over today." She stood up, too, since it seemed rude not to.

"Me too."

He was standing close to her, and she watched his

gaze lower to her mouth. But he wouldn't kiss her goodbye because she'd told him she wanted to hit the brakes. After three days of not seeing him, though, she didn't want brakes. She wanted going too fast, skidding through corners, barely in control.

She closed the gap between them, and put her hand on his arm. It was all the invitation he needed, and he lowered his mouth to hers. He was gentle at first, almost tentative, but when she put her hand on his neck and slid her fingertips into his hair, he deepened the kiss. His tongue slipped between her lips to dance over hers. And as her knees got shaky and she couldn't stop the small sound of need from deep in her throat, Laney wondered how she was supposed to resist this man. Hell, she wondered why she was even trying to.

He kissed her until the sound of the four-wheelers got too close to ignore anymore. Then he broke it off and smiled at her.

"I should go. Tell everybody I said hi, though, okay?"

"Yeah. I hope you have a nice dinner with your family."

He started to walk away, but then he turned back. "You could come, you know. To dinner. My mom wouldn't mind."

Meeting his family was too much and her stomach knotted, but she wasn't sure how to say no when he was looking at her like that. And part of her really wanted to meet them because she knew Ben and his parents were close, and she couldn't help but be curious about them. "I...are you sure she wouldn't mind? Unexpected dinner guests are one of my mother's worst nightmares."

"I'm sure she wouldn't mind."

"Okay." When he grinned, she felt the knot of anxiety loosen a little. It was dinner. It wasn't *that* big a deal. "So a little before five?"

"Sounds good. You remember how to get there?"

She nodded, turning her head as the ATVs grew louder. "They're almost here. You should run if you're going to get out of here before they see you."

When Ben winked and then took off at a jog toward his SUV, Laney sighed. First the kiss, and now dinner with his parents. She was *not* good at braking.

WHEN BEN HEARD Laney's Camaro pull into the driveway, he restrained himself from jumping up off the couch and running to the door, but only because his dad was watching him. He was trying to keep everything as casual as possible, so Laney wouldn't feel uncomfortable.

As casual as it could be when a man told his mom he was bringing a woman home for dinner, anyway.

He didn't regret inviting her, and he was damn glad she'd come, but it hadn't seemed like that big a deal when he was standing outside of her camper, with the taste of her mouth still on his lips. But now with his parents eager to meet her, and Jimmy and his wife and kids there, it seemed like a much bigger deal. He didn't mind, but he was worried about what Laney would think.

He met her out in the driveway, and he couldn't help but notice she'd showered and changed before coming over. Her hair was hanging loose around her shoulders, and she was wearing capris with a summery blouse and sandals. She looked beautiful, and he was touched that she'd seen dinner with his parents as a reason to get dressed up.

"Thank you for coming," he said, giving her a quick kiss hello. "You're gorgeous."

She blushed. "Thank you. I figured dinner at a friend's house was a good excuse to get out of my shorts and T-shirts for a little while."

Dinner at a friend's house. Ouch. "Come on in and meet everybody."

His mom had come out of the kitchen when she heard the car, so they were all in the living room when Ben led Laney inside. "Laney, those are my parents, Alan and May. My brother Jimmy. His wife, Chelsea, and their two boys. The one in the Batman T-shirt is J.J. and the little one is Zach. Everybody, this is Laney."

She was gracious and friendly, and Ben relaxed as he watched his family warm up to her. They all moved into the dining room when his mom told them, too, and he pulled her chair out for her. When he sat down next to her, he realized it had been a very long time since he'd had somebody with him at his mother's table. It was always his parents, Jimmy and Chelsea and their boys, and him.

There was the usual small talk as they started eating, until Laney leaned close to whisper in his ear. "These are the best Swedish meatballs I've ever had."

He nodded, but he also caught the speculative glance his mom sent their way. Ben knew he and Laney had a strong enough chemistry so most of the Kowalskis had pegged them for a couple even before they were one, so they certainly weren't going to slip anything by his mother.

"Have you been home to visit this summer, Laney?"

his mom asked when there was a break in the conversation. "Rhode Island, isn't it?"

"Yes, home is Rhode Island, but I haven't gone back. They're keeping me pretty busy at the Northern Star."

Ben knew there was a lot more to it than being busy, but he also knew she wouldn't want to talk about her former marriage or her relationship with her family while eating dinner with his parents for the first time. She'd talked to him enough about them to know it was a painful subject, since they'd sided with their former son-in-law in the divorce. Maybe not publicly, but emotionally, and it was them Laney had needed a break from, not her ex.

"What will you do when the summer's over?" his mom asked. "You can't stay in a camper during snowmobile season, can you?"

Laney laughed. "I don't know about *can*, but I definitely don't intend to. I'll be gone before the snowmobilers start showing up."

"Gone? You're going back to Rhode Island?"

"Probably. Working at the Northern Star is just a temporary job for me."

"Oh." Ben watched his mom frown at her plate, stabbing a piece of meatball with her fork. He willed her to let it go. He wasn't sure if she was disappointed the first woman Ben had been interested in for a while was leaving, or if she was afraid he'd run off to Rhode Island with Laney, but he could practically hear the wheels turning in her mind. "You should stay until the leaves turn at least. The fall foliage is beautiful around Whitford."

"We don't really have a hard end date, so it's possible. It depends on how busy it stays after Labor Day, I guess."

"That's a nice car you've got," Jimmy said, and Ben could have jumped across the table and kissed him for changing the subject. "Six or eight cylinders?"

Laney snorted. "Eight. I'm not sacrificing power in a muscle car to save a little gas."

Jimmy swallowed the bite he'd popped in his mouth and pointed his fork at Laney, though he spoke to Ben. "I like her."

They all laughed and talked cars for a while, until the meal was over. Chelsea took the boys back to the living room since they were getting fidgety, and everybody else helped clean up.

Ben tried not to dwell too much on how it felt to watch Laney moving around the kitchen with his mom. They talked easily—something about Nola promising to teach Laney how to knit—while they worked, and it felt right to him. It was too easy to imagine their kids playing with Jimmy's kids in the other room, or all sitting around Grandpa and Grandma's Christmas tree, waiting to open presents.

With his throat feeling tight all of a sudden, he went to the fridge and grabbed a water bottle. He needed to take a page from Laney's book and put the brakes on. Not even an hour ago, she'd made it pretty plain she planned to be back in Rhode Island before the snow flew, so there would be no little cousins to hang out with J.J and Zach anytime soon.

"I really should get back to the Northern Star," he heard Laney say, though he'd missed what she was responding to. His mother had probably offered to make dessert or offered her an after-dinner drink. "But dinner was amazing. Thank you so much for having me over on short notice."

"You're welcome anytime, honey. You don't need an invitation."

Ben walked through the house with Laney as she said goodbye to everybody. "It was nice to meet you all."

"If we're here the next time you visit Ben, pop in and say hello," his dad said.

Ben wondered if Laney caught the fact his parents knew she'd spent some time in his apartment. Not that it mattered, but there were no keeping secrets in a town like Whitford.

It was almost a relief to close the door behind them, even though it meant she was leaving. He took her hand in his as he walked her to her car, and tried to think of something to say.

"Your family's really nice," she said, leaning against her car door without letting go of his hand.

"They are. And they liked you." He smiled. "Which isn't a surprise."

"They're not watching us out the window right now or anything, are they?"

He laughed, but he also looked. "They don't seem to be. Why?"

"Because I want you to kiss me good-night, but maybe not with an audience."

He ran his thumb over her lower lip, inhaling deeply. "You do, huh?"

"I do. I think my brakes are slipping." She laughed. "Or something like that. Basically, I'm not very good at not wanting you."

"Good." He lowered his mouth to hers, kissing her

until she had his T-shirt bunched in her free hand and moaned against his lips. Then he forced himself to remember they were in his parents' driveway and put a little space between them.

"I hope you get a chance to visit the lodge again soon," she said in a low voice, her mouth curved into an inviting smile.

"Oh, I will." When she stepped out of the way, he opened her car door for her, but kissed her again before she could slide into the seat. "Text me when you get there."

"Good night, Ben." She started the car and reached for the handle to pull the door closed. "Sweet dreams."

Before he could say anything else, she closed the door and put the car in Reverse. He gave her a little wave as she backed out onto the road and watched until her taillights were out of sight.

He was going to need a minute or two before he went back inside. Or maybe a cold shower from the garden hose.

FIFTEEN

Emma

THEIR TIME IN WHITFORD was almost over, and the closer it got to time to say goodbye, the more anxious Emma became. She felt at any random moment the conversation would turn to the lodge and Sean would finally say it. *I'd like to raise my son here.*

She loved Whitford. She loved the Northern Star. But she didn't want to live there. They lived in the house she'd been raised in—the house she'd fought so hard to keep—so she knew the pull a house and its history could have on a person. And while he had his aunt and uncle and his cousins in New Hampshire, the fact Rosie and his brothers and sister were here probably added to that pull.

The camper door opened and Sean stepped inside. "Are you going to come have breakfast? There are roughly a thousand pancakes, but you know how fast the bacon goes."

"Yeah, I was just cleaning up a bit. Where's Johnny?"

"He's helping Rosie with the syrup."

Emma winced. That cleanup was going to require copious amounts of hot water. "I'll be out in a minute."

"What's going on with you, Em? Are you feeling okay?"

"Yeah." She gave him a smile, but she didn't have to see his face to know it had been a weak attempt.

"Talk to me. Something's been wrong most of this trip, and it's time to talk about it because it's getting worse. Is it Paige and Katie being pregnant?"

She shook her head. "No. I mean, I'm jealous. I really want another baby."

"We'll keep trying, Emma. And if it doesn't happen, we can talk about other options. I know it's important to you that Johnny have a brother or sister. Or two, even. I want that, too."

"I know. And maybe you were right the other day. Maybe we'll have a Northern Star baby."

He tilted his head, frowning a little. "Okay, I don't know what it is, but I know we're hitting close on whatever it is. You had a weird tone, but I can't figure out why conceiving a child here would be a bad thing."

"It wouldn't." She knew Sean wasn't going to let it go now. He was worried and he wouldn't leave the camper without an answer. "When I watch you here, with Rosie and your brothers and Liz, I feel like you *belong* here. And when you talk to Johnny about the house and the land, and show him where you did things when you were a kid, I… I don't know. I feel like you want to raise *your* son here."

"Is that what's been bothering you this whole time?"

"Not bothering me, exactly. It's just something I've noticed." When he didn't respond, she finally gave a little shrug of one shoulder. "Okay, maybe it's been bothering me a little."

"This isn't the first time we've been here. Why now?"

She tried not to focus on the fact he hadn't denied it. "It's the first time we've been here long enough to really relax and settle in. And Johnny's getting older now. He holds your hand and walks with you and you look so proud when you're showing him around."

"I *am* proud. I walked away from this place for a long time, but now that I'm older and wiser—or older, at least—I'm glad we didn't sell it. I'm grateful my brothers busted their asses bringing it back to what it used to be and then expanding it. It's part of who I am and, yes, I'm proud to share it with my son. And with my wife."

Emma blinked, but the tears welling up and blurring her vision didn't go away. "You're so happy here."

He used his thumb to gently wipe away a tear that spilled over onto her cheek. "Emma, come on, honey. What is this? Of course I'm happy here. We're on *vacation*."

"You want Johnny to have a pirate ship."

"You're freaking right I do. Who *wouldn't* want a pirate ship in the backyard? I wish my brothers and I had a pirate ship when we were kids. We could have tied Katie to the mast and held her hostage until Liz pillaged cookies from the house to ransom her." She gave him a look and he stopped talking for a second. "Okay, I might have digressed there for a minute."

"See? You can see your son growing up here like you did."

"No, Emma. I see my son spending vacations here and being a pirate and riding a four-wheeler so fast I want to puke and stealing cookies from Rosie's kitchen. I might even see him staying here an extra couple of weeks each summer when he's old enough. But I don't see us *moving* here. Is that what you think I want?"

"Sometimes it seemed like you want to and it scares

me. I love our home, but I want you to be happy and… I've been worried that for the first time, what makes you happy and what makes me happy weren't going to be the same thing."

"We've built a life together, you and me. We have a son. We have businesses. I don't want to walk away from that. And I know how much that house means to you. You made up an imaginary fiancé to keep your grandmother from selling it."

"You weren't imaginary—"

"Just uninformed," he finished for her, and she blushed at the memory of the day she'd knocked on his door and asked him to not only pretend he was engaged to her, but to move into her house. "You keep calling this my home and I guess it always will be because this is where I'm from. It's where I was raised and where my family lives. But it's not *our* home."

"Do you love our home like you love this place?"

He cupped her chin in his hand and tilted her head back so she was looking into his eyes. "You and Johnny are my *home*. Always. But yes, I love our house like I love this place. Honey, I ate broccoli with a smile on my face to help you keep that house. I ain't leavin' it."

Emma laughed at the memory of how she'd launched her plan to convince her grandmother she and Sean were engaged with celebratory Chicken Divan, not knowing the fake love of her life loathed broccoli. And he'd eaten it for her. "I'm being silly, aren't I?"

"You do a lot of silly things, Emma Kowalski, but loving me and worrying about my happiness isn't one of them."

She held his chin and kissed him because he was so sweet. But also wrong. "I don't do a *lot* of silly things."

"There was the time you put flannel sheets on the bed and then tried to get into it wearing flannel pajamas. I thought you were going to set the house on fire. And the time you tried to change the faucet without shutting the water off first. And the—"

She kissed him again, just to shut him up. This time he cupped her neck and kept kissing her until she softened against him. When he broke it off and looked into her eyes, she sighed. "I love you, Sean."

"I love you, too." After taking a deep breath, he raised his eyebrows. "You know what else I love? Bacon. Let's go."

As he was about to open the screen door, she said his name and then waited until he turned to face her again. "You know, we can get a pirate ship for our own backyard."

The grin lit up his face. "You're a damn good woman, Emma. And maybe sometimes, after the kid's asleep, we can sneak out there and you can shiver me timbers."

She frowned. "I'm not sure what that means."

"Yeah, I don't actually, either. We should find out before I ask you to do that to me."

"Just don't search for it on the internet without a porn filter."

He almost fell off the camper step, which made her laugh. "What the hell does that mean?"

"Long story." She grinned and nudged him to get moving because she could smell the bacon now. "Ask Aunt Mary about it sometime."

LANEY CLOSED THE dryer door on what was hopefully the last load of laundry and pondered the feasibility of hiding in the basement for a little while longer. She hadn't slept well the night before because she'd been too busy tossing and turning and dissecting dinner with Ben's family.

It was also a hot and humid day, and being in the cool basement didn't help kill her desire to dump a pile of clean laundry onto the floor, curl up on top of it and take a nap.

"Laney?" she heard Rosie call from the top of the stairs. "Are you down there?"

And there went that idea. "Yes, but I'm on my way up."

"It seems like you've been doing laundry all day," Rosie said once she'd closed the basement door behind her.

"I think I have. Since Ryan and Lauren left after yesterday's ride, I was doing their bedding. And between dust and mud, everybody was changing clothes more than they anticipated so I offered to do a few loads for them."

"That's nice of you. But you should have told them where to find the washer and dryer and let them do it themselves."

Laney laughed and sat down at the table, since Rosie had put a sandwich down and pointed to it. "That's not exactly your usual hospitality."

"They're not exactly paying guests." Pulling out a chair, Rosie sat down with her own sandwich, along with a third plate that she set in front of an empty chair. "Not that we'd take their money even if they tried, but they can do for themselves, if you know what I mean."

Laney bit into the chicken salad sandwich, wondering what had precipitated this surprise lunch meeting. And who was running late.

She'd barely finished the thought when the back door opened and Mary walked into the kitchen. "I swear, I need a vacation from this vacation."

"I told you to take one of the rooms upstairs," Rosie said. "I'll tell nobody where you are."

"Trust me, they'll find me." She sat down in front of the third sandwich. "Hi, Laney."

"Hi. Rough day?"

"I swear I'm going to line them all up and whack each of them with the wooden spoon. You can tell when it's almost time to go home because there's been too much together time and the bickering starts."

"Whack them with a wooden spoon?"

Rosie shook her head. "She's not talking about the children, Laney. She's talking about the grown men."

"The Kowalski men have thick skulls," Mary added. "Trust me, sometimes the only way to get their attention is a quick thump with the spoon."

"Speaking of men," Rosie said. "How was dinner with Ben's parents last night?"

Laney froze with the sandwich halfway to her mouth. The way Rosie asked the question—with obviously fake nonchalance—and Mary's expectant look told her why she was being fed lunch today. The grapevine needed fertilizing.

"How do you know about that?"

Rosie gave her an *oh, honey* look. "May was in the market and mentioned it to Fran. Then Fran had to run to the library to return some movies and she told Hailey. Hailey told Matt, who had to call Josh about something related to the club and he told him. And Josh told Sean while Andy was standing nearby. Andy told me."

"Seriously? And all that happened this morning?"

"There's not a lot to do in Whitford, in case you haven't noticed. This is like a sport for us, really."

"So, how was it?" Mary asked.

"It was good, I guess. The best Swedish meatballs I've ever had." Both women looked as if they wanted to argue that point, so she kept talking. "His nephews are adorable. Maybe Johnny's age and a little older."

"I wasn't asking how the meal was," Mary said. "How did you get along with his parents?"

"Fine. They're nice. His brother and his sister-in-law are nice. It wasn't a big deal, really."

Rosie looked skeptical. "When a man brings a woman home to his mother, it's a big deal."

Laney wanted to push back against that line of thinking, since she didn't *want* it to be a big deal, but she suspected she'd be wasting her breath. Instead, she took a big bite of her sandwich and took her time chewing it.

When they got the hint she wasn't going to say any more about dinner, the two women ate their own lunches. The talk turned to the daunting task of getting the belongings spread all over the campground back into the correct campers, the way they had come out.

Just as she was about to excuse herself, the back door opened again and Josh walked in. "Hey, Rosie, have you seen some papers rolled up with a rubber band on them?"

"When I find papers, I put them on your desk. Like I have been for years."

"I'll check there. Ben just drove up and I want to go over some maps with him. We've been marking every location he responds to, and we've got a remote cluster. We'll never get permission to cut a road in from that many landowners, but one guy owns a big chunk and Matt suggested we approach him about cutting in a clearing for a helicopter. I want to get Ben's take on it."

He was walking as he talked and he was stepping out of the kitchen as he said the last words. Laney turned back to find both women staring at her and she didn't have to guess why. But she wasn't going to admit anything, either. "What?"

"Ben sure does spend a lot of time here," Mary said.

"Because Sean and the others are here. And because he's always talking to Josh and Andy about the trails. Plus, he said starting from here cuts down his response time, so he can visit you guys while still doing his job, instead of sitting in the fire station." Laney got up and rinsed her plate. "I'm going to go check the laundry."

"That dryer's not done," Rosie said. "I'll check it in a bit and they can come haul their own clothes up the stairs."

"Okay, then I'm going to go…do something."

She had her hand on the door when Mary spoke. "Tell Ben we said hi."

They were both laughing when she walked out in the hot sun, and she couldn't help smiling. Yes, she wanted to see Ben. Maybe he had logical reasons for being there, but that didn't stop her from remembering the way he'd looked at her when he'd said he'd be stopping by to see her. The intensity of it still made her shiver.

She spotted him right away, since he hadn't made it as far as out back. He was leaning against the barn, talking to Andy, but as soon as he saw her, he stood up straight. His smile made Andy look over, and then he smiled, too.

"I think I might know where those papers are that Josh is looking for. I'll be back in a minute."

It was such an obvious move to leave them alone, Laney almost laughed out loud. And judging by the way he grinned and shook his head, Ben was aware of it, too.

"I'd kiss you," he said," but I have a feeling we're being watched."

If Laney was sure of one thing, it was that they weren't hiding anything from anybody. "Do you care?"

"No. Do you?"

"Not really."

He closed the distance between them and kissed her. It didn't last long, because maybe they did care a little, but the small sound of appreciation he made when his mouth met hers made up for it.

"That definitely makes up for looking at more maps with Josh," he said, lacing his fingers through hers. "That man loves maps."

"I noticed you didn't ride over on your ATV."

He shrugged. "It's quiet today. I asked around and most of the lodging establishments around the trail system have vacancies. There's usually a lull right after a holiday weekend, and it doesn't take me that long to get back to the station if I need the four-wheeler."

When he looked at something over her shoulder, she turned to see Josh and Andy walking toward them. "I guess it's map time."

"If nothing comes up, you want to go for a walk later? You told me you try to walk every day, so I was hoping to keep you company."

"Sure." She squeezed his hand before releasing it.

"*Mom*, there's something in the pool!"

"That sounds like Brianna," she said. "I should go see what's going on."

"Holler if you need help," Josh told her.

She laughed. "I'm sure it won't be bad. Johnny's been trying to toss things over the fence since he got here. A personal challenge, I think."

As she walked away, she heard Josh start talking about the maps in his hand and almost laughed out loud. He really did love his maps. But it made sense. The ATV trail system had changed all of their lives, so the care and maintenance of it was a priority for him.

And in a little while, maybe she and Ben would get to walk one of those trails. They'd have some peace and quiet and—most importantly—privacy. He owed her a much more thorough hello kiss.

Sean

"WHO DOES THIS belong to?" Sean held up a T-shirt that had been draped over one of the support arms for the RV's awning.

Emma stared at it for a few seconds before shrugging. "It's a man's Red Sox T-shirt, Sean. I think you *all* have that one."

"So it's mine?"

"I don't know. Take it and when we're home and all the laundry's done, if you have two, you owe somebody an apology. And a T-shirt."

"Next year we need to write our names on everything with a laundry marker or masking tape, like we're going to summer camp."

"Or maybe you could all learn to pick up after yourselves instead of leaving your clothes wherever you happen to take them off." She pulled a marshmallow out of a chair's cup holder, grimacing. "I'm going to give you the benefit of the doubt and guess this is Johnny's."

"Did we really bring this much stuff with us?" It didn't seem possible, even though he and Russell had moved the original pile from the lawn to the RV. "It'll be nice when Johnny's a teenager and all he needs is a phone and a charger cord."

"Do those pirate ships come with outlets?"

He laughed, and then looked over to where Johnny was playing with his trucks. He was sharing with Gabe, while Lily and Brianna pretended to sing karaoke with plastic microphones. Brian and Bobby had been assigned the task of going through all the four-wheelers and making sure no food or damp clothing had been left in the cargo boxes and bags. In the summer heat, that could lead to finding nasty surprises when they finally got around to cleaning them out at home.

"Do you think Gram and Russell will house-sit and lend us their RV again next summer, or should we think about buying our own?" he asked.

Emma laughed. "We haven't even left yet and you're thinking about next year?"

"You know, if we made a Northern Star baby, we could have a three-month-old." He gave up on trying to figure out where the sleeve for Johnny's little camp chair disappeared to and pulled his wife close. "That would be an adventure."

"Remember when Kevin and Beth did that with Lily? I'm not Beth. *If* we should have an infant this time next year, Gram and I will stay home with the baby, and you and Russell can bring Johnny with you."

He kissed the side of her neck. “There’s no way I’m leaving you for two weeks. A long weekend, maybe. We might have to consider changing the weeks we vacation, though. Us being here for a holiday cost the family money.”

“It would probably be easier for us all to just pay, like we did at the campground in New Hampshire. And you should talk to your brothers and Liz and see if they enjoyed this. I mean, *they* didn’t actually get to go on vacation for two weeks, if you know what I mean.”

“I’ll bring it up next time we have a meeting. I don’t want today to be about business.”

She looped her arm around his waist and leaned her head against his chest. “I found your sticky note, by the way.”

He chuckled, sliding his hand down her back. “Did you?”

“Terry found it, actually, when she ran into the RV to grab Johnny a banana.”

“Oops. But you did read it, right?”

Tonight. Our bed. Being quiet optional.

“I did. And the sooner you get your hand off my ass and start packing up, the sooner we can leave.”

Sean slapped her on the butt before going back to trying to find the sleeves for the camp chairs. He was ready to go home. It was always tough saying goodbye, especially to Rosie, but it would be good to be back in their routine. Dinner and dishes after work. Some quick evening chores. And then reading to Johnny before he went to bed. Snuggling on the couch with his wife in front of the television. Maybe it didn’t sound like much, but there was nothing like being away from home for two weeks to remind him it was actually everything.

"Why are you looking at me like that?" Emma asked, tucking loose wisps of hair behind her ear.

"Saying yes to your crazy plan was the best thing that ever happened to me."

She laughed and wrapped her arms around his neck to kiss him. "I think the words you used at the time were *batshit crazy*."

"If you two don't stop fondling each other and get a move on, Josh will have to start charging you rent," Kevin said as he walked by with a basket of pool toys.

"Let's get a move on," Sean said, though he kissed her again before he let her go. "I want to take you home."

A few hours later, they were ready to go, and he saw Ben pull his SUV into the grass so he wouldn't be blocking the line of campers parked in the drive. His friend couldn't have timed it any better if he'd tried. He'd get to say goodbye to everybody, but packing up the campsites and loading the four-wheelers was done.

The family was gathered on the porch and the front lawn, and Ben veered to where Sean was talking with the other guys.

"Good timing," he said, arching an eyebrow at Ben.

"I know, right? So sorry I missed trying to fit all that stuff back in the campers." He looked at the long line of vehicles. "And strapping down all those machines."

Joe shook his head. "If the women don't stop talking and start actually saying goodbye pretty soon, you can help put everything back for another night."

"Hell, no," Sean said. "Emma and I have a date with our own damn bed tonight."

"So we heard," Kevin said.

"Your sister has a big mouth. But I'm serious. I'll

get the tractor and some chains and drag you guys out from in front of us if I have to."

They all laughed, but he wasn't kidding. He'd miss his brothers and Liz and the others. And he'd enjoyed the hell out of spending time with Ben again. But he was ready to take his wife and son home.

"Thirty seconds," he yelled, like his uncle often did on the ATV trail to make everybody scramble to get ready.

It took another half hour for the hugging and tears to subside, plus get everybody in the RV or truck they were supposed to be in. After another round of shaking hands, he climbed up into the cab and closed the door.

Johnny was strapped into his car seat, riding shotgun, and he smiled. "Home, Daddy!"

SIXTEEN

"I'M NEVER GOING to get the hang of this." Laney held up a badly misshapen square that was supposed to be a dishcloth. "And I use a sponge. Why am I knitting a dishcloth, anyway?"

Nola laughed. "I wouldn't exactly call that knitting. But dishcloths are fun because you can play with borders and colors, and they don't take forever, so you don't get bored. Plus, once you've done a few, you don't need a pattern, so they're good for knitting while watching TV at night."

"You told me knitting would be relaxing."

"It's only relaxing if you actually relax."

"I came over the first time the week the Kowalski family left, so it's been almost a month now." Laney sighed. "I'm not getting any better."

"That's because you worry too much about the fact you're *not* getting any better. When you're tense, your stitches are too tight and whatever *that* is happens."

"I love you, but I hate knitting." She set the sorry excuse for half a dishcloth on the coffee table and picked up her iced tea. "I don't enjoy it, so I'll visit and watch *you* knit."

"I guess not everybody likes it." Nola chuckled. "At least your conversation will consist of more than muttering bad words under your breath now."

"Your knitting lessons have definitely expanded my vocabulary."

"Your mom was asking about you again. I guess she and my mom talked on the phone yesterday, because my mom called me after."

Laney bit back the urge to show off some of that new vocabulary. "I talked to her a few days ago. I told her everything's great and, to be honest, it was one of the better conversations we've had in recent years."

"I don't think she believed you when you told her you're happy and enjoying your job and, you know, living in a camper. She thinks you're suffering and lying about it just to spite her."

Laney laughed, but it was mostly due to her cousin's theatrical eye roll. The fact her own mother was so resistant to the idea her daughter could be happier living alone in a camper than she'd been in a big, expensive house with a husband wasn't as funny.

"HAVE YOU TOLD your mom about Ben yet?" Nola asked. "I'm guessing you haven't because my mom hasn't mentioned it and that's prime gossip, if you know what I mean."

"I haven't said anything about him yet."

"You're going to soon, though, right? Aren't things getting serious between you two?"

She mentally shied away from the word *serious*. It was a word that made her anxious on some level because she couldn't deny they spent a lot of time together. In the weeks since the Kowalski family left, Laney had gotten in the habit of hanging out with Nola and knitting—or trying to, anyway—since the town hall closed early on Tuesdays and it was a slow day at the lodge. And she'd also gotten in the habit of leaving Nola's and going to Ben's, where she'd spend the evening. They'd cook together and watch some television until the cuddling and the touching got heated, and then they'd end up in his bed.

And despite not having the convenient excuse of being a friend of the guests for spending time at the Northern Star, Ben was still a frequent visitor. When he could get there early enough, he'd often walk with her, holding her hand. Or they'd sit in her chairs and talk about the day. And they'd made love in her bed a few times, too, though she preferred his place. Campers weren't the best at soundproofing.

They enjoyed each other's company, but they didn't put a label on it. He didn't push her for more than the easy companionship between them and she didn't overthink it. She was happy and Ben seemed to be, so she didn't feel a need to define what they had for anybody else.

"I'd prefer to keep my mother out of it for now. You know how she can be."

Nola made a sympathetic noise, nodding. "I don't blame you. My mom's not quite as bad as yours, but you can definitely tell they're sisters."

"Enough about moms," Laney said, since it would also change the subject away from Ben. "When are we going to make the drive to see a movie in an actual theater?"

"Oh, I need to see what's coming up so we can plan a trip. But you also have to come to the next movie night. They're usually the first Saturday of every month, though it gets messed up a lot in the summer. All the women get together at somebody's house and watch a movie. There's food and drinks and no men or kids."

She listened to Nola talk about some of the movies they'd watched in the past, and then she shared some funny stories about the women who attended, but Laney's attention kept wandering to the clock. Ben would probably be home soon, and it had been a few days since she'd seen him. Texting and phone calls were nice, but definitely not the same.

"I should probably go," she said when Nola's conversation had run its course. She knew her cousin liked to spend some time in her garden before starting dinner, and this was about the time she usually left.

"Going to see Ben?"

"Probably. He hasn't sent me a message saying he's busy, so he'll probably be home by the time I get there." Last-minute cancellations were part of being in Ben's life, but she didn't mind. As much as she missed seeing him when he was busy, she knew what he was doing was more important than throwing together dinner with her.

But when she pulled into his driveway, Ben's SUV wasn't there. And his mother was.

May was watering the petunias that draped out of boxes lining the windowsills on the front of the house. She was using an old-fashioned metal watering can, which made Laney smile since she knew there was a hose coiled up and hanging on a bracket on the side of the garage.

"Hi, Laney," she called when Laney got out of her car. "How are you today?"

"I'm good, thanks. Your flowers look beautiful. The

colors are so cheerful." The bright pinks and purples would match her chairs, she thought.

"Thank you. I don't have the patience for big flower beds, but I do like a little pop of color around the house." She set the watering can down and pinched a dying blossom off the plant. "I haven't seen Ben yet."

"I don't know if he's just running late or if he's out on a call and hasn't had a chance to text yet."

"Since he's not here yet, would you mind helping me in the backyard for a few minutes? I'm trying to convince Alan we need to enlarge the patio and put in a hot tub, but he says we don't have room. I found a hundred-foot tape measure in the garage and some dimensions on the internet, and now I need help proving him wrong."

Laney laughed. "That sounds like fun. I'd be happy to help."

BEN HAD ABOUT had his fill of four-wheelers, idiots and his cell phone ringing. The first call of the day had been a couple of local kids playing in a sand pit they knew was off-limits. Rolling his ATV over on himself had scared the crap out of one of the teenagers, but he was lucky enough to escape with a broken leg.

The second call had been a couple of guys from Connecticut up for the week who'd gotten lost. They didn't have any food or water with them, and they didn't want to spend all day waiting, so they'd faked a suspected head injury to get a faster response. They'd gotten a faster response. They were also going to get a hefty bill if Matt Barnett had his way, since Maine allowed billing for rescues if the rescue was caused by the victims being idiots.

So Ben wasn't thrilled to get a third call. He hadn't yet had a day he regretted taking the job, but riding through the woods for no good reason got old fast. Especially on a Tuesday, when it was supposed to be slow and he'd get to see Laney. He'd put together a homemade pizza earlier so they could just pop it in the oven and have some extra time on the couch. As much as he enjoyed cooking with her, he enjoyed her being in his arms a lot more.

If he lost out on that extra time because some dumbass did something stupid, he'd be pissed.

But until he knew exactly what he was dealing with, every minute could mean the difference between life and death, so he tore through the woods until he spotted a rider standing in the middle of the trail, waving his arms.

It wasn't a nuisance. The rider and his wife had been riding double on a two-up machine, with no helmets, and he'd hit a water bar badly. Sometimes shallow trenches were dug across trails for drainage, since the alternative was water washing out the trail itself. This particular water bar was marked, but the rider either hadn't seen the sign or hadn't taken it seriously. The front end of the machine had hit the ditch, the ass end had come up, and his wife had been thrown off the back, straight into a tree.

She was unconscious with an obvious head injury and probably trauma to her neck and spine. Ben immobilized her the best he could and had his hands full just keeping her breathing until the rest of the guys showed up.

Thanks to the shortcuts he and Josh had managed to finagle, they only had to get her three miles to a nearby house, where an ambulance would take her to the closest hospital. The medical helicopter was already en route to pick her up there and take her either to Maine Med or to Boston because she needed a top-notch trauma team.

He rode beside the rescue sled secured in the side-by-side, monitoring her vitals and ready with the defibrillator, while Dave kneeled backwards, leaning over the front seat to squeeze the bag and keep her breathing as regular as possible.

Due to the seriousness of her condition, he chose to ride in the ambulance with the EMT, leaving the fire department guys to deal with her husband. There was no sense in Drew or one of the game wardens driving him to the local hospital, so they'd get him back to town and calm him down while they waited for the chopper's final destination.

And even though it was the nature of his job and something he'd been doing for many years, Ben had a hard time letting this patient go when the medical flight's paramedic took over. They knew each other from the job, but other than a brief hello, it was just a recitation of facts and stats on Ben's part and a confirmation on the other guy's. Then they were gone and Ben was left standing in a hallway, the adrenaline fading.

And no way back to Whitford.

Dammit. He took out his phone and wasn't surprised there were no text messages from Laney. She'd told him once she assumed he was dealing with an emergency and didn't want to distract him, trusting him to reach out to her when he had a chance. While he appreciated that, since he'd dated women in the past who weren't so patient, he could have used the boost.

There was a bad one, he typed into a message for her. I'm at the hospital and have to get a ride back. Don't know how long I'll be. Sorry.

It's okay. Do you want me to come get you?

As exhausted as he was, that made him smile. I'll see who's around, but probably not. If I do, I'll let you know.

If you get a ride, let me know when you'll be home. I found the pizza in the fridge and I'll put it in the oven so it'll be ready when you get here.

She was at his place. She was waiting for him, and ready to put dinner in the oven so he'd have a hot meal when he got there. Ben closed his eyes for a moment, soaking in the feeling of having the thing he'd come to want more than anything—not only a woman at home who cared, but Laney.

Until the afterglow wore off and she got dressed and went back to her place.

But he'd take what she was willing to give him, just as he'd told her he would. Thanks. I'll let you know.

Before he could start making calls, looking for a state trooper or a game warden out patrolling the region who could extend that patrol to Whitford with him riding shotgun, his phone rang and Drew's number came up.

"Hey," Drew said. "I heard on the radio the patient's on her way to Boston. Just wanted to give you a heads-up that Butch is on his way in the tow truck. He was listening to his scanner and left shortly after the ambulance to give you a ride back. He's probably about twenty minutes behind you."

Ben laughed, feeling his good spirits being restored with every passing minute. First Laney, and now Butch, coming to get him in the tow truck. "That's good news. I didn't have much hope of finding a ride in a hurry on a Tuesday evening. How's the victim's husband?"

"He's a wreck, but they were up here with some friends. They didn't ride with them today, but they can drive him to Boston so he's on his way."

"Good. She'll definitely want him there if she pulls through. If you hear anything else, let me know, okay?"

"Will do. And good work out there."

He wasn't sure he felt the same, but he said his thanks before he hung up. He supposed the fact she'd been alive when she was put in the helicopter meant he'd done a good job, but he always wished he could do more.

After letting Laney know Butch was going to give him a ride home and promising to give her an update when he had a better idea of what time he'd be home, Ben went in search of something to drink. The slight headache let him know he was dehydrated and it would only get worse if he ignored it.

Ten minutes later, he was still wandering around when he ran into one of the guys who'd met the ambulance in the emergency bay. "Where the hell are they hiding the damn vending machines?"

"From here, it's faster to run into the gift shop. They have basically the same kinds of snacks and drinks, but it's easier to get to and you don't need change."

After getting directions, he hurried to the gift shop because Butch would probably be there any minute and he didn't want to keep the man waiting when he was doing him a huge favor. He wasn't sure yet if it was a favor that would be paid for by the fire department or some other town fund, but that wasn't Ben's problem.

As he grabbed a bottle of water and a soda from the cooler on the back wall of the small gift shop, movement in the window caught his eye. Lined up on a shelf across the bottom of the glass were a bunch of plastic toys that appeared to be dancing. And right in the front was a silly pink flamingo that made him smile.

"What are those?" he asked the cashier.

"They're solar powered and they wave or dance or whatever. They cheer people up, I guess."

The flamingo flapped its wings up and down, so he wasn't sure if it was dancing or pretending to fly, but it looked ridiculous.

Laney would love it.

"I'll take the flamingo."

LANEY HEARD THE low rumble of Butch's tow truck pulling up outside and closed the book she'd been reading on her phone. The pizza had come out of the oven five minutes before and the timing couldn't have been more perfect. All she had to do was cut it and they could eat.

It had been weird, emotionally, sitting in his apartment and waiting for him. She'd almost decided to head home, but May had suggested she go ahead upstairs and wait for him since Ben never locked his door. And she'd been looking forward to seeing him all day, so the temptation was too strong to resist.

It wasn't long before he'd sent her a text message,

and she told him she'd cook the dinner he'd prepared for them. Now she was listening for his footsteps on the stairs, and it was a glimpse into what a normal day could look like if their relationship lasted beyond the summer. Waiting with dinner warming on the stove was something she was familiar with, since she'd done it for her entire marriage.

The delicious sense of anticipation simmering under the strangely conflicted feelings was new, though. Even though he must have had a hard day if he'd ridden to the hospital with the patient and she had her own misgivings about getting too comfortable in their relationship, Laney wanted to see him.

When his footsteps finally reached the top step and the door opened, Laney was in the process of cutting the pizza into slices. He smiled when he saw her, and she could almost see some of his exhaustion fade away as their gazes locked.

Hi honey, how was your day? She killed the impulse to ask the question out of habit and held up the pizza cutter. "Perfect timing."

"I'm starving." He kicked off his shoes and dropped his wallet and keys, along with a small paper bag, on the coffee table before crossing the room to pull her into his arms. "But first I want a kiss."

She dropped the pizza cutter on the counter so she could wrap her arms around his neck. He smelled like sweat and the inside of a twenty-plus-year-old tow truck, but his mouth tasted like mint and she would have smiled against his lips, but his tongue slid over hers as he deepened the kiss. His hands gripped her waist, pulling her hard against his body before he sighed against her mouth. After breaking off the kiss, he rested his forehead against hers for a moment.

"I needed that," he said, giving her another smile.

"Bad day?"

"It was a rough one," he said, and she knew that was all he'd say about the call that had kept him out late. "I need a shower, but the pizza's ready, so let's eat first."

He didn't wait for her to serve him, but instead grabbed a couple of plates and put a slice on each. While they ate, he told her some of the funny stories Butch had shared with him during the long ride back from the hospital. He didn't pay a lot of attention to the gossip Fran shared with him, but when Butch did decide to tell a story, he did it with good old Yankee flair. By the time they'd eaten their fill of pizza, all traces of his day had seeped from Ben's face except for some tiredness around his eyes.

"Before I jump in the shower, I got you something today." Laney watched him grab the paper bag off the coffee table. He gave her a sheepish grin as he handed it to her. "It's kind of silly, but I saw it in the hospital gift shop when I was buying a drink and it made me think of you."

Intrigued, she opened the bag and pulled out a little pink flamingo. Its tiny wings were moving and she noticed the little solar panel right away. Given enough sun, the bird would keep flapping its wings like it was flying, and she smiled at the thought of it dancing in front of a window in her camper.

Ben brushed his thumb over her bottom lip. "I hoped it would make you smile like that. The same way you do when you look at the flamingo outside your door."

"I love it," she said, cupping the back of his neck and

giving him a long thank-you kiss. "How can a person not be happy watching it dance?"

"Watching you smile makes me happy." Before she could say anything, he kissed her again and then gave her a light slap on the behind. "And now I'm going to make us both happy by taking a quick shower."

She set the flamingo on the counter so she could clean up after dinner, which consisted of tossing the paper plates and napkins, and leaving the baking sheet for him to wash tomorrow. It was a small but important-to-her boundary she'd established right away. She'd cook with him and if he washed the dishes, she'd keep him company and dry them, but she didn't clean up after him. Spending time with him was one thing, but taking care of him was another and she didn't let herself cross that line.

The pink flamingo caught her eye as she was wiping down the table and she couldn't stop herself from smiling at it again. Tired and thirsty, Ben had still taken the time to buy her a toy just to make her happy, and her heart seemed to beat a little faster in her chest. He'd said it was silly, but it wasn't. Nobody had ever really done that for her before.

"You're smiling again," Ben said from so close behind her, she felt his breath on her neck, and she jumped.

"I didn't even hear the shower shut off."

"I told you it would be a quick shower."

When she turned around to find him naked except for a towel wrapped around his hips, she laughed. "You're still damp, Ben."

"I was in a hurry." He pulled her hard against his

body, so she could feel the proof of his urgency against her hip. “I missed you today.”

“Part of you did, anyway,” she teased.

“All of my parts,” he replied before claiming her mouth.

The words should have made her pull back, but instead they just inflamed her. He was never shy about what he was feeling. He’d missed her. He wanted her. And she wanted him. For now it was all that mattered.

She ran her hands over his bare chest, stopping just short of the towel, before sliding them around his waist and up his back. His skin was still warm from the shower and he made a growling sound against her mouth when she skimmed her fingernails up his spine.

When he tugged at her T-shirt, she lifted her arms. He broke off the kiss and pulled it over her head. She unbuttoned her shorts and tugged them down so she could step out of them as his hands cupped her breasts through the thin fabric of her bra.

When his thumbs brushed over her nipples, she moaned, knowing his mouth would follow. But first he turned her and backed her toward the bed. The towel fell off halfway across the floor, but he didn’t seem to mind. And Laney sure didn’t.

Her knees hit the edge of the bed, and he kissed her again while his fingers made short work of unclasping her bra. She slid her hands over the curve of his ass, holding him close enough so she felt the hard length of his erection against the front of her panties. But when she moved one hand between them to stroke him, Ben moaned and dropped his head to her shoulder.

“I thought about this—about *you*—all the way home

and if you touch me like that, this isn't going to take long."

It was heady stuff, being wanted that much, and Laney closed her fingers around him just to hear him make that sound again. He bit gently at her neck while rocking his hips, slipping his hand under the elastic waist of her panties.

Her breath caught when his fingers brushed her sensitive flesh, and she knew it wouldn't be very long before she either needed to be lying on the bed or Ben would have to hold her up. She didn't know if he could read her mind or if he felt the same way, but after stroking her for another moment, he withdrew his hand and then held her wrist until she released him.

"I want to be inside you," he murmured against her lips before he kissed his way down her neck. As she pushed her panties down far enough so she could step out of them, his mouth closed over her nipple, sucking hard enough to make her gasp.

He lifted his head and grinned before setting her on the mattress. She pushed back toward the center as he got a condom from his nightstand and rolled it on, and was unable to keep from smiling as he moved over her.

"You look pretty happy for a woman who hasn't come yet," he said, settling between her thighs.

"Maybe because I'm confident you're about to make me *very* happy." She reached between their bodies, guiding him into her.

They moved together, her hips moving to meet his as he pushed deeper with each stroke. Laney scraped his back with her fingernails before taking his face between her hands and pulling his head down so she could kiss him.

His mouth was fierce against hers, his tongue sliding over hers until he bit her bottom lip, holding it between his teeth. Then he lifted his head so he could look into her face. His gaze was so intense, Laney shivered.

"You're so beautiful."

She *felt* beautiful when he looked at her like that, and when he said the words in that low, earnest voice. "You make me feel beautiful."

"Good." He kissed her again and it was less forceful and more emotion-filled this time—almost electric with the connection between them. "I like making you feel good, Laney."

He quickened his pace, which felt *really* good, and she dug her fingertips into his hips. Each thrust came deeper and faster, until the delicious tension in her body exploded in a burst of pleasure. She might have said his name, or maybe she was incoherent. She didn't know. All she knew was the orgasm rocking her world and the feel of Ben's body.

"Laney," he said a moment later, his voice raspy as he found his own release. When the tremors faded, he collapsed on top of her with a guttural groan, his face pressed to her breast.

"I swear you are everything I've ever wanted, Laney," he mumbled against her skin.

She tightened her arms around him and kissed the top of his head before closing her eyes. A moment later, he rolled away and disposed of the condom before curling up against her body and throwing his arm over her. Ben was a cuddler, which she loved about him, and he always pressed little kisses to her hair or behind her ear as he nodded off.

When she felt her eyelids getting heavy, though, she lifted his arm off of her and slid out of the bed. She thought he'd be tired enough to sleep through her gathering her clothes, but when she turned back to the bed after getting dressed, he was awake. Barely.

"Are you leaving?"

"Yeah, it's getting late. And I don't know if I'll be able to get away for the rest of the week. We have a big group coming in and it's some kind of guys' trip. That means a lot of drinking and who knows what, so it'll probably take all of us to keep things under control without making them feel babysat, if you know what I mean." She leaned over the bed to kiss him, and he put his arm around her, as if to hold her there.

"If it's quiet tomorrow afternoon, I'll ride over on the four-wheeler and let Sam know I'll be responding from the lodge." He paused, pushing her hair away from her face. "If that's okay. If you think you'll be too busy or you want some alone time, that's cool, too."

Maybe telling him another night would be for the best, she thought. After tonight, she should probably put a little distance between them. But that's not what she wanted, so she shook her head. "I don't think I'll be too busy. And they have to sleep eventually, right?"

"I'll try not to keep you up too late," he said, but the way his lips kicked up at the corners told her he didn't mean it.

"Speaking of being up past my bedtime, I need to get back so I can get some sleep."

She saw the amusement fade and felt in her gut that he was about to ask her to stay the night. But then his expression cleared and he kissed her. "Drive safely. Text me when you get there."

One more kiss good-night, and then Laney picked up her present and went down to her car. She winced as she fired the engine and tried to pull out of the driveway and head up the road while giving it the least amount of gas possible. Hopefully his parents were sleeping.

For the entire drive back to the Northern Star, she tried not to look at the flamingo on the passenger seat and cursed herself for not staying in bed with Ben. She knew he'd wanted her to. It was only his promise not to ask for more than she was willing to give that kept him from saying the words, but she hadn't considered how *she* felt about it until the moment had passed.

She wanted to be in his bed right now, her back pressed to his chest and his breath warm on her hair. And that scared the hell out of her because she felt as if she was losing herself in him, and she wasn't even sure she'd found herself yet.

SEVENTEEN

Ben bolted upright in bed, almost knocking himself out on the cabinet that hung over the bed. Laney's bed, he thought, as she sat up beside him.

He was in Laney's bed, and somebody was pounding on the door.

"Ben! Come on, dammit!"

It was Josh's voice, and the urgency in it had Ben on his feet. He pulled on his underwear, but didn't bother with the rest. He unlocked the door and had barely released the door latch when Josh yanked it out of his hand.

"Something's wrong with Katie."

Ben looked back at Laney, who was sitting on the edge of her bed with the sheet wrapped around her. "Keys are in the pocket of my pants. The one with the black plastic head opens the big cargo box on the back of the ATV. Can you grab my jump bag?"

As soon as she nodded, Ben grabbed his phone off the counter and took off across the lawn on Josh's heels. There were a few small rocks in the grass and he'd probably regret the bare feet in the morning, but he followed Josh through the kitchen door and through the house to their bedroom.

Katie was lying on her side, clutching her stomach and grimacing with pain. Rosie sat next to her, smoothing her daughter's hair back from her face. She looked up when they came in and Ben spared her only a quick glance before he leaned over the bed.

"Hey, Katie. What's going on?"

"She started—" Ben cut Josh off with a wave of his hand.

"Tell me what's happening, Katie," he repeated, because her ability to speak would help him gauge her pain level. "And we're going to roll you to your left side, okay?"

She nodded, and he was relieved she was able to roll to her other side without too much assistance from him. "I felt fine when I went to bed. And then I woke up and my stomach hurts really bad. I have antacids next to the bed, but they didn't help."

Laney ran into the bedroom, her face almost as flushed as the patient's. She'd pulled on shorts and a hoodie, and she had his bag in her hand. He took it from her and started checking Katie's vitals.

"Can you check the baby's heartbeat?" Josh asked.

"I don't have the equipment for that. Hearing a fetal heartbeat with a stethoscope is almost a miracle under the best of conditions and takes too long. Katie, has your doctor expressed any concern through your pregnancy? Any risk factors?"

"No. We're both doing great."

"Do you feel any pressure low in your abdomen? Between your legs?"

"No. No pressure. And the pain's higher." She rubbed her sternum, above the baby bump. "It's like a knot."

Ben relaxed. Not a lot, but some of the tension eased from his muscles. "How are those cravings going for you lately?"

She made a face, but it was Josh who answered. "Cravings? She's even eating stuff she never has before. And I swear she turns into a raccoon at night."

"What have you eaten tonight?"

"We had pork chops and mashed potatoes for supper."

"Which you dumped ranch dressing on because your taste buds are weird now," Josh added.

"I had mint chocolate chip ice cream before we went to bed."

"On top of the egg salad you begged me to make while you were watching television?" Rosie shook her head and Ben had to bite back a smile when she stood and picked up the small wastebasket under the bedside table.

"Sit up here on the edge of the bed for me, Katie." He helped her up, watching her face. She looked miserable and her level of discomfort rose, but he didn't see signs of severe pain. After making sure Katie was able to sit, he nodded for Rosie to move a little closer. "So, to recap, you had pork chops and potatoes with ranch dressing, egg salad *and* ice cream?"

Katie made a keening sound of distress and her mom was there, wastebasket at the ready. Ben supported her shoulders to make sure she didn't fall, while she wrapped her arms around her stomach and threw up.

Josh disappeared, and Ben wondered if he had a weak stomach, but he was back in less than a minute with a wet washcloth. Once Katie nodded, Rosie removed the basket while Ben helped her roll back onto her left side. Her husband wiped her face, smoothing away the clamminess and making her smile.

"I hate throwing up."

"Everybody does, honey." Josh kissed her forehead. "Do you feel better now?"

"I think so. And the baby's awake."

Ben watched as Katie ran her hand over her stomach. She looked relieved and exhausted, but her mouth curved into a smile as the baby kicked her hand.

"I know your muscles will feel sore after that," he said, "but do you have any pain?"

"No. Everything feels more normal now. Well, pregnant-normal, anyway." She sighed, already looking sleepy again. "But I'm never eating pork chops, mashed potatoes, ranch dressing, egg salad or ice cream again."

Ben chuckled. "Maybe not all in the same evening, anyway."

"I might have panicked," Josh said. "She's had heartburn, but nothing like this and when the antacids didn't help, I thought it might be the baby."

"Always better to be safe than sorry." Ben checked Katie's vitals again. They were good, and she looked relaxed. "I think you're going to feel better now, Katie, but I can give you a ride to the hospital so they can check you out more thoroughly if you want."

"I still feel a little bit queasy but other than that, I don't feel like anything's wrong. Are you going to be close by?"

Ben glanced at Laney and she nodded. "Yes, I'll be close by. If you or Josh have any concerns, I'll come running."

"You could probably take the time to put pants on next time," Rosie said. "I'm doing my damnedest not to look because you're my daughter's age, but the less worried I am for her, the harder it gets not to notice."

"Yeah, when you were running here in your underwear and bare feet to save my wife and child, it was awesome," Josh said. "But now you can get out of my bedroom."

Laughing, Ben packed up his bag and gave Katie a last visual exam. Her smile was sleepy, but she looked content and he had no doubt she'd be asleep by the time he reached the back door. "Get some rest and I'll see how you're doing in the morning."

"Thank you," she said.

Josh held out his hand, which Ben shook. "Thanks, man. I'd hug you, but you're practically naked."

Bag in hand, Ben left the room with Laney. He put his hand on her back as they walked through the lodge and out the back door. "Thanks for getting my bag."

"I'm glad you were here tonight. That was scary."

"Do you mind if I stay the night, or would you be more comfortable if I grabbed one of the beds in the lodge?"

She looked confused for a few seconds. "You were in my bed when Josh knocked, remember?"

"Yeah, I definitely remember being in your bed, but we kind of nodded off together. That's different than deliberately spending the night."

"Ben, I want you to stay."

Once they were back in her camper, he set his bag on her dinette table and tossed his pants on the bench seat, just in case. Responding to an emergency in his underwear was a first and he knew that once the fear from the night faded, it was going to be a long time before he heard the end of it.

Once he was back in Laney's bed, her back pressed to his chest, he pulled her hair back so he could kiss her neck. "I've been wanting to ask you something."

"Mmm?"

"Next Saturday we're having a party for my parents, to celebrate their sixtieth birthdays and fortieth wedding anniversary."

"Really? You mean like a date you picked to celebrate all three?"

"No, they have the same birthday. And they got married on that day. It's kind of a milestone, so we're having a party for them in the late afternoon and I'd like for you to go with me."

"That sounds fun, and I like your parents. I'll have to make sure it's okay with Rosie and Josh, but it shouldn't be a problem."

Ben smiled and kissed her neck again before laying his head on the pillow. Having the woman he was falling in love with—even if she wasn't ready for him to tell *her* that yet—at his side to celebrate his parents' long, happy marriage would mean the world to him.

LANEY HAD ASSUMED when Ben said they were having a party for his parents, that *they* meant Ben and his brother, sister-in-law and nephews. She'd been wrong.

It didn't measure up to the Fourth of July barbecue at the lodge, but there were still a lot more people than she'd expected in the Rivers' front yard. A couple of large canopies had been erected for shade, and it looked like a *bring your own lawn chair* memo had gone out with the invitations. Ben had neglected to mention that.

"Laney!" May beckoned her over to where she was talking to a few other women.

At least Ben's mother was a nice lady, she thought as she made her way to her. Laney had made the mistake of answering the phone fifteen minutes before she had to leave her camper, when her own mother called.

It hadn't been a good conversation. One of her dad's agents had quit abruptly and wasn't that the perfect opportunity for Laney to give up on her silly little camping thing and join her father in business?

When that hadn't worked, her mom had changed her tactic from a very strong suggestion to some blatant emotional manipulation. Her dad hadn't been feeling well, according to her mother, and he needed to have a stress test.

Layne had finally told her she was losing cell service, which her mom believed because in her mind, her daughter was living in the wilderness. She'd promised to call her dad when she got a chance, though she had no intention of going to work for him. Then she'd cranked the stereo in her Camaro and done her best to shake off her mood on the drive over.

"I'm so glad you came," May said, giving her a warm hug. "These are my good friends, Denise and Michelle. Ladies, this is Ben's girlfriend, Laney."

Laney felt her face freeze and hoped it had frozen in a reasonably friendly expression. *Ben's girlfriend.* "It's nice to meet you."

They'd heard of her, of course. Everybody in Whitford knew she was working at the Northern Star, even if they hadn't actually met her yet. She made small talk for a few minutes, until Alan interrupted to say hello. He hugged her, too, and then so did Chelsea. Jimmy kissed her cheek, and then told her Ben was in the house, finishing up a few things in the kitchen.

"I'll go find him and see if he needs any help, then."

It seemed as if it took her forever to get to the house,

since she knew just enough people so she had to stop and chat a few times. But finally, she went in the side door and found him in the kitchen, dumping bags of cut vegetables onto a disposable platter.

"Hey, there you are," he said, his face lighting up when he saw her. She remembered wondering what would happen if he looked at her like that on the day they met, but she couldn't put her finger on when it had started happening—when Ben looked at her as though her walking into the room was the best thing to happen to him all day.

"Need some help?" She walked around the island to stand next to him. "Are you doing this all yourself?"

"Oh, Jimmy and I are smarter than that. The magic words are *bring your favorite potluck dish*. In a town like this, trying to outdo each other is practically a sport. You must not have seen the tables lined up along the garage wall, in the shade."

"No, I didn't. Do you have dip?"

"In the fridge, if you don't mind grabbing them. I got two and we might as put them both out."

She found the jars of ranch dip and popped the lids. He rummaged in a cupboard and found two plastic spoons.

"Thanks. That's it, I guess."

"Before we go outside," she began, and she could tell by the way he moved closer that he thought she was going to kiss him. "Your mom's introducing me to people as your girlfriend."

"Okay." He leaned his hip against the island and took her hand in his. "I haven't used the word myself, but we've been dating all summer, Laney. It hasn't been a secret."

"I know." And she did. "I'm not mad or anything. It was just a bit of a shock. It makes everything seem… defined. It's a word that comes with expectations, you know?"

He gave her one of those smiles that didn't reach his eyes. "You and I are the only ones who know what we're doing, and even that's a little fuzzy at times. To everybody else, it looks like you're my girlfriend."

"You're right."

"I *feel* like you're my girlfriend, Laney. You must know that."

"I know. I just feel…" She felt off-balance because her mother had called so close to May introducing her as his girlfriend, and she couldn't help but feel like people were trying to put her in a box again.

"Hey." He tipped her chin up. "Don't let it bother you. It's a party and there's a bunch of people here. Things will be said, but just smile and know that you and I are okay. And there's cake."

She smiled, but she knew they weren't okay. She knew he wanted a family of his own—that he wanted marriage and babies and a big backyard—and he had to be losing patience with her inability to commit to him. She wasn't sure she could trust herself in a forever relationship and asking him to keep waiting wasn't fair. But she couldn't bring herself to walk away, either. "I like cake."

"I know you do." He kissed her, then. Quick and light, but it was enough for now. "Somebody's coming or I'd do better."

She was laughing when Tori walked in, carrying her baby. Chessie was a cute little blonde, about seven months old. She was named after some railroad thing, since Max was a huge rail fan, and her smile was one of the cutest things Laney had ever seen. "Is there a place I can change this little stinker? And I mean that literally, so maybe not on any surface that requires professional cleaning."

"I'll grab you a towel and you can change her in the guest bedroom," Ben said.

Laney picked up the veggie platter. "I'll take this outside, and see you out there."

He smiled at her before disappearing down the hallway, but it was nothing like the smile he'd given her when she first walked into the room.

BEN WATCHED FAMILY and friends milling around the yard, enjoying good food and good company. The entire time, he was aware of Laney. Sometimes she was at his side, but others she roamed through the crowd, talking to friends she'd made in Whitford.

And the entire time, he could only think about the fact the woman he was pretty sure he was in love with hadn't liked being called his girlfriend. And this was happening at a celebration of forty years of his parents being in love with each other. It felt wrong.

He could tell himself he understood her reservation. She'd felt diminished by her first marriage—almost erased somehow—and she hadn't felt strong enough to let another man in. But the pull had been too strong between them and now he was stuck half in and half out of her life.

All summer, he'd told himself to be patient. If he gave her the space she needed to feel like herself again, she'd realize they had a really good thing together. It hadn't been easy, but she was worth it.

But even now, she was thrown by being called his girlfriend. And it hurt. He hadn't been prepared for the emotions that had swept through him in the kitchen. Disbelief. Anger. But most of all, more hurt than he was sure he could handle.

"They're getting ready to bring the cakes out."

Ben turned to Jimmy, surprised to see him there. He'd been watching Laney talking to Matt and Hailey, idly scratching behind their black Lab's ears. "Is it time already?"

"Are you okay?"

"Sure. It's just been a long day."

"Bullshit. Are you and Laney having problems?"

Ben wasn't sure there really *was* a him and Laney, but he didn't want to get into it standing in the middle of his parents' yard with a bunch of people around them. "We're just kind of...casually dating or whatever. It's not a big deal."

"To which I say bullshit again, but I can see you don't want to talk about it right now. I guess the next best thing is cake."

"I want a corner piece since I'm going to have to listen to you sing."

They were laughing when Chelsea and Denise carried the cakes out. One was a traditional three-layer cake with birthday wishes across the top. The other was a large sheet cake wishing them a happy anniversary and covered with a photo from their wedding day. As they all gathered around to sing, Ben wasn't surprised to see tears in his mom's eyes. And when his dad put his arm around his wife's shoulders and kissed her cheek, Ben thought he might get a little choked up himself.

They'd argued, of course. They'd lived out both sides of their wedding vows. The sickness and the health. The better and the worse. But there had never been a day in Ben's life he doubted his parents loved each other.

That's what he wanted.

When Laney appeared at his side, he managed a smile, but he didn't reach for her hand as he usually would. She knew, he thought. He could tell by the way she looked at him, with questions and uncertainty in her eyes, that she knew their relationship had shifted today.

He was looking at the amount of food left on the folding tables next to the garage, debating on bringing the cold items inside, when she appeared beside him and put her hand on his arm. There didn't appear to be anybody within earshot, since most of the remaining guests were under the canopies.

"I think I'm going to go," she said quietly. "I don't think there's anything I can say to fix whatever's happening right now."

"There is, but you won't trust yourself to say it. Or maybe I'm seeing things that aren't really there because I want to so badly. I don't know."

Her lips pressed together, and he hoped like hell she wasn't going to cry, because he wouldn't be able to stand that. "You once told me you'd give me whatever I wanted, but *only* what I wanted."

"I did. And I meant it at the time. But I can't keep doing this, Laney. I can't pretend I'm okay with you keeping me at arm's distance and the fact you're still determined to go back to Rhode Island when the season's over. I'm more than a rebound guy. I'm more than a summer fling. But you can't accept that and I'm not going to stand here and pretend I'm okay with it on a day dedicated to the love and commitment my parents have shared with each other for forty years."

"I'm scared, Ben."

"I know, but I don't know what else I can do. If you're not willing to stay here and take the chance, there's nothing else I can say."

"I don't want to stay for you. I need to want to stay for *me*."

"And I don't want you to stay for me, either. I want you to stay for *us*."

"My mother called today. It wasn't a good conversation and she just assumed I'd go back to Rhode Island. And then your mom assumed I wanted to be introduced as your girlfriend and it all just threw me off. I won't let anybody make decisions for me, and I won't let anybody push me into making decisions."

"I haven't pushed you. I've waited. I've hoped." He took a deep breath. "Every day I fall more in love with you. Every day it gets harder to imagine my life without you."

She looked as gutted as he felt, but she didn't say anything. And in that moment of silence, his cell phone rang. He wanted to ignore it—just this once—but he couldn't. And when he glanced over and saw Matt unclipping his cell phone from its holster, Ben knew it would be bad.

One glance at the screen confirmed it. "Dammit. I have to go."

"Ben, you can't leave like this. We need to talk—"

"No, I *need* to go do my job because somebody's life

might depend on it. You should go home when you're ready. Don't wait for me."

He turned without giving her a chance to say more—or giving himself time to look into her eyes and see if the emotion in her voice was reflected there. After waving a goodbye to his parents as he jogged across the street to his SUV—which was parked, like Matt's truck, in such a way it couldn't be blocked in—he tried to put Laney out of his mind. He needed to focus.

But as he hit the lights and sirens and pulled away from the curb, he caught a glimpse of Laney, still standing where he'd left her.

EIGHTEEN

TWO WEEKS. BEN parked his SUV in front of the lodge's parking area and killed the engine. It had been two weeks since he'd been to the Northern Star. Two weeks since he'd seen Laney.

He'd called her that night, not trusting himself to swing by the campground and talk to her in person. She'd told him she needed time to think—to process what had happened—and he'd been honest with her. He couldn't wait anymore.

"I'm sorry," she'd said.

That was the end of the conversation. And every day of his life since they'd ended the call had sucked. So he'd avoided the lodge. He'd avoided the diner. He'd more or less been avoiding any place he might run into her until he was sure he could handle seeing her and knowing she wasn't his anymore. That she maybe never had been.

But Josh was in the preliminary stages of planning a big ATV event for the following year and he needed Ben and Drew to look over the rough map of the event area, possible activities and the projected attendance to get an idea of what they'd need in the way of emergency personnel on-site. And Ben was an adult with a job to do, so he'd put on his game face and made the drive.

He went around the side of the house to the back door because he wasn't really "company" any more, and wasn't surprised to find Rosie in the kitchen. She had something that smelled amazing in the slow cooker.

"Well, look who's here. Come on in."

He'd been nervous about his reception from Rosie for the entire drive. He'd known her his entire life, but she'd taken a strong liking to Laney and practically made her part of the family. If she knew things had gone bad between them and took sides, he could have found himself having meetings with Josh in the barn.

"Things have been busy," he said, feeling a need to explain his absence after he'd spent so much time there, but she gave him a look that made it clear she knew *exactly* why he hadn't been around. "How is she?"

"If you want to know how Laney is, you can find her out back. She's probably not doing so well right at the moment because one of our guests in a rented RV didn't pay attention to the part about dumping tanks and everything's backed up in their shower. She's helping them take care of it, so I'd probably give her a few minutes."

"You know I love her, Rosie. This isn't what I wanted."

"I know that. But maybe you were ready to fall a little faster and a little harder and she needed a little extra time to catch up." She sighed and nodded toward the table. "Sit down and I'll give you a brownie."

He knew he should ask if Josh was in his office and head back there, but he sat and took the brownie on a napkin she handed him. "I feel like I gave her time."

"She married a guy who loved her, but then turned out to maybe not love her that much after all and spent ten years trying to make her into what he wanted. And her parents did their part, too."

Rosie was doing something at the counter while she talked and when she turned, she had a wooden spoon in her hand.

He pointed at her. “Don’t even think about hitting me with that.”

She looked confused for a few seconds, and then she laughed. “I was going to stir my sauce with it, but now that you mention it, a good whack upside the head probably wouldn’t hurt you any.”

“Nothing can hurt more than I already do.” His voice was raw and he probably wouldn’t have said the words out loud, but Rosie was the kind of woman a person could talk to.

“Son, I can tell you there are more painful things in life than what you’re going through. But I also know this isn’t just any breakup for you. And it’s not for her, either.”

“I’m afraid if I talk to her, I’ll convince myself I can wait longer.”

“And can you, if that’s what she needs?”

“Hey, I thought I heard you pull in.”

Ben turned to see Josh walking into the kitchen, saving him from having to answer Rosie’s questions. He didn’t know what to say, anyway. He loved Laney. He wanted Laney to love him—to be willing to put everything else behind her and share her life with him.

“I’ve got the map here,” Josh said, pulling a folded piece of paper from his back pocket.

“You have a map? I’m shocked.”

“That gets funnier every time I hear it.” The straight face and dry tone made Ben laugh, which he hadn’t done a lot of lately. “You want to sit here or go to my office.”

"Here's fine if we're not in Rosie's way. Where's Drew?"

"He's on his way. He has Jackson and there was a diaper incident that required turning around for fresh clothes and the spare car seat. I didn't ask any more questions."

"I can look at a map without him for now."

Anything to keep his mind off the fact the woman he loved was so close his body ached with the need to see her.

LANEY KNEW BEN was at the Northern Star. She'd caught a glimpse of his SUV through the trees and her breath had caught up in her throat so hard she'd stopped walking for a few seconds.

God, she missed him.

But she forced herself to keep walking to her camper. She cleaned up because some jobs in a campground were a little more unsavory than others. Then she sat at her dinette and asked herself what the hell she was going to do.

Option one was to hide in her camper until she was sure he was gone, sneak into Rosie's kitchen and steal some cookies, and then crawl into her bed and cry.

Option two was to go find some physical labor to do or maybe take a long walk so her body would be so exhausted her thoughts couldn't torment her anymore.

Option three was to go find Ben and tell him she loved him.

The third option scared the hell out of her, but she'd spent the last two weeks missing him desperately. She learned that loving Ben didn't take over her life. It didn't diminish her. He made her life better, and she was stronger and happier with him.

If she went to him and he rejected what she had to say…it would be crushing. But she'd hurt so badly the last two weeks, she knew it was worth the chance. And if he turned her away, she'd survive. She'd keep doing what she was doing. Working. Walking. She'd get through it, and at least she'd know she'd tried.

Movement caught her eye and she looked at the little dancing pink flamingo sitting on the windowsill at the end of the dinette. It had been sunny for days, and he was flapping his wings like he really believed he could fly, with that goofy smile on his face.

It made *her* smile, and that broke her. Ben knew her. He knew what made her happy and what made her smile. And, tired and stressed after a hard medical call, he'd taken the time to buy a silly dancing flamingo just because he knew it would make her smile.

It was tempting to spend a little more time in her camper. She could put on a little makeup to hide her tired eyes. Or rehearse what she wanted to say. But if she went out there and he was already gone, she might not have the courage to get in her car and go after him.

She was halfway across the lawn, her hands balled into fists so tightly her fingernails were pressing into her palms, when the kitchen door opened and Ben stepped out. Stopping in her tracks, she watched him close the door and then take a deep breath, as if he was steadying himself.

Then he started walking, not toward his SUV, but toward her. And he slowed when he saw her, but kept moving. His eyes never left hers, and she exhaled a slow, shuddering breath. His look was questioning, and she realized he might not know she hadn't been on her way to the lodge, but was specifically looking for him.

"I came to tell you I'm in love with you," she said, not wanting there to be any doubt.

The lines in his face softened, and his lips curved into a smile. When he reached her, he took her hand and uncurled her fingers so he could lace his with hers.

"I think I miss holding your hand more than anything else," he said. "That connection. The reassurance of touching you. It grounds me somehow."

"I'm sorry I hurt you," she whispered. "I panicked and it was stupid and—"

"It wasn't stupid. You weren't ready."

"I'm ready now. I want to make my life here, in Whitford, with you. If you still want me."

He kissed her, his mouth crushing hers as his hand squeezed hers. When she was breathless, he broke it off and smiled at her. "I will always want you. We have what it takes, Laney. You just have to trust in me. Trust in *us*."

"I trust you. I don't know if I've ever trusted anybody in my life the way I trust you. But I needed to trust myself. I felt like I had to know that I would do what was best for *me*, not to make anybody else happy. And I got so hung up on finding myself, whatever that's supposed to mean, that I almost missed finding myself happiness."

With his free hand, he tucked her hair behind her ear and then traced the line of her jaw. "Laney Caswell, will you be my girlfriend?"

Laughter bubbled up through the tears and she nodded. "I want to be your girlfriend more than anything."

"I love you," he said, his expression growing more

serious. "I love everything about you. I love your laugh and your questionable taste in TV shows and that bright pink makes you happy. There's nothing about you I would change."

She kissed him this time, slowly and relishing every second of it. "We can paint one of my chairs blue if you want. His and hers."

"Not a chance. The pink makes you smile and when you smile, I smile. Forty years from now, we'll be sitting in those pink chairs, holding hands, and I'll still feel like the luckiest man alive when you smile at me."

"You're talking your way into an invitation to spend the night with me, you know."

"And Rosie didn't even have to hit me with a wooden spoon."

She grinned. "I wonder if they come in pink."

EPILOGUE

October

"KEEP YOUR EYES CLOSED. No peeking."

"I'm either going to fall asleep or get carsick if you don't let me open my eyes soon, Ben," Laney said. They'd been a few minutes from the lodge when he'd told her to close her eyes, though she couldn't imagine why. The party at the Northern Star wasn't a surprise, and it wasn't for her. They had babies to celebrate.

She felt the Camaro slow and then make a left turn, which confused her. The turn off to the lodge was a right from this direction. Then it came to a stop and the engine went silent.

"Don't look. I'm coming around to get you."

She played along because Ben was obviously excited, and kept her eyes closed as he opened her door and took her hand to help her out. His other hand went to her back as he guided her. Autumn leaves crunched under their feet and her pulse quickened as the pieces started falling into place in her mind.

"Open your eyes," he said.

It wasn't the cream-colored cape with blue shutters and deep porch that made tears spring to her eyes. They'd looked at the house—with its two-car garage, three bedrooms and white picket fence—several times, and she'd fallen in love with it. But the owners were offering it for rent with an option to buy, and it had access to the ATV and snowmobile trails, so there had been some competition for the property.

But today, sitting in the shade of the porch, were two bright pink Adirondack chairs. *Her* chairs, which they'd put in Josh's barn when they winterized her camper and she'd moved into Ben's apartment.

"We got it?" she asked, almost afraid to believe it. "Really?"

"Welcome home, Laney." She threw her arms around his neck and he kissed her. Then he laced his fingers through hers and led her across the lawn to the front steps. "They're still moving out, but they said I could put the chairs here because I couldn't wait to tell you. And I know how much you wanted this house, so I set up the appointment for us to sign the papers and get the keys for next week."

"Thank you, Ben." She would have thrown her arms around him again and sobbed into his shirt, but he nudged her toward one of the chairs and she sat. "This is perfect."

When he sat in the other chair, which was close enough so he could hold her hand across the distance, Laney breathed in the crisp fall air and looked out over their yard. Yellow and orange leaves danced in the breeze, and she could picture the kids they would have diving into piles Ben raked up.

"Close your eyes again," he said. "There's more."

"Seriously? More than our house?"

He grinned and nodded. "The house we chose together. But I have a surprise, too. Now close your eyes."

Once she had, she could tell by the tug on her hand

that he'd stood up. And it was only a few seconds before he told her to open her eyes again.

He was on one knee in front of her, her hand still in his. In the other was a small velvet box, open to show a beautiful diamond solitaire. When their eyes met, he exhaled shakily and she realized he was nervous.

"I love you, Laney. I love this life we're making for ourselves and I want you to be my wife." He paused for a second, swallowing hard. "Maybe I should have waited so it wouldn't seem like marrying me goes with the house, because it doesn't."

"Yes." She pushed forward in the chair, wanting to be closer to him. "Yes, I'll marry you."

He'd barely gotten the ring on her finger before she threw her arms around him. He was off-balance and ended up on his back on the wooden floor, with her straddling him. Once she'd kissed him until his fingers curled in her hair and he moaned against her mouth, she broke it off and smiled down at him.

"If we already had keys to our house, I'd take you inside and show you just how much I love you."

"I see how much you love me every time you smile at me like that," he said. "And we have a party to get to."

She'd forgotten they were supposed to be on their way to the lodge. "I hope they don't mind me sharing our big news at their baby party because there's no way I can keep it a secret."

"Trust me, when it comes to family, the more they have to celebrate, the happier they are."

As she stood and then helped Ben to his feet, she thought about what he'd said. *Family.* She was already a part of the Northern Star family, even though she'd only been there for a summer. And the connection would only get stronger, since Josh had asked her to stay year-round. They couldn't pay her a lot, but she didn't need a lot and it was enough. She'd learned you couldn't put a price on the kind of happiness that made you fall asleep with a smile every night.

As they walked back to the car, she looked over her shoulder. "I can't believe it's really ours."

"Those chairs weigh a ton. They're staying." He lifted her hand to kiss the ring on her finger. "And next week, we'll spend our first night together in it."

She was still smiling when they pulled up to the lodge. Because of the babies, the party was inside, but the doors and windows were open and they could hear the chatter of happy voices as they walked up to the porch.

"Laney!" Rosie saw her as soon as they stepped through the door and wrapped her in a hug before doing the same to Ben. "I was wondering where you two were."

"We were sitting on the porch of our new house."

Rosie clapped her hands to her chest, her eyes wide. "So we don't have to keep it a secret?"

Ben laughed. "No, we stopped over there first because I knew Josh would tell you and I didn't want you to have to suffer."

"You're a good boy. Keeping secrets is hard on me, you know."

Laney held up her left hand. "I won't ask you to keep this one, then."

Rosie squealed and then Laney and Ben were swallowed up by hugs and congratulations. But after a few minutes, she was able to extract herself and head to the couch, where there were two little bundles of joy she was there to meet.

Paige and Katie each had an end of the couch. Sarah was curled up against her mom, looking ready for a nap, but she perked up when she realized she had a fresh audience.

"I have a baby sister," she told Laney and Ben, pulling at the pink blanket.

"Easy, honey." Paige lifted the baby's head, so they could see her little face.

"Her name's Charlotte," Sarah told them. "She's going to play dolls with me. But not 'til she's bigger because she was only borned three weeks ago and she can't hold them yet."

"She's beautiful," Laney said. "Just like her big sister."

"Look at Nate, too! He's my cousin and he was just borned, so he can't play dolls, either."

Katie looked exhausted, but she laughed as she folded back the blue blanket, which had obviously been knit by Rosie. The newborn was asleep, and Laney kept herself from touching him so she wouldn't risk waking him.

"He's such a handsome boy," she said in a quiet voice. "Congratulations."

Katie smiled. "He looks like his daddy. And congratulations back at you. Your ring is gorgeous!"

Laney felt a rush of happiness and wondered if, at some point, the thought of marrying Ben would stop making her feel like that. She hoped not. "Thank you.

I don't want to take any attention away from these babies, though."

Katie laughed. "More reasons to celebrate are never a bad thing. And Mom's probably baking you a cake right now."

"I am not," Rosie said, and Laney jumped. She hadn't realized she was standing so close. "Because there was room to write in Ben and Laney's names on the big sheet cake."

"Did you tell her the rest of the good news?" Paige asked.

"Not yet." Rosie was already beaming, but her face seemed to light up even more. "Emma's expecting. And she didn't say, but I think she and Sean conceived that baby while they were here. They've been trying for so long, and that just makes it even more special."

She didn't even hesitate to wrap her arms around Rosie and give her a big squeeze. "I'm so happy for them. And for you."

"So many babies. And a wedding." She sniffed and dabbed at her eyes. "I didn't think one woman could be this happy."

"Uh-oh," Josh said as he squeezed past the women to sit on the arm of the couch next to his wife. "I told Mitch we should have boxes of tissues on every flat surface. Like party favors."

Laney felt Ben's hand at her back and leaned into his touch. There was a lot of talk—about babies and houses and goings on in the family—as the party went on, and they milled around, making sure they talked with everybody. There was food and cake and a lot of laughter, and Laney knew they would gather like this to celebrate for her and Ben, too. Their wedding. Maybe a baby.

There would be visits to Rhode Island, too. She'd been talking to her mom on the phone more often, and they were making progress. And she and Ben had met her parents in Boston for lunch so they could meet him. It had gone better than she'd hoped. She knew, when the time came for them to throw her a bridal shower, Rosie would make sure her mother was invited, and she was actually excited for her mom to see how happy she was in this unexpected place.

The sampler Sarah Kowalski had stitched so many years ago caught her eye. *Bless This Kitchen.* And it was. Filled with family and love and laughter, the kitchen of the Northern Star was definitely blessed.

"Are you okay?" Ben asked. "You look like you're going to get weepy on me."

"I should stitch one of those for our house."

He followed her gaze and then smiled. "You should. But instead of those dove things at the corners, you should make pink flamingos."

How lucky was she to find a man who loved her enough to embrace things just because they made her happy? Whether it was her pink chairs or her dancing flamingo or the radio station they listened to in the car, he was all for anything that made her smile.

"You're getting that look again," he said.

"What look?"

"Like maybe Josh was right about party favor tissues. I'm hoping those are happy tears you're trying to hold back."

"I never could have dreamed this life for myself,"

she said, her voice a little hoarse from the unshed tears. “Not without you.”

“We’re going to have an amazing life together, Laney.”

His eyes were full of promise, and she squeezed his hand. “We already do. And I’m going to love every day of it, because I love you.”

* * * * *

ACKNOWLEDGMENTS

I CAN'T ADEQUATELY express my gratitude to Angela James and the entire Carina Press team, as well as my agent, Kim Whalen, for everything they do for me. So many people have worked hard to make the Kowalski series the best it can be and I appreciate each and every one of them more than I can say.

And, as always, none of these books would be possible without the love and support of my husband, Stuart, and my BFF Jaci. It takes both of you to get me through the day, and I love you both for being here with me.

Meet the Men of Boston Fire. Tough. Dedicated. Devoted to their women. Read on for an excerpt of Book 1, HEAT EXCHANGE now available from Shannon Stacey and Carina Press in digital, print and audio.

ONE

LYDIA KINCAID COULD pull a pint of Guinness so perfect her Irish ancestors would weep tears of appreciation, but fine dining? Forget about it.

"The customer is disappointed in the sear on these scallops," she told the sous-chef, setting the plate down.

"In what way?"

"Hell if I know. They look like all the other scallops." Lydia had a hairpin sticking into her scalp, and it took every bit of her willpower not to poke at it. Her dark hair was too long, thick and wavy to be confined into a chic little bun, but it was part of the dress code. And going home with a headache every night was just part of the job. "Ten bucks says if I wait three minutes, then pop that same plate in the microwave for fifteen seconds and take it out to her, she'll gush over how the sear is so perfect now."

"If I see you microwaving scallops, I'll make sure the only food you ever get to touch in this city again is fast food."

Lydia rolled her eyes, having heard that threat many times before, and accepted a fresh plate of scallops from the line cook. The sous-chef just sniffed loudly and dumped the unacceptable batch in the garbage, plate and all. She was pretty sure the guy spent all his off time watching reality television chefs throw tantrums.

Three hours later, Lydia was in her car and letting her hair down. She dropped the bobby pins and elastic bands into her cup holder to fish out before her next shift and then used both hands to shake her hair out and massage her scalp.

She hated her job. Maybe some of it stemmed from the disparity between the cold formality of this restaurant and the warm and loud world she'd come from, but she also flat-out wasn't very good at it. The foods perplexed her and, according to the kitchen manager, her tableside manner lacked polish. Two years hadn't yet managed to put a shine on her. The tips were usually good, though, and living in Concord, New Hampshire, cost less than living in Boston, but it still wasn't cheap.

She'd just put her car in gear when she heard the siren in the distance. With her foot still on the brake, she watched as the fire engine came into view—red lights flashing through the dark night—and sped past.

With a sigh, she shifted her foot to the gas pedal. She didn't need to hold her breath anymore. Didn't need to find the closest scanner. Nobody she loved was on that truck so, while she said a quick prayer for their safety, they were faceless strangers and life wasn't temporarily suspended.

And that was why she'd keep trying to please people who wouldn't know a good scallop sear if it bit them on the ass and taking shit from the sous-chef. That job financed her new life here in New Hampshire, including a decent apartment she shared with a roommate, and it was a nice enough life that she wasn't tempted to go home.

Her life wasn't perfect. It had certainly been lacking in sex and friendship lately, but she wasn't going backward just because the road was longer or harder than she'd thought. She wanted something different and she was going to keep working toward it.

Thanks to the miracle of an apartment building with an off-street parking lot, Lydia had a dedicated parking spot waiting for her. It was another reason she put up with customers who nitpicked their entrées just because they were paying so much for them.

Her roommate worked at a sports bar and wouldn't be home for another couple of hours, so Lydia took a quick shower and put on her sweats. She'd just curled up on the sofa with the remote and a couple of the cookies her blessed-with-a-great-metabolism roommate had freshly baked when her cell phone rang.

She knew before looking at the caller ID it would be her sister. Not many people called her, and none late at night. "Hey, Ashley. What's up?"

"My marriage is over."

Lydia couldn't wrap her mind around the words at first. Had something happened to Danny? But she hadn't said that. She said it was over. "What do you mean it's over?"

"I told him I wasn't sure I wanted to be married to him anymore and that I needed some space. He didn't even say anything. He just packed up a couple of bags and left."

"Oh my God, Ashley." Lydia sank onto the edge of her bed, stunned. "Where did this even come from?"

"I've been unhappy for a while. I just didn't tell anybody." Her sister sighed, the sound hollow and discouraged over the phone. "Like a moron, I thought I could talk to him about it. Instead, he left."

"Why have you been unhappy? Dammit, Ashley,

what is going on? Did he cheat? I swear to God if he stepped out—"

"No. He didn't cheat. And it's too much for me talk about now."

"If you had been talking to me all along, it wouldn't be too much now. You can't call me and tell me your marriage is over and then tell me you don't want to talk about it."

"I know, but it's…it's too much. I called to talk to you about the bar."

Uh-oh. Alarm bells went off in Lydia's mind, but there was no way she could extricate herself from the conversation without being a shitty sister.

"I need you to come back and help Dad," Ashley said, and Lydia dropped her head back against the sofa cushion, stifling a groan. "I need some time off."

"I have a job, Ashley. And an apartment."

"You've told me a bunch of times that you hate your job."

She couldn't deny that since a conversation rarely passed between them without mention of that fact.

"And it's waiting tables," Ashley continued. "It's not like I'm asking you to take a hiatus from some fancy career path."

That was bitchy, even for Ashley, but Lydia decided to give her a pass. She didn't know what had gone wrong in their marriage, but she did know Ashley loved Danny Walsh with every fiber of her being, so she had to be a wreck.

"I can't leave Shelly high and dry," Lydia said in a calm, reasonable tone. "This is a great apartment and I'm lucky to have it. It has off-street parking and my space has my apartment number in it. It's literally *only* mine."

"I can't be at the bar, Lydia. You know how it is there. Everybody's got a comment or some advice to give, and I have to hear every five minutes what a great guy Danny is and why can't I just give him another chance?"

Danny really *was* a great guy, but she could understand her sister not wanting to be reminded of it constantly while they were in the process of separating. But going back to Boston and working at Kincaid's was a step in the wrong direction for Lydia.

"I don't know, Ash."

"Please. You don't know—" To Lydia's dismay, her sister's voice was choked off by a sob. "I can't do it, Lydia. I really, really need you."

Shit. "I'll be home tomorrow."

"WE GOT SMOKE showing on three and at least one possible on the floor," Rick Gullotti said. "Meet you at the top, boys."

Aidan Hunt threw a mock salute in the direction of the ladder company's lieutenant and tossed the ax to Grant Cutter before grabbing the Halligan tool for himself. With a fork at one end and a hook and adze head on the other end, it was essentially a long crowbar on steroids and they never went anywhere without it. After confirmation Scotty Kincaid had the line, and a thumbs-up from Danny Walsh at the truck, he and the other guys from Engine 59 headed for the front door of the three-decker.

Some bunch of geniuses, generations before, had decided the best way to house a shitload of people in a small amount of space was to build three-story houses—each floor a separate unit—and cram them close together. It was great if you needed a place to live and didn't mind living in a goldfish bowl. It was less great if it was your job to make sure an out-of-control kitchen fire didn't burn down the entire block.

They made their way up the stairs, not finding trouble until they reached the top floor. The door to the apartment stood open, with smoke pouring out. Aidan listened to the crackle of the radio over the sound of his own breathing in the mask. The guys from Ladder 37 had gained access by way of the window and had a woman descending, but her kid was still inside.

"Shit." Aidan confirmed Walsh knew they were going into the apartment and was standing by to charge the line if they needed water, and then looked for nods from Kincaid and Cutter.

He went in, making his way through the smoke. It was bad enough so the child would be coughing—hopefully—but there was chaos in the front of the apartment as another company that had shown up tried to knock down the flames from the front.

Making his way to the kid's bedroom, he signaled for Cutter to look under the bed while he went to the closet. If the kid was scared and hiding from them, odds were he or she was in one of those two spots.

"Bingo," he heard Cutter say into his ear.

The updates were growing more urgent and he heard Kincaid call for water, which meant the fire was heading their way. "No time to be nice. Grab the kid and let's go."

It was a little girl and she screamed as Cutter pulled her out from under the bed. She was fighting him and, because his hold was awkward, once she was free of the bed, Cutter almost lost her. Aidan swore under his breath. If she bolted, they could all be in trouble.

He leaned the Halligan against the wall and picked up the little girl. By holding her slightly slanted, he was able to hold her arms and legs still without running the risk of smacking her head on the way down.

"Grab the Halligan and let's go."

"More guys are coming up," Walsh radioed in. "Get out of there now."

The smoke was dense now and the little girl was doing more coughing and gasping than crying. "My dog!"

Aidan went past Kincaid, slapping him on the shoulder. Once Cutter went by, Kincaid could retreat—they all stayed together—and let another company deal with the flames.

"I see her dog," Aidan heard Cutter say, and he turned just in time to see the guy disappear back into the bedroom.

"Jesus Christ," Scotty yelled. "Cutter, get your ass down those stairs. Hunt, just go."

He didn't want to leave them, and he wouldn't have except the fight was going out of the child in his arms. Holding her tight, he started back down the stairs they'd come up. At the second floor he met another company coming up, but he kept going.

Once he cleared the building, he headed for the ambulance and passed the girl over to the waiting medics. It was less than two minutes before Cutter and Kincaid emerged from the building, but it felt like forever.

They yanked their masks off as Cutter walked over to the little girl and—after getting a nod from EMS—

put an obviously terrified little dog on the girl's lap. They all smiled as the girl wrapped her arms around her pet and then her mom put her arms around both. Aidan put his hand on Cutter's shoulder and the news cameras got their tired, happy smiles for the evening news.

Once they were back on the other side of the engine and out of view of the cameras, Kincaid grabbed the front of Cutter's coat and shoved him against the truck. "You want to save puppies, that's great. If there's time. Once you're told to get the fuck out, you don't go back for pets. And if you ever risk my life again, or any other guy's, for a goddamn dog, I'll make sure you can't even get a job emptying the garbage at Waste Reduction."

Once Cutter nodded, Kincaid released him and they looked to Danny for a status update. They had it pretty well knocked down and, though the third floor was a loss and the lower floors wouldn't be pretty, the people who lived in the neighboring houses weren't going to have a bad day.

Two hours later, Aidan sat on the bench in the shower room and tied his shoes. Danny was stowing his shower stuff, a towel wrapped around his waist. He'd been quiet since they got back, other than having a talk with Cutter, since he was the officer of the bunch. But he was always quiet, so it was hard to tell what was going on with him.

"Got any plans tonight?" Aidan finally asked, just to break the silence.

"Nope. Probably see if there's a game on."

Aidan wasn't sure what to say to that. He didn't have a lot of experience with a good friend going through a divorce. Breakups, sure, but not a marriage ending.

"If you want to talk, just let me know. We can grab a beer or something."

"Talk about what?"

"Don't bullshit me, Walsh. We know what's going on and it's a tough situation. So if you want to talk, just let me know."

"She doesn't want to be married to me anymore, so we're getting a divorce." Danny closed his locker, not needing to slam it to get his point across. "There's nothing to talk about."

"Okay." Aidan tossed his towel in the laundry bin and went out the door.

A lot of guys had trouble expressing their emotions, but Danny took it to a whole new level. Aidan thought talking about it over a few beers might help, but he shouldn't have been surprised the offer was refused.

He'd really like to know what had gone wrong in the Walsh marriage, though. He liked Danny and Ashley and he'd always thought they were a great couple. If they couldn't make it work, Aidan wasn't sure he had a chance. And lately he'd been thinking a lot about how nice it would be to have somebody to share his life with.

A mental snapshot of the little girl cradling her dog filled his mind. He wouldn't mind having a dog. But his hours would be too hard on a dog, and he wasn't a fan of cats. They were a little creepy and not good for playing ball in the park. He could probably keep a fish alive, but they weren't exactly a warm hug at the end of the long tour.

With a sigh he went into the kitchen to rummage for a snack. If he couldn't keep a dog happy, he probably didn't have much chance of keeping a wife happy. And that was assuming he even met a woman he wanted to get to know well enough to consider a ring. So far, not so good.

"Cutter ate the last brownie," Scotty told him as soon as he walked into the kitchen area.

Aidan shook his head, glaring at the young guy sitting at the table with a very guilty flush on his face. "You really do want to get your ass kicked today, don't you?"

"MAYBE I SHOULDN'T have called you. I feel bad now."

Lydia dropped her bag inside the door and put her hand on her hip. "I just quit my job and burned a chunk of my savings to pay Shelly for two months' rent in advance so she won't give my room away. You're stuck with me now."

Tears filled Ashley's eyes and spilled over onto her cheeks as she stood up on her toes to throw her arms around Lydia's neck. "I'm so glad you're here."

Lydia squeezed her older sister, and she had to admit that coming back was about the last thing she'd wanted to do, but she was glad to be there, too. When push came to shove, her sister needed her and when family really needed you, nothing else mattered.

When Ashley released her, Lydia followed her into the living room and they dropped onto the couch. About six months after they got married, Danny and Ashley had scored the single-family home in a foreclosure auction. It had gone beyond *handyman's special* straight into the rehab hell of *handyman's wet dream*, but room by room they'd done the remodeling themselves. Now they had a lovely home they never could have afforded on their salaries.

But right now, it wasn't a happy home. Lydia sighed and kicked off her flip-flops to tuck her feet under her. "What's going on?"

Ashley shrugged one shoulder, her mouth set in a line of misery. "You know how it is."

Maybe, in a general sense, Lydia knew how it was. She'd been married to a firefighter, too, and then she'd divorced one. But the one she'd been married to had struggled with the job, tried to cope with alcohol and taken advantage of Lydia's unquestioning acceptance of the demanding hours to screw around with every female who twitched her goods in his direction.

That wasn't Danny, so other than knowing how intense being a firefighter's wife could be, Lydia didn't see what Ashley was saying.

"He's just so closed off," her sister added. "I feel like he doesn't care about anything and I don't want to spend the rest of my life like that."

Lydia was sure there was more to it—probably a lot more—but Ashley didn't seem inclined to offer up anything else. And after the packing and driving, Lydia didn't mind putting off the heavy emotional stuff for a while.

"I should go see Dad," she said.

"He's working the bar tonight. And before you say anything, I know he's not supposed to be on his feet that much anymore. But you know he's sitting around talking to his buddies as much as being on his feet, and Rick Gullotti's girlfriend's supposed to be helping him out."

Rick was with Ladder 37 and Lydia had known him for years, but she struggled to remember his girlfriend's name. "Becky?"

Ashley snorted. "Becky was like eight girlfriends ago. Karen. We like her and it's been like four months now, which might be a record for Rick."

Lydia looked down at the sundress she'd thrown on that morning because it was comfortable and the pale pink not only looked great with her dark coloring, but also cheered her up. It was a little wrinkled from travel, but not too bad. It wasn't as if Kincaid's was known for being a fashion hot spot. "And Karen couldn't keep on helping him out?"

"She's an ER nurse. Works crazy hours, I guess, so she helps out, but can't commit to a set schedule. And you know how Dad is about family."

"It's Kincaid's Pub so, by God, there should be a Kincaid in it," Lydia said in a low, gruff voice that made Ashley laugh.

Even as she smiled at her sister's amusement, Lydia had to tamp down on the old resentment. There had been no inspirational *you can be the President of the United States if you want to* speeches for Tommy's daughters. His two daughters working the bar at Kincaid's Pub while being wonderfully supportive firefighters' wives was a dream come true for their old man.

Lydia had been the first to disappoint him. Her unwillingness to give the alcoholic serial cheater *just one more chance* had been the first blow, and then her leaving Kincaid's and moving to New Hampshire had really pissed him off.

Sometimes she wondered how their lives would have turned out if their mom hadn't died of breast cancer when Lydia and Ashley were just thirteen and fourteen. Scotty had been only nine, but he was his father's pride and joy. Joyce Kincaid hadn't taken any shit from her gruff, old-school husband, and Lydia thought maybe she would have pushed hard for her daughters to dream big. And then she would have helped them fight to make those dreams come true.

Or maybe their lives wouldn't have turned out any different and it was just Lydia spinning what-ifs into pretty fairy tales.

After carrying her bag upstairs to the guest room, Lydia brushed her hair and exchanged her flip-flops for cute little tennis shoes that matched her dress and would be better for walking.

"Are you sure you want to walk?" Ashley asked. "It's a bit of a hike."

"It's not that far, and I won't have to find a place to park."

"I'd go with you, but…"

But her not wanting to be at Kincaid's was the entire reason Lydia had uprooted herself and come home. "I get it. And I won't be long. I'll be spending enough time there as it is, so I'm just going to pop in, say hi and get the hell out."

Ashley snorted. "Good luck with that."

It was a fifteen-minute walk from the Walsh house to Kincaid's Pub, but Lydia stretched it out a bit. The sights. The sounds. The smells. No matter how reluctant she was to come back here or how many years she was away, this would always be home.

A few people called to her, but she just waved and kept walking. Every once in a while she'd step up the pace to make it look like she was in a hurry. But the street was fairly quiet and in no time, she was standing in front of Kincaid's Pub.

It was housed in the lower floor of an unassuming brick building. Okay, ugly. It was ugly, with a glass door and two high, long windows. A small sign with the name in a plain type was screwed to the brick over the door, making it easy to overlook. It was open to anybody, of course, but the locals were their bread and butter, and they liked it just the way it was.

Her dad had invested in the place—becoming a partner to help out the guy who owned it—almost ten years before his heart attack hastened his retirement from fighting fires, and he'd bought the original owner out when he was back on his feet. Once it was solely Tommy's, he'd changed the name to Kincaid's Pub, and Ashley and Lydia had assumed their places behind the bar.

After taking a deep breath, she pulled open the heavy door and walked inside. All the old brick and wood seemed to absorb the light from the many antique-looking fixtures, and it took a moment for her eyes to adjust.

It looked just the same, with sports and firefighting memorabilia and photographs covering the brick walls. The bar was a massive U-shape with a hand-polished surface, and a dozen tables, each seating four, were scattered around the room. In an alcove to one side was a pool table, along with a few more seating groups.

Because there wasn't a game on, the two televisions—one over the bar and one hung to be seen from most of the tables—were on Mute, with closed-captioning running across the bottom. The music was turned down low because Kincaid's was loud enough without people shouting to be heard over the radio.

Lydia loved this place. And she hated it a little, too.

But in some ways it seemed as though Kincaid's Pub was woven into the fabric of her being, and she wasn't sorry to be there again.

"Lydia!" Her father's voice boomed across the bar, and she made a beeline to him.

Tommy Kincaid was a big man starting to go soft around the middle, but he still had arms like tree trunks. They wrapped around her and she squealed a little when he lifted her off her feet. "I've missed you, girl."

She got a little choked up as he set her down and gave her a good looking over. Their relationship could be problematic at times—like most of the time—but Lydia never doubted for a second he loved her with all his heart. Once upon a time, he'd had the same thick, dark hair she shared with her siblings, but the gray had almost totally taken over.

He looked pretty good, though, and she smiled. "I'm glad you missed me, because it sounds like you'll be seeing a lot of me for a while."

A scowl drew his thick eyebrows and the corners of his mouth downward. "That sister of yours. I don't know what's going through her mind."

She gave him a bright smile. "Plenty of time for that later. Right now I just want to see everybody and have a beer."

A blonde woman who was probably a few years older than her smiled from behind the bar. "I'm Karen. Karen Shea."

Lydia reached across and shook her hand. "We really appreciate you being able to help out."

"Not a problem."

Lydia went to the very end of the back side of the bar

and planted a kiss on the cheek of Fitz Fitzgibbon—her father's best friend and a retired member of Ladder 37—who was the only person who ever sat on that stool. She supposed once upon a time she might have known his real first name, but nobody ever called him anything but Fitz or, in her father's case, Fitzy.

There were a few other regulars she said hello to before getting a Sam Adams and standing at the bar. Unlike most, the big bar at Kincaid's didn't have stools all the way around. It had once upon a time, but now there were only stools on the back side and the end. Her dad had noticed a lot of guys didn't bother with the stools and just leaned against the polished oak. To make things easier, he'd just ripped them out.

About a half hour later, her brother, Scotty, walked in. Like the rest of the Kincaids, he had thick dark hair and dark eyes. He needed a shave, as usual, but he looked good. They'd talked and sent text messages quite a bit over the past two years, but neither of them was much for video chatting, so she hadn't actually seen him.

And right on Scotty's heels was Aidan Hunt. His brown hair was lighter than her brother's and it needed a trim. And she didn't need to see his eyes to remember they were blue, like a lake on a bright summer day. He looked slightly older, but no less deliciously handsome than ever. She wasn't surprised to see him. Wherever Scotty was, Aidan was usually close by.

What did surprise her was that the second his gaze met hers, her first thought was that she'd like to throw everybody out of the bar, lock the door and then shove him onto a chair. Since she was wearing the sundress, all she had to do was undo his fly, straddle his lap and hold on.

When the corner of his mouth quirked up, as if he somehow knew she'd just gone eight seconds with him in her mind, she gave him a nod of greeting and looked away.

For crap's sake, that was Aidan Hunt. Her annoying younger brother's equally annoying best friend.

He'd been seventeen when they met, to Lydia's twenty-one. He'd given her a grin that showed off perfect, Daddy's-got-money teeth and those sparkling blue eyes and said, "Hey, gorgeous. Want to buy me a drink?"

She'd rolled her eyes and told him to enjoy his playdate with Scotty. From that day on, he had seemed determined to annoy the hell out of her at every possible opportunity.

When her brother reached her, she shoved Aidan out of her mind and embraced Scotty. "How the hell are ya?"

"Missed having you around," he said. "Sucks you had to come back for a shitty reason, but it's still good to see you. I just found out about an hour ago Ashley had called you."

"She just called me last night, so it was spur-of-the-moment, I guess."

"It's good to have you back."

"Don't get too used to it. It's temporary."

She'd always thought if she and Scotty were closer in age than four years apart, they could have been twins, with the same shaped faces and their coloring. Ashley looked a lot like both of them, but her face was leaner, her eyes a lighter shade of brown, and her hair wasn't quite as thick.

Scotty was more like Lydia in temperament, too. Ashley was steadier and liked to try logic first. Scott and Lydia were a little more volatile and tended to run on emotion. Her temper had a longer fuse than her brother's, but they both tended to pop off a little easy.

They caught up for a few minutes, mainly talking about his fellow firefighters, most of whom she knew well. And he gave her a quick update on their dad's doctor not being thrilled with his blood pressure. It didn't sound too bad, but it was probably good Ashley had called her rather than let him try to take up her slack.

Then Scotty shifted from one foot to the other and grimaced. "Sorry, but I've had to take a leak for like an hour."

She laughed and waved him off. "Go. I'll be here."

He left and Lydia looked up at the television, sipping her beer. She only ever had one, so she'd make it last, but part of her wanted to chug it and ask for a refill. It was a little overwhelming, being back.

"Hey, gorgeous. Want to buy me a drink?" What were the chances? She turned to face Aidan, smiling at the fact she'd been thinking about that day just a few minutes before. "What's so funny?"

She shook her head, not wanting to tell him she'd been thinking about the day they met, since that would be an admission she'd been thinking about him at all. "Nothing. How have you been?"

"Good. Same shit, different day. You come back for a visit?"

"I'll be here awhile. Maybe a couple of weeks, or a

month." She shrugged. "Ashley wanted to take some time off, so I'm going to cover for her. You know how Dad is about having one of us here all the damn time."

His eyes squinted and he tilted his head a little. "You sound different."

"I worked on toning down the accent a little, to fit in more at work, I guess. Even though it's only the next state over, people were always asking me where I was from."

"You trying to forget who you are?" It came out *fuh-get who you ah.* "Forget where you came from?"

"Not possible," she muttered.

He gave her that grin again, with the perfect teeth and sparkling eyes. They crinkled at the corners now, the laugh lines just making him more attractive. "So what you're saying is that we're unforgettable."

She laughed, shaking her head. "You're something, all right."

Aidan looked as if he was going to say something else, but somebody shouted his name and was beckoning him over. He nodded and then turned back to Lydia. "I'll see you around. And welcome home."

She watched him walk away, trying to keep her eyes above his waist in case anybody was watching her watch him. Her annoying brother's annoying best friend had very nice shoulders stretching out that dark blue T-shirt.

Her gaze dipped, just for a second. And a very nice ass filling out those faded blue jeans.

TWO

Aidan was just having a beer. Shooting the shit with the guys. Figuring out when they could get in some ice time at the rink. What he *wasn't* doing was checking out his best friend's sister.

That was Lydia over there, for chrissake. Scotty's sister. Tommy's daughter. She was bossy and sarcastic and pretty much the last woman on Earth he could mess around with. Except Ashley, who was all of those things *and* married to Danny, which put her one rung higher on the off-limits ladder. But he'd never been attracted to her the way he was to her sister.

Last he knew Lydia didn't even like him very much.

So why had she given him a look that said she might have mentally stripped him naked and was licking her way down his body?

He took a slug of his beer, trying to work it out in his head. She'd definitely been looking at him. The only other person in range had been Scotty, and she sure as hell hadn't been looking at *him* like that. And he hadn't imagined the heat, either. That woman had been thinking some seriously dirty thoughts. About him.

Yanking his T-shirt out of his jeans in the hope it would be long enough to cover the erection he was currently rocking seemed a little conspicuous, so he turned his body to the bar and rested his forearms on it. He seriously needed to get a grip.

He couldn't disrespect Tommy Kincaid by lusting after his daughter. The man was not only a mentor of sorts and a second father to him, being his best friend's dad, but he was the reason Aidan was a firefighter.

He'd been eleven years old when his family's minivan got caught up in a shit show involving a jackknifed 18-wheeler, two other cars and a box truck full of building supplies. His memories of the accident itself were hazy. Screeching tires. Shattering glass. His mother screaming his father's name.

But the aftermath imprinted on his memory so clearly it was like a movie he could hit Play on at will. A police officer had gotten them all out of the vehicle and Aidan had held his little brother's hand on one side and kept his other hand on his little sister's baby carrier.

A firefighter was working on his dad, whose head had a lot of blood on it. Aidan's mom was dazed and sat leaning against the guardrail, holding her arm. When his little brother called out to her, she didn't even look at him.

Then a woman started screaming and there were a lot of shouts. The firefighter who was holding some bandaging to his dad's head looked over his shoulder and then back to his dad. Aidan could tell he wanted to go help the woman who was screaming, so he stepped forward.

"I can hold that," he told the firefighter. "Just show me how hard to press."

The firefighter hadn't wanted to. But the screaming and the voices grew more urgent and he had Aidan kneel down next to him. After making sure Bryan put his hand on Sarah's carrier and wouldn't move, Aidan took over putting pressure on his dad's head wound.

"You're okay, Dad," he said, looking into his father's unfocused gaze. "Just keep looking at me and we'll wait for an ambulance together."

He'd been the one to give the paramedics their information and tell them his father took a medication for his blood pressure. Then he'd given them a description of his mom's demeanor since the accident. After asking them to retrieve Sarah's diaper bag from the van, he'd cared for his siblings until his aunt arrived.

The firefighter had shown up at the hospital and given him a Boston Fire T-shirt. "You did good, kid."

Aidan hadn't really known what praise and pride felt like until he looked into the man's warm eyes. "Thank you, sir."

"Some people are born to take charge in emergencies. It's a special thing and not everybody's got it. When you grow up, if you decide you want to save lives, son, you look me up. Tommy Kincaid. Engine Company 59."

Aidan rubbed the Engine 59 emblem on his T-shirt and smiled. He'd been only sixteen the first time he showed up at the old brick building that housed Engine 59 and Ladder 37, looking for Tommy. He met Scotty that day and together they'd never looked back. Friendship. A little bit of trouble here and there. Training. Testing. They'd been inseparable. Aidan didn't know if it was a favor to Tommy or if Fate played a hand, but when the station assignments went out, they'd even been assigned to the same engine company.

His extremely white-collar parents hadn't been able to reconcile their hopes for their oldest son with his drive to serve the public, and things were still rough between them. And maybe his old man was embarrassed to only have one of his sons working with Hunt

& Sons Investments—Sarah being destined for more feminine pursuits, like marriage and motherhood, according to their father—but Aidan wouldn't be swayed.

Tommy had become his father figure. Scotty and Danny and the rest of the guys were his brothers. This was his family, and he knew they had his back, anytime and anyplace.

Messing around with Lydia Kincaid was a bad idea. Like a *sticking a fork in a toaster while sitting in a bathtub cocked off your ass* kind of a bad idea.

"Earth to Hunt," Scotty said, and Aidan felt an ugly jolt of guilt for even considering messing around with Lydia while standing right next to her brother, for chrissake. "What the hell's wrong with you?"

"Nothing. Wicked tired is all."

"What's her name?"

Aidan snorted. "I wish."

"Piper's got a friend I could hook you up with. Her name's Bunny, and she's not bad."

"I'm too old for chicks named Bunny."

Scott shrugged. "I don't think that's her real name. At least I hope it's not. But whatever, man. Your loss."

Aidan didn't exactly wallow in regret. He was tired of it. He was tired of women who saw his face and didn't look any further. He was sick of women who got off on banging firefighters and the women who saw him outside the rink with his bag and wanted to spend a little time with a hockey player.

He didn't mind at all if a woman wanted to use him for hot, dirty sex. But he also wanted her to laugh with him and enjoy a quiet evening on the couch. And he needed her to stroke his hair when the day was shitty and to hold him when the nightmares came.

Lydia's laughter rose above the noise of the bar, but Aidan didn't turn to look. He just knocked back the rest of his beer and kept his eyes on the television.

THE OVERLY CHIPPER chime sound that indicated an incoming text made Lydia very reluctantly open her eyes the next morning. Ashley's guest room mattress had seen better days and it had taken her forever to fall asleep.

With a groan, she reached over to the nightstand and felt around until she found her phone. She had just enough charger cord to read the message without picking her head up off the pillow.

What the hell, girl?

She had no idea what the hell, since she wasn't even awake yet. But then she realized it was a group text, the group being her two best friends, Becca Shepard and Courtney Richmond. With Ashley as their fourth, they'd been inseparable growing up, and there was a group text going on more often than not.

This time it was Becca, and Lydia wondered which of them the message was aimed at. Probably her.

Before she could respond, another text from Becca came through.

Heard you were at KP last night. Ninja visit?

Lydia didn't have time to compose a reply before a response from her sister popped up.

I'm taking some time off. L's home to cover for me.

How long?

Don't know.

Since Ashley was not only awake, but able to type coherently, Lydia dropped the phone onto the blanket and closed her eyes again. Kincaid's didn't open until eleven, so she didn't have to jump out of bed.

But when the phone chimed again she realized that, even if she didn't join in the conversation, the alerts would drive her crazy. After a big stretch, she picked up the phone again.

GNO!

That was Courtney, and Lydia rolled her eyes. While a girls' night out was appealing, she barely had her feet under her. She hadn't even worked a shift at the bar yet, so trying to get time off would be tough.

Soon. Stop at KP & say hi if you can.

That might hold them off for a while. Long enough to get coffee into her system, at least.

That turned out to be the end of the messages, but Lydia knew she'd tipped past the mostly awake point and wouldn't be able to go back to sleep now. After unplugging her phone, she made a quick stop in the bathroom and then headed downstairs.

Once she reached the top of the stairs, she could smell the coffee and followed the aroma to the kitchen. Ashley was sitting at the table, her phone in hand, and she looked up when Lydia walked in.

"Hey, how did you sleep?"

"Like a baby." It was a lie, but Ashley already felt bad about asking her to come home. No sense in piling on guilt about it. And even a crappy mattress was better than staying at her dad's.

Once she'd made her coffee, she sat down across from her sister and sipped it. If it wasn't so hot, she'd guzzle the stuff. Lydia was a better cook than Ashley, but her sister was definitely better at making coffee.

After a few minutes, Ashley put down her phone and looked at her. "It's been ten days."

"Ten days?" A week and half had gone by before her sister bothered telling her that her marriage was over?

"I thought he'd come back, you know? Like maybe he'd blow off some steam and then we'd talk about it. But he didn't come back. And when I called him, he just closed up and it was like talking to a machine." Ashley stared at her coffee, shaking her head. "More than usual, even. So the more I hope we can work it out, the more he does the thing I can't live with anymore."

Lydia took the time to consider her next words carefully. She had her sister's back, 100 percent, but sometimes having a person's back wasn't as cut-and-dried as blindly agreeing with everything they said. "He's always been quiet. I don't know how many times I've heard the other guys call him the ice man. It's not just with you."

"He can be however he wants with other people, especially the other guys. I'm his *wife*. If I'm upset and worried or pissed off, I need to feel like he at least cares."

"Have you thought about counseling?"

Ashley shrugged. "I mentioned it once and he

changed the subject. I'm not sure what the point would be in talking to somebody when he doesn't talk."

"That *is* the point. A professional can help you guys communicate, including helping him break through whatever block he's got up and talk to you."

"I left a message on his voice mail, asking him if we could set up a time to meet somewhere for coffee. If he shows up, I'll mention it."

"Just don't make it about him—that *he* needs help because he can't communicate. Make it about you feeling like it would be good for your marriage."

She nodded. "Assuming he even calls me back. He keeps texting me, but I want him to stop taking the easy way out and actually talk to me. I want to hear his voice."

"Where's he staying? With his parents?" Ashley's mouth tightened and Lydia leaned back in her chair. "No. Don't even tell me."

"He's staying with Scotty."

"Of course he is." Lydia's hand tightened around the coffee mug and it took supreme will not to chuck it at the wall. "Is Scott working today?"

Ashley looked at her, and then slowly shook her head. "Don't, Lydia. You'll only make it worse."

"It's not right. You're his sister."

"It's better than not knowing where Danny is or having him shack up with God knows who."

"There are plenty of other guys who could offer him a couch," Lydia argued. "He could crash with Aidan or Rick. Jeff. Chris. Any of them. It didn't have to be *your* brother. In our father's house."

When Ashley just gave a small shrug, Lydia wanted to shake her. As far as she was concerned, Scott had crossed a line and she wanted her sister to be pissed off about it. To demand the respect and loyalty the Kincaid men should be showing *her*, and not Danny.

But she knew Ashley wasn't wired the same way she was and it took a lot to make her angry. Just like their mother, once she'd had enough, she could give Lydia and Scott a run for their money, and that's what Lydia wanted to see.

"Did I really jam you up by asking you to come back?" Ashley asked. "I'm sorry about what I said about your job, by the way. I was so desperate to get out of being at the bar, but that was dirty."

"I forgive you because God knows I've vented at you often enough. That's what sisters are for. And you didn't jam me up at all. You were right about me hating that job and, when I go back, I'll find one I like more."

"You should go back to bartending. You're a natural."

Lydia shrugged. Bartending was something she was good at and she honestly enjoyed it, but she'd taken the waitressing job because she wanted something different. Tending a bar that wasn't Kincaid's Pub had seemed at the time like it might be too painful for her.

"I thought about going to school," she said. "But I spent weeks looking at brochures and stuff online and nothing jumped out at me. If I'm going to invest that time and money, I want it to be for something I *really* want to be, you know?"

"If I had the chance to go to college, I'd go for office or business stuff. I don't even know what it's called, but I think it would be awesome to work in a medical clinic, like for women's health."

"Have you thought about going to the community college?" They'd both been thrown into work young and college had never been a big deal in their family, but if Ashley wanted to go, she should.

"Danny and I talked about it a while back. He was supportive, but Dad made a big deal out of needing me at Kincaid's and you were getting a divorce. Plus working around Danny's hours would be a pain. It was easier to forget about it."

Lydia shoved back at the guilt that threatened to overwhelm her and make her say something stupid, like offering to stay in Boston so Ashley could go to college. Her dad had accused her of being selfish when she'd taken off, and maybe she was, but she couldn't be responsible for everybody's lives. She was still working on her own.

"I'm going to take a shower," Lydia said when it became clear Ashley had nothing else to say at the moment. "We should go out for breakfast."

"I already made pancake batter. I was just waiting for you to get up."

Her sister wasn't the best cook in the world, but she made amazing pancakes. "I hope you made a lot. I'm starving."

Ashley's face lit up with a real smile. "I know you and my pancakes. I practically had to mix it in a bucket."

AIDAN HELD UP a metal rod and looked over at Scotty. "What is this? Does this go somewhere?"

They both looked at the piece of playground equipment they'd spent the past hour assembling, and then Scotty shrugged. "It doesn't look like it goes anywhere."

"I don't think they said, 'Hey, let's throw a random metal rod in there just to mess with the idiots who have to put it together,' do you?"

"I don't know. If you set something on fire, I know what to do with it. Building things? Not my job."

Chris Eriksson joined them, scratching at a slowly graying beard. "I don't think you're supposed to have extra pieces. A bolt maybe. A few nuts. That looks important."

"Where did the instructions go?" Aidan asked, scanning the playground to see if they'd blown away.

"There were instructions?"

"Funny, Kincaid." Eriksson shook his head. "My kid's going to climb on this thing. If we can't figure it out, we're breaking it down and starting over."

Aidan stifled the curse words he wanted to mutter as he started circling the playground structure. They were surrounded by an increasingly bored pack of elementary students and a photographer waiting to snap a few pictures of the kids playing on the equipment the firehouse had donated and built. When Eriksson had come to them, looking for some help for his son's school, they'd been all-in.

And they still were. This was their community and they all did what they could. But it would have been nice if somebody had been in charge of the directions. After a few minutes, one of the teachers—a pretty brunette with a warm smile—moved closer and beckoned him over.

"We built one of these where I did my student teaching, and I think it's a support bar for under the slide," she whispered. "If you look up at it from underneath, you should see the braces where it bolts on."

"Thank you."

"No, thank you. We really appreciate you volunteering your time."

He gave her his best public relations smile, secure in doing so because of the ring on her finger and lack of *I'm hitting on a firefighter* vibe. "Just doing our part for the children, ma'am."

She nodded and went back to her students, leaving him relieved he'd judged the situation correctly. Having a teacher flirt with him in front of her students would be a level of awkward he didn't care to experience. He'd learned fairly quickly that, for whatever reason, there were women out there who really liked men in uniform, with police and fire uniforms ranking right up there. Fake kitchen fires were rare, but not unheard of, and it seemed like every firehouse had a story about busting through a front door to find the lady of the house wearing little to nothing.

For a few years, he'd been like a kid in a candy store, so to speak, but it had gotten old after a while. He'd grown to hate not being sure if a woman was attracted to him or his job, so one time he'd actually told a woman he was interested in that he was a plumber. It was a lie he kept going for several weeks, until she suffered a plumbing emergency and he was forced to admit he had no idea why disgusting water was backing up into her bathtub.

That had been his longest relationship, surviving his confession and lasting about a year and a half. He'd even been thinking about an engagement ring, but she struggled with his job and in the end, she opted out. Or rather, she opted for a guy who worked in a bank and was home by five and never worked weekends.

There had been a few almost-serious relationships since then, but they always fizzled out under the strain of his job. Flipping back and forth between day tours and night tours was something that came naturally to him at this point, but it was a lot harder on the people in his life.

He tried to stay hopeful, but sometimes it was hard to be optimistic about finding a woman he'd spend the rest of his life with. Even Scotty's sisters—who'd grown up with Tommy Kincaid and surrounded by firefighters—hadn't been able to make their marriages to firefighters work. Sure, there were a lot of strong marriages if he looked around enough, but it got discouraging at times.

"Hey, Hunt, you gonna stand around yank—" Scotty bit off the words, no doubt remembering just in time they had a young audience. "Doing nothing, or are you gonna help?"

Once they'd gotten the metal rod bolted into the proper position, Chris Eriksson turned testing it out into a comedy skit that made the children laugh and then, finally, it was time for some press photos. The kids gave them a handmade thank-you card that the firefighters promised to hang on their bulletin board, and then it was time to get back to the station. Several guys had agreed to cover for them, but only for a few morning hours.

Once they were on their way back, in Eriksson's truck, Chris looked over at Scott. "Hey, I heard Lydia's back."

Aidan was glad he'd been too slow to call shotgun and was wedged into the truck's inadequate backseat because he felt the quick flash of heat across the back of his neck. He was going to end up in trouble if he didn't figure out how to stifle his reaction to hearing Lydia's name.

But the way she'd looked at him at Kincaid's last night…

"Yeah," Scotty said. "She's going to help out at the bar so Ashley can take a little time off while she and Danny figure out what the hell they're doing."

"I heard Walsh was staying with you. That's cozy."

Aidan wondered if Lydia knew that part yet, because he couldn't imagine she'd take it well. He'd known the Kincaid family almost a decade and a half, and he knew that Ashley was the older sister, but Lydia was the junkyard dog. If you messed with the family, Ashley would try to talk it out with you, but Lydia would take your head off your shoulders.

"Lydia can worry about the beer and burgers and stay out of the rest of it," Scotty said.

Aidan laughed out loud. "I wouldn't recommend you tell *her* that."

"Hell, no. I'm not stupid."

As they got close, Eriksson sighed. "Fun time's over. Chief says we've gotta clean the engine bays today. And everything else that needs cleaning."

"That's bullshit," Scotty said. "I swear to God, the guys on night tour last week were all raised in barns. We should go drag their asses out of bed and make *them* clean up."

Aidan didn't mind the thought of filling the time around any runs with cleaning. It was mindless work that would keep him from having to look his best friend in the eye until he'd gotten a handle on thinking dirty thoughts about the guy's sister.

He didn't think the *she started it* excuse would cut it with Scott Kincaid.

Buy HEAT EXCHANGE now wherever Carina Press books are sold.